The Season
of Secrets

DE McCluskey

D E McCluskey

The Season of Secrets
Copyright © 2025 by
DE McCluskey & Dammaged Productions

ISBN 978-1914381072

Dammaged Production

www.dammaged.com

For Kelly Rickard
Best proofreader ever
and an all-around nice person to go with it
Happy days … chicken

D E McCluskey

1.

A WINTERY WISCONSIN wind blew along the Wolf
River. As it did, it dropped the temperatures to somewhere around
twenty.

It was Christmas Eve, and it was already full dark. It was a
peculiar kind of darkness, an almost complete velvety obsidian. The
kind that only seems to settle in small, rural locations. Kitchowa,
Wisconsin, is almost the definition of a small rural location. It's a
slowpoke of a town situated, as the locals would tell you, *just a skip
and a jump* from the lesser travelled Highway 55. Snow had been
falling for what felt like months, and the huge drifts had long been a
nuisance, having lost their picturesque charms weeks ago. They were
a cause of constant consternation to travellers along the county road,
as the piles on either side grew taller than some of the houses dotted
along it. Of the few streetlights that serviced the road one of them
was out. This had the effect of casting one of the houses into shadow.
If ever there was a house that welcomed or perhaps suited the
shadows, it was this one. The house was the same as the other houses
on the sparse street, but to generations of local school children, this
house had always had *the* reputation that at least one house possesses
in every small town.

This was the boogieman's house.

Harry Sharpe was that boogieman.

He'd lived alone in that very same shadowed house for most
of his life. He'd been the one chosen to be the outcast, the pariah, by
the children and most of the adults.

A lot of them thought they had good reason, although most of them didn't even know what that reason was.

He'd seen enough winters in this small town to have grown savvy to the harshness of them, and he had purchased enough provisions to see him through his annual self-imposed hibernation. He'd spent the latter parts of the fall gathering and storing wood in his shed and had enough to see him through until April if he needed it. This wasn't his first rodeo—another of the locals' favourite sayings—regarding surviving the clawing, intense cold of the dark end of the year. The talk between the old timers, the ones who frequented Not Bob's Bar and Grill, had been optimistic about this winter after the humdingers they'd endured two years on the bounce. 'This one should be a doozy,' they'd say without explaining to anyone what a doozy was.

Harry didn't listen to the old timers, mostly because he avoided Not Bob's Bar and Grill like the plague. If the feeling took him, which it seldom did, he might venture into downtown Kitchowa for essential provisions only, but mostly, he kept himself to himself, at home, alone, just how he liked it. He had everything he needed to lead a self-sufficient lifestyle, and after everything that this life had thrown at him, it was good enough for him. During the winter, he could be mostly found laid up in his bed, content in his own company.

The many books that adorned his shelves told of his one true passion. He seldom watched anything on TV, mostly because he enjoyed using his imagination more than the TV shows would allow their target audiences or even give them credit for. He loved losing himself in lost and distant lands filled with mystique and adventure. Fiction was always preferable to the reality of the slog of living in the middle of nowhere, where it was below freezing about half the year, while the other half ran away far too fast to keep up with.

And all of this in a town where he was seen as nothing more than a pariah at best.

Since he'd lost his job at Kitchowa High School, he'd never bothered much with the comings and goings of the narrow-minded townsfolk. He thought if he left them alone, then they might leave him alone.

He'd been wrong about that.

Over the years, he'd found out how wrong he'd been.

Christmas Eve was always the bleakest of nights for Harry Sharpe. It was a far cry from how he used to love the holidays. As a child, and even a young man, he would look forward to the twenty-fourth day of December, counting the days down from Thanksgiving. He loved everything about the myth of Santa Claus, the elves, and the flying reindeer. He had tried to instil his love of the innocence of the happiest day of the year to the children he taught, imparting to them the importance of the works of Charles Dickens and Clement Moor, to name but two.

Now, Christmas was nothing to him other than a hateful time. All Santa Claus brought him these days was melancholy and a longing for days that should have been filled with mirth, joy, and laughter, not misery, tears, and self-loathing.

'Maybe I should read more Seuss,' he chuffed to himself on numerous occasions as the overproof moonshine he brewed for his own personal consumption overpowered the meagre food rations he'd consume and the bitterness of the season dragged him further from the light, towards the gloom.

These days, Santa's sleigh was pulled not by eight tiny, delightful reindeer but by one huge black dog, whose eyes were deep voids of … nothingness!

Tonight would be no different, he feared.

In a moment of weakness, he'd succumbed to nostalgia and attempted to cheer himself up by venturing out to the new mall downtown. He yearned for some Christmas cheer, for the decorations in the shops to lift his spirits. However, what had happened, what had greeted him there, steeled his resilience to block out the rest of the world. He'd come away from that place vindicated, so much so that when he shored up his home for the winter on his return, it was with a deep foreboding of the season.

He closed his well-thumbed copy of his current read, *Jimsy, The Christmas Kid,* and reached for the bedside lamp, killing its dim illumination. The wind howled against the eaves of his home, keeping their own Christmas chorus … *The Angels heralding the birth of our Lord and Saviour,* he thought with a wry smile. Even though it was a nice thought, an uplifting one, a shiver ran through him, and goosebumps rose over his exposed flesh. It caused the hairs on the back of his neck to wake up too. *A Christmas goose walking over my grave,* he thought. This made him smile, that small thought feeling more fitting than the last.

The room was colder than it should have been, considering he'd stoked the old cast iron wood stove right before retiring. He made sure there was enough wood to keep burning until the morning, when he'd return to the woodshed to collect more.

In keeping with his literary traditions, as he hadn't completely forgotten about the season, and being a huge fan of Dickens, he always looked forward to treating himself to a traditional English Christmas feast, mostly consisting of a healthy portion of goose, keeping the rest of the bird for later and the bones for boiling for soup. After this celebration, there would be an equally healthy helping of plum pudding for dessert. All of this was before making a dent in the home-brewed hooch he always made in the warmth of his home. *To Christmas,* he'd toast, raising a lonely but full glass to the world.

So, it felt strange having a chill wrap its cold fingers around him, caressing him with its icy embrace. 'There's no way that fire could have gone out,' he mumbled to himself as he slipped out of the grey bedsheets. They had once been white and freshly changed at least once a week; now, he was lucky if he changed them once a month—he no longer saw the point.

As he slipped into the carpet slippers he knew would be waiting for his feet at the side of his bed, he drew in a sharp whoosh of air as his eyes widened. They crunched as his toes slipped into them. He pulled them out again as fast as he could, as frost bit into his digits. 'What the …' he gasped as the unexpected iciness passed up through his legs, causing them to throb. He lifted up his reading lamp, illuminating his bedroom. There were a few photographs on the side table, mostly old black-and-white pictures of his parents. He ignored them as the yellowing glow continued around the room.

The dim light caused more shadows than it eliminated.

He shivered. As he did, he watched his breath plume out of his mouth.

The noise was small, almost innocuous. However, to his over-sensitive ears, it might as well have been a crescendo of instruments heralding the crashing end of a rousing symphony. His head whipped to the side, bringing the illumination with it.

The room was still.

The only other sound was coming from outside. It was the wail of the wind picking up again, screeching past his window. This was a normal occurrence, something he'd heard a million times before, but this one caused the stubborn goosebumps on his arms to raise even further. He didn't know if the room had gotten colder or if it was just his overactive imagination, but he grabbed the bathrobe that was currently hanging on the back of a chair and pulled it over his shoulders, tugging it tight across his waist, to combat the dramatic change in temperature.

The small sound came again.

As it did, his lamp flickered.

Coincidence, he thought, feeling somewhat like the character of Ebenezer Scrooge, convincing himself there was no such thing as ghosts. The noise was different this time, like there was a structure to it, a weight, even.

It was something he recognised.

His already thumping heart upped its tempo just a notch. The cold that had enveloped his body was now aided by the sheen of sweat that suddenly covered him as the noise came for a third time.

This time, he knew what it was.

It was music.

He'd always loved music. He played his extensive record collection often, spinning his blues and rock albums time and time again. He loved the crackle and hiss of the old vinyl being picked up by the needle. He also loved his radio. Even though he'd attempted to limit any contact with the rest of the world, it didn't mean he wanted *nothing* at all to do with it. Back in the day, before everything changed, he'd been something of a social animal. He'd courted many a young lady in his time; however, all of them, every last one, had broken contact with him, shunning him, as did all his friends and even most of his family.

Ever since …

The strange music came again. It snapped him out of this horrible and sad reverie. He smiled at the realisation that the disembodied, mysterious music, issuing from an esoteric source, was preferable to his own thoughts. *The wallowing of a pathetic old man,* he thought. *What a great book title that would make.*

The music was coming from his living room. This house had once been a beautiful, warm, and inviting place. *Perhaps it had been too inviting,* he pondered. But now it felt like a prison. Like the four walls were there to keep him inside, keeping him in solitary confinement as the world continued to spin … outside.

The song issuing from the room was not clear, but the greasy sweat that was covering the palms of his hands, mixed with the palpitations of his heart as it hammered against his chest, told him otherwise.

He knew the song.

It was how he knew the music wasn't coming from the radio. Ever since it had happened, he'd stopped listening to radio stations that played Christmas music. Just in case he heard it. Originally, he'd enjoyed the popular old song. Johnny Plaid, the old crooner with the silky voice, had released his own version of the classic, and it had been a hit for years. However, it brought back too many memories, too many ghosts of Christmases long, long ago.

'*Do you believe the magic?*' Mr Plaid's smooth voice was asking all over the house. The chorus girls echoed him. '*Do you believe the magic?*'

His blood was ice in his veins. His knuckles cracked as he gripped the shaft of his faltering lamp. His feet felt as if someone had glued them to the floor.

I haven't heard that song since …

'*A bright and blinding light!*'

He wanted nothing more than to turn the lamp off, to crawl back into the darkness of his bed, to pull the covers over his head, and block the whole of the world out forever.

'*Do you believe … in the promise and the awe!*'

The haunting melody had always given him shivers, even when he was a child and his mother would play it on repeat, singing along with the tenor of Johnny Plaid's vocal track. Hearing it now gave him the same feeling. Only this time, it wasn't nostalgia. It was something else.

'Mr Sharpe?'

The pain in his left arm began at the crook of his elbow. He could feel it as it shot up his arm at an alarming rate. It left a numbness and the tingle of pins and needles in its wake.

'Mr Sharpe?'

He knew the whispered voice.

He knew it intimately.

He'd heard the same sweet innocence in his head over and over again for years.

'Mr Sharpe?' The voice was barely a whisper, yet it cannoned through his head; it deafened him. It's thin, raspy scratch caused more shivers to run through him. 'Can you hear me, Mr Sharpe? *Do you believe in Christmas magic?*'

He couldn't tell if the voice was mocking him, taunting him. If it was forcing him to relive those events, *those damned events!* Or if the innocence he could hear in the words was genuine. Either way, it was alien to this environment, and it was terrifying.

'*That sings to us this day.*'

The voice was no longer in his head; it was here, with him, inside his room. *That's impossible,* he thought. That didn't help. He knew exactly what she was going to say next. He closed his eyes and willed her to go away, to leave him alone, and to stop singing *that* song. However, he knew, as certain as he knew his speeding heart would not last the night, what she was going to say next.

'Can you help me, Mr Sharpe?' she whispered.

The voice, even though it was only a thin whisper with all the weight of crepe paper, it screamed in his head. The words bounced from one side of his skull to the other, taking chunks of his brain with it. They felt like mini sledgehammers battering him from the inside.

The volume of the song increased. It rang in his ears. It was louder than the bells of Big Ben in London, than St Peter's, than the bells of St Nicholas Cathedral in New York. It was the loudest noise he'd ever heard in his life. The *thud, thud, thud* of his heart kept perfect time with the crashing rhythm of Johnny Plaid and his perfect, silky voice.

'Do you believe ... Open hearts, open door.'

The pain in his arm was back, and suddenly, he found himself on his knees, clutching the lamp to his chest. It slipped from his moist fingers as the agony in his arm invaded his body. The lamp smashed, sending the room into complete darkness.

'Let ... all ... your ... love ... soar!'

Harry felt as if he was about to explode. The music was deafening, the sledgehammer words smashing through the confines of his head, obliterating all other thought. The sudden darkness was making his weakening heart work overtime.

Then everything stopped.

The song, the pain, the thrashing in his head, even the numbness in his arm. Everything went away at once, and he found himself immersed in a world of darkness and silence.

He closed his eyes, hoping this was nothing but a dream. He prayed that this personal ghost of Christmas Past would allow him to continue his life unburdened by their appointment. He held his breath for a few moments before releasing it slowly. He could only imagine the mist emanating from him, as it was too dark to see.

As he opened his eyes, they widened, as the breath he was expelling was glowing like a million radiant jellyfish swarming in a dark, dark sea.

'Mr Sharpe?' the little girl's voice continued, disembodied in the darkness. 'I have something to tell you.'

He was able to move but not in the direction he wanted to go. He had lost control of his functions and found himself turning to where he thought, where he *knew* the voice was coming from. Although it was dark and all he could see was his own pluming, glowing breath, he knew he was facing the door between his bedroom and the hall.

That was where he saw her.

She was just a small thing, beautiful in the innocent way girls were before the ravages of puberty and time took them. She was small, timid, trusting.

'I've come to tell you something, Mr Sharpe.'

Her face became clear in the darkness. She looked exactly as she had the last time he'd seen her, the last time anyone had seen her. The only difference was she was smiling.

She hadn't been smiling then.

'I've come to tell you … I forgive you, Mr Sharpe.'

'Lisa!'

This gasp was his last.

Harry Sharpe, a teacher at Kitchowa High School and the town of Kitchowa's very own boogieman for as long as most could remember, died alone on the floor of his bedroom.

2.

I DON'T THINK any of us had ever really known loss until the year Mother fell sick over Christmas. Yes, we'd lived through the passing of our father, but we were only children then and had never understood what was happening. This was different in almost every way imaginable.

She had always been my rock, my brother Anthony's too. When we'd grown and flown the nest, she had never once tried to guilt us into staying close. She allowed, even encouraged us to spread our wings, to find our own nests, with the true grace of a real strong, independent woman. We both moved from Kitchowa within a few years of each other. I didn't go *too* far, having been accepted into the college of my choice. There, I met a boy. It became serious, and when school finished, we moved to Minnesota. Anthony pretty much did the same. He got a job out of town, met a boy, but he ended up moving a little further afield. He made it all the way to Toronto, where he stopped and settled. Even though he wasn't really *that* far away from her, she could never see over the US/Canadian border. To her, he was a whole country away.

He found himself a nice house, an easy commute to work, and all the freedom he and Richard needed to enjoy their life together, plus a fantastic view over a picturesque lake to boot.

Even though we'd both moved away, we always knew our hearts had never really left Kitchowa.

We'd enjoyed a loving childhood growing up in the small but tight community. The summers had been warm, the winters long and cold, but the beautiful springs and colourful falls in between were always worth the slog. There was always enough to do and enough friends to do it with. But as life moved on and our friends began to drift away, dreaming their own dreams of the big, bad city, the pull for us became too irresistible to ignore.

Mom stayed.

I'd invited her to come to Minnesota with me for a few weeks. This was done surreptitiously, with a view to her moving out and living in the city, where life wasn't so harsh and I was less than a mile away. She came, she enjoyed herself, and then she left, saying that city life was just too fast for her.

Since Dad died, she had done everything around the house, gardening, maintenance, and everything in between, so living in an apartment overlooking a coffee house chain was never going to work for her. The noise was just too much for her. Cars driving by all hours of the night and the sirens of emergency vehicles racing backwards and forwards. Even my apartment, which, for the city, was a good size, was just not to her liking. She was always complaining that there was just no room to breathe.

She returned to Kitchowa, grumbling and mumbling. 'How the hell do city folks get by?' she asked for the entirety of the four-and-a-half-hour drive home.

City life wasn't for her, and on my return with her, I knew county life was no longer for me.

We agreed that the journey wasn't as long as it seemed, that it wasn't a taxing drive to see each other, and I did my best to make it at least once a month. Anthony would see her when he could, not as frequent as I did but enough, for a boy anyway.

Then marriage came for me.

The boy I met in college didn't turn out to be the boy he promised to be, but his cousin did. I married at the age of twenty-six and a fresh-faced recruit at a dream job. Life was treating me fine as I passed from being Alison Wynne to Alison Dickinson.

Anthony married too. Although it wasn't official—as same sex marriages were still not legal in Canada—in his eyes, his husband's eyes, and the eyes of me, our mom, and all our friends, it was the most legitimate marriage anyone had ever seen.

We were a close family, living nicely in each other's pockets, albeit hundreds of miles apart. We still looked out for each other and could be there in less than half a day's drive if needed.

Except maybe in winter.

From personal experience, I knew Wisconsin winters could be harsh and unforgiving, so from October through to March, I would worry almost constantly about how Mom was dealing with the cold and the snow. Whenever there was a break in the weather, either me or Anthony would go to see her, taking her food and anything else she might need to see her out until the melt.

Then I fell pregnant.

That was also the year I found out my first real boyfriend's cousin was not the boy he promised to be either. He was having an affair. Apparently, it was my fault. I'd become so stuck in my ways and so boring that he'd had to find excitement elsewhere.

I was devastated.

I'd made many friends in Minnesota, but the only real people I wanted in my life after the breakup were my mother and my brother.

They both came, and they got me through it.

Grace was born in July. She was my reason for continuing and my little bundle of joy.

Alan, Grace's father, wasn't present at the birth. His new girlfriend wouldn't allow it.

It was his loss.

I brought Grace up as a single parent. I'd left a big fat *blank* in the box on her birth certificate where it asked for the father's information. It stayed that way. Alan had made his choice. He didn't want to be a part of her life, and she never once missed what she never had.

Life was good for a while. I moved out of the apartment; it wasn't convivial for life with a small child. I found myself a beautiful, comfortable little two-story, two-bedroom house on the outskirts of town. Because it was a foreclosure repo, I manged to get it at a steal. The money I was earning was more than enough to pay the mortgage, and I was shocked when I found out the payments worked out cheaper than renting.

Even without a man in our lives, we were on the up.

Christmases came, and Christmases went, and everything moved along at pace.

I got a promotion and was allowed to work from home some to cater to my growing child. Anthony and Richard set up a website company, and it blossomed due to their sterling work, allowing them the freedom to come and go as they pleased. My brother and his husband were a constant presence in Grace's life.

It worked out well for all involved, as Anthony doted on his niece and the feelings were returned in abundance.

Then came the phone call, the one that both of us had been silently dreading for a few years.

It was Doc Browning in Kitchowa.

The man was nearly as old as the town. He was the doctor who'd brought both me and my brother into the world. He was also the doctor who kept my father out of pain's way when his turn to leave us was at hand.

'Ali, it's your mother …'

His gravelly voice hadn't changed one bit, not since I was a little girl and he'd treated me for the colds, flus, and any other maladies that children suffered, and Anthony for every scrape and bang he got himself into. The only deviation from his normal rich voice was the touch of melancholy in his words.

I knew instantly what the call was about.

'How long has she got, Doc?' I asked, my head bent low. The plastic case of the phone was slick in my tightened fist.

The gravelled sigh on the other end of the line told me everything I needed to hear. 'Well, little one …'—he'd always called me that; a small term of endearment that still made me gush—'she might see out the winter. But I'll tell you this … this will be her last Christmas.'

I smiled. It was the only thing I could do to combat the sadness spreading within me. 'In that case, it looks like Kitchowa will have a few extra visitors this Christmas, Doc. Can you inform the police and the fire department that Anthony will be coming too?' I said, attempting to lift the mood.

As Doctor Browning and my mother had been close friends since school and he was as close to us as a beloved uncle, this news seemed to cheer him up, and I noted a slight inflection in his voice. 'I will, little one. I will!'

~~~~

When Anthony came out as gay, it surprised everyone. In a small town like Kitchowa, things like that were usually picked up early, while in school or playing sports. With Anthony, it came out of the blue, and it broke a lot of the girls' hearts in the process. He was part of the jock crowd, playing on the football team in the fall and running track during the spring. This afforded him with a very healthy female following.

I was more shocked than anyone when he told me. I'd been in college for three years and he was in his freshman year when I got the phone call.

'Alli!'

I remember the terror in his voice on the other end of the line as if I was on the phone with him right now. I also remember my heart dropping into my stomach as five thousand awful scenarios danced through my head, each worse than the last.

'Alli,' he stuttered again. I could tell just by those two words that he had been drinking heavily. 'I've got something I need to tell you.'

These words deepened my dread. I gripped the phone, sat down, and readied myself for him to tell me the worst thing a brother could tell his sister.

'It's something I've been wanting to tell you for a … a while.' He paused then, and I could hear the sloshing of whatever bottle he was drinking from pass by the phone. 'But I just haven't known how.'

The Christmas holidays were days away, and I was due to go home to see Mom. Anthony had already informed us he wouldn't be home this year, as he'd picked up a part-time job for the holidays, and there was just too much money to be made. I hadn't heard him sound so serious since the time he'd spent a weekend in county jail for a fight in a bar he shouldn't have been in the first place. I knew something was wrong, and my hands were almost dripping as I gripped the phone receiver. 'What is it, Ant? You're scaring me. Are you in some kind of trouble?' I asked, not sure I really wanted to know.

'Kind of,' came his reply.

I swallowed. My heart was tapdancing in my chest. I'd always been protective towards my little brother, even though he towered over me and outweighed me by maybe fifty pounds. 'Ant, tell me what it is,' I demanded, not enjoying this conversation.

I was replied to with silence. Loud music was playing in the background, so I knew he was at some kind of party but was far enough away from the action to allow a phone call. Then I heard a small sob. I'd never heard him cry before, not since we were kids, anyway. My hackles were already up, but when I heard that pitiful sound, I wished beyond all wishes that I could have closed my eyes and travelled the distance between us through the phone lines to be there with him, ready to wrap my arms around him, to comfort him.

'Ant, come on, now, I'm terrified here. What is it? What have you done?' Then a thought occurred to me, one that wasn't abhorrent but could have messed up his academic plans. 'Did you get someone pregnant? Is that what this is all about?'

His laugh told me that wasn't it, but it also told me that the situation maybe wasn't as bad as I had originally thought.

'No sis, I haven't gotten anyone pregnant. That's kind of hard to do when you're gay.'

'It's not. I've seen programmes on TV and read about people who are gay. It didn't stop them ...' It was that precise moment—I remember it distinctly—when I realised what he'd just told me. The world stopped for just a few moments. My mouth was dry, and I felt as if I couldn't speak.

Finally, 'You're what?' was the only thing I could push out of the desert in my mouth. I couldn't believe what I was hearing. It couldn't be Anthony telling me this; he wasn't the type. *But then what is the type?* I thought. I began to laugh. I think it broke the barrier between us, the one he'd artificially erected to hide his sexuality. 'Ant, that's … erm, unexpected,' I replied, still laughing and still at a loss of anything else to say.

I could sense the relief on the other end of the phone. 'You … you're OK with this? You're not going to judge me?' he asked. I could hear him swallowing tears.

I tutted and wiped away the tears that were tickling my cheeks. I never knew then, and I still don't today, if they were tears of happiness that he had chosen to tell me, or relief that he wasn't going to prison for doing something characteristically stupid. 'Anthony, it's 1998. I think the world has moved on a little bit by now. You know I love you no matter what.'

There was a shaky sigh over the phone, followed by another sob. 'Alli, you … you don't know what that means to me.' He was crying again, but I knew now they were happy tears. 'You know I won't be home for Christmas this year. Would … would you tell Mom for me? I really don't know if I have it in me to break it to her.'

We spent another hour on the phone. We laughed and we cried. I told him all about the man I had been seeing, telling him it was nothing serious, and he told me all about Richard, who he was in a relationship with.

It was a beautiful chat.

I broke it to Mom over a quiet Christmas dinner. It was just the two of us, and it was lovely. All she did was shrug her shoulders and laugh. 'As long as he's happy,' was her only comment.

That was Mom all over.

3.

'ANT, WHAT DID you have planned for Christmas?'

'Hey, sis, I'm fine, thanks for asking. How are you?' There was a hint of sarcasm in his voice, but I knew it was in jest. There had never been any animosity between us.

'Anthony, I need to know.'

There must have been something in my voice, something that told him I wasn't joking, that this was not really a social call. His voice lost all its joviality in an instant. Maybe it was because I called him Anthony.

'Erm …' He paused for a moment—to me, it felt like an eternity. 'We've don't have anything special planned as yet. We're upgrading the company systems over the holidays, but nothing is written in stone. Why? What's the urgency? What's going on?'

I could tell he was holding something back. There was something he wasn't telling me, but I didn't have time to pry.

'It's Mom. Doc Browning was just on the phone. She has cancer, and it's bad.' I thought I'd have trouble telling him. I thought my voice would crack or an escaping sob would steal my words, but it didn't. They came out as clear as day.

'Shit,' was his only reply.

I sighed down the line; it was *my* only reply.

'Did he say how long?'

'Months, at best, maybe weeks. He said if we wanted to get another Christmas with her, this would be the one.'

'OK. Right.' I could hear the panic in his voice; it was akin to what I heard on his phone call when he came out years before.

'I'll work it out with Richard. He'll have to stay here to look after the upgrade. I'll, erm … I'll be there. I'll drive up on the … shit, what date is it today?' I could hear him flicking through the pages of a book, and my heart swelled. I knew exactly how he was feeling, as I was feeling the same. 'I can be there on the twenty-second. I'll drive over in the morning. That'll be OK, won't it?'

I could hear the Canadian in his voice, and it made me smile a little, even through the weight of the conversation. 'That'll be great. I was looking at the twenty-second too. It's a shame Richard won't be able to make it. We could have had a proper family get-together.'

'He'll be disappointed too, but we've had these, erm, upgrades planned for a while. I'll see if he can drive up in-between, and maybe we can celebrate New Year's together.'

'Grace would love that. She loves and misses you guys,' I said, tears filling my eyes.

'We miss her too, and you.'

'OK,' I said, taking a deep breath. I wanted to hide the shaking but knew I was failing miserably. 'I have to go. I need to call Mom. Let her know the good news.'

'Tell her I'll call tonight. I love you, sis.'

'I love you too …' As I hung up, the feeling of separation, of the vast miles between us with Mom languishing sick somewhere in the middle, was overwhelming. The fat tears that had been threatening finally flowed.

'Mommy, what's the matter?'

I turned to see a face that I knew could always make me smile. Grace, my seven-year-old daughter. Her blonde hair in pigtails caused my heart to swell. I broke a genuine smile and wiped away the tears. 'Nothing's the matter, honey.' I sniffed. 'Come here and give me one of those big old hugs you're so good at.'

She did.

'Don't cry, Mommy, everything's gonna be all right. You'll see.' She spoke in that delightfully cute way that children who are nearly eight are so good at—the slight mispronunciation of letters, and you can no longer be mad or sad at anything anymore.

'I'm not sad, honey,' I little-white-lied to her. 'I'm happy. We're going to be spending Christmas with Grandma and Uncle Anthony.'

Her face lit up. Her smile brought out the dimples in her cheeks that I hoped would never leave. 'When do we go?' she shouted as she rushed towards the stairs. 'I'm going to pack. Will Uncle Richard be there too?'

'No, honey, but he might get there for New Year's,' I shouted after her.

There was another, distant squeal of joy as I heard her bedroom door crash open.

With my sadness passed, or at least paused, I thought I'd built up enough courage to call Mom. I took a few deep breaths before gripping the phone while I pondered the buttons. I could see the correct ones, the ones I needed to use to make the call connect, but still, I procrastinated.

Growing up, Mom had been the rock that both mine and Anthony's lives were built upon. Dad had died when we were both very young, so she had been both parents to us. She'd been loving and caring, cooking, cleaning, and washing; she had also been the breadwinner and was fiercely defensive of our family unit. Not that we needed much defending. We were always so independent.

Now, in her hour of need, I felt myself lacking in the skills required to call her, the one person I loved in equal measure only to my daughter and brother. *What if she sounds sick?* I thought. *Or, worse than that, what if she starts to cry?* I didn't know if I could handle either of those scenarios. *Does this make me a bad daughter?* I was overthinking how Grace might react if she ever got the news about me being sick.

That thought gave me all the motivation I needed.

Mom was sick and needed me to be strong and to be there for her. Christmas or not, it was my responsibility, least of all as the eldest child. I dialled the number from memory and sat on the small chair beneath the phone base on the wall.

I had more flashbacks to the phone call with Anthony years before. My heart was pounding, and even though the heater was doing a fantastic job of warming the room, I was suddenly freezing. The line rang and rang, and this is awful to admit, but I was relieved, thinking no one was going to answer. Then suddenly, a confident, healthy voice boomed out a solid, 'Hello?'

She sounded good, she sounded like Mom, and that was enough for me.

'Mom, it's Alison. How are you feeling?' It was a good enough opening, but I could already guess her next defensive move.

'Has Doc Browning been calling you? Telling his tales? He's an interfering old fart if ever there was one.'

I had guessed correctly.

I exhaled slowly. Deep down, I was happy she sounded like her old self, but I was also more than a little disgusted at myself for my hesitancy to call. *It's only human,* I thought. *After all, she's been your role model for thirty-one years. It's only natural to not want to see the demise of the strongest person in your life.*

'Yes, Mom, he has. I don't believe they're tall tales, though. So, back to my original question. How are you feeling?'

There was silence for a couple of moments. Then I heard the breath. That was when I knew for sure. She needed me. Not only me, but she needed Anthony, and Grace too. We all *had* to be there for her. If this was to be her very last Christmas, then she needed, no she deserved, us all to be with her.

'It's cancer, Alli. Doc says it's everywhere.'

'Is there anything they can do? Any therapy?' I asked this even though I was a believer that chemotherapy was nothing more than a series of experiments the medical industry performed on sick people. Not normally one for conspiracy theories, but I had seen too many people wither away and be in agony while on this therapy.

23

'Oh, you know what that chemo shit does to your body. I'd rather take my chances with the cancer than have those chemicals running around, making me sicker than I already am. No, I'm just going to deal with it all the old-fashioned way.'

'What's that, Mom? Booze?' I don't know why I got angry with her then, but I did. The last comment was supposed to cut her, to make her realise she was being silly, that she should take the chemotherapy and get herself another six months of life. But then I thought of the quality of that last six months. Vomiting, uncontrollable shaking, too weak to get out of bed. All of this along with the knowledge of what was inevitable hanging over her head.

I instantly regretted my retort.

It seemed she hadn't acknowledged the snide remark anyway. 'I hadn't thought of that. It doesn't sound too bad, actually,' she laughed down the line. 'No, I'm going to take a regimen of painkillers and spend the last months of my life enjoying myself to the max. I might even go dancing.'

I smiled. I wished she could have seen it, as it was all for her. I wiped a rogue tear from my cheek as I envisioned her in her old, comfortable chair, sitting by the window, gazing out into the fields while she talked to me.

'We're coming for Christmas, Mom. All of us. Me, Anthony, and Gracie.'

'No, list—'

I didn't allow her to finish her protest.

'We're coming, and that's that. We'll all be there on Wednesday. That's the twenty-second. I'll get some decorations, and Anthony will get a tree. We can decorate the house together and have a big family Christmas like we used to. We can unleash the ghosts of the McEvoy family once and for all. OK?'

I felt the smile, probably the same one I sent to her, coming at me down the line. 'Oh, so all the ghosts are on my side of the family, are they? Not your father's? What about Richard? Is he coming too?' Mom had always loved Richard, as he always made a big fuss of her, and she revelled in the attention.

'He won't be there for Christmas, but he should be for New Year's,' I replied.

'New Year's?' she shouted. 'You mean I'm going to have to put up with you all for a full week?'

'Yes, Mom, maybe more than that. You won't have to do a thing. Just relax, put your feet up, and let your kids and grandkid look after *you* for once.'

We talked then for another half hour, mostly about how I was doing, how Gracie was doing in school, how busy Anthony was these days, about if there was a man in my life yet. In the end, I put the phone down feeling so much better about myself and about Mom's condition. The rest of the day, even though tinged with sadness, was a good day. It felt like an already healthy relationship had just gotten a little better.

'Grace, where are you?' I shouted up the stairs. There was no reply, although I could hear her banging about in her room. 'Gracie, what are you doing?'

As I got to the top of the stairs, I saw her sitting on the floor, a suitcase open before her. It was filled to the brim with teddy bears and dolls. She looked up at me as I stood in the doorway. 'I'm all set to go to Grandma's,' she announced with wide eyes and the biggest smile I'd seen for a long time.

'Do you think you maybe should have left some room for clothes in there?' I asked.

She looked at the suitcase and ruffled her brow, and she looked so much like Mom at that moment that I had to look twice. 'No.' She shook her head as if this was the most logical decision in the world. 'I'll take another one for them.' I couldn't argue with that, so I sat next to her and began rummaging through the contents of the case.

'Mommy?' she asked. Her voice was so serious at that moment that I thought she might have picked up on the conversation I'd just had over the phone.

'Yes, honey?' I replied, ready to answer any question she might have had with whatever lie would keep her away from the ugly truth, maintaining her innocence for another few months, at least until the inevitable happened.

'If we're going to be at Grandma's for Christmas, will Santa know I'm there?'

This was a good question. It was a seven-year-old's question, a Gracie question. I leaned in to tickle her. 'Of course he will, honey-pie. His elves know every move you make.'

She looked physically relieved, like a great weight had been lifted off her shoulders. I made a mental note to pack another suitcase filled with gifts.

Later that evening, when Grace was asleep, I called her dad and told him the good news: that he didn't have any responsibilities towards his daughter over the holidays. He protested a little, but I could hear the relief in his voice. 'I'll pop over on Tuesday with her present,' he said.

Don't bother, I thought, remembering the garbage dime store gifts he got her last year due to the hefty down payment he'd had to make on his new car. Thankfully, this conversation was over within a few minutes. I was shaking my head as I replaced the receiver. *Everything is set,* I thought, bringing my smile back. *We're going home for the holidays.*

I made myself a cup of hot chocolate and sat on the couch, ready to watch some banal TV. I found myself drifting after about ten minutes, so I turned everything off, washed my cup, and made my way up the stairs.

That's when I heard the voices coming from Grace's room.

I stopped in my tracks and leaned against the door. The hairs on the back of my neck stood to attention, and all thoughts of sleep vanished just like that. It was only a whisper, but in the silence of the house, it carried. 'I can't wait!' It was unmistakably Grace's voice, and she sounded excited. 'It's going to be such fun meeting you. Are you *really* the Spirit of Christmas?'

I grasped the handle of the door and was surprised to find it cold. So cold, in fact, that my instinct was to let it go. And then the whispering stopped. My heart was once again pounding. This time, it was for a different reason. Despite the chill and my cold hand, the rest of my body was suddenly clammy, damp with sweat.

Did she say Spirit of Christmas? I had to ask myself, even though I knew she had. It was this *exact* phrase that made me determined to go into the room. I pulled the sleeve of my nightshirt over my hand and touched the handle again, steeling myself for another frost burn. To my surprise, it was normal temperature. I realised this was something I would have to think about later, because now, I needed to get inside to see if Grace was OK and to see who she was talking to.

The room was dark and filled with shadows. The night-light in the corner was doing its job admirably, casting a gentle glow over the room, making it a cosy ambiance. I quickly noted Grace was in her bed, her covers rising and falling in time with the rhythm of her breathing. I scanned the room but could find nothing out of place.

Everything was normal.

Who could she have been talking to?

I made my way over to her. Her blonde hair was poking out of the covers, spreading over her pillow, but that was all. She always slept with the blankets pulled over her head. A light snore reassured me everything was fine. I sucked in my cheeks as I looked at her in the twilight of the room. The whispering must have been her talking in her sleep, obviously excited about her Christmas trip to Grandma's. As I smiled and leaned in to kiss the top of her head, I became aware that the room was uncomfortably cold. I was surprised to see breath pluming before my face on each exhale. I looked around again, wondering what could have caused such a dramatic drop in temperature. I checked that the windows were closed and that the air blowing from the vent in the ceiling was on, keeping the room warm. Everything was normal.

So why is it so cold?

A small movement in my peripheral vision caught my attention, and I spun around, my heart suddenly hammering, attempting to escape the confines of my chest. However, everything was as it should be. It was just the door settling back into its natural position. My heart, still beating a solid rock song in my chest, was making me feel dizzy. I needed to get out of the room, but I didn't want to leave Grace.

Then, as suddenly as the oppressive feeling had come, it went. The room was its usual nighttime temperature again, and everything seemed normal.

I sighed as I began to calm down, realising the conversation with my mother must have affected me more than I'd thought it had. I checked Grace once more, stroking her head, happy to see her fast asleep. After one more glance around the room, I was satisfied there was nothing amiss. *I need to get to bed. It's been a long day,* I thought, leaving the room, closing the door behind me.

As it shut, a voice passed through my head. 'Alli …'

I closed my eyes, attempting to block out my vivid and obviously overworked imagination. I made it to my bedroom, wrapped myself in the covers, and closed my eyes.

~~~~

I must have gotten a good few hours of solid sleep because I was awakened by Grace.

'Mommy,' the voice hissed in my ear.

I was instantly awake. The dream I was having, where I was trapped inside an iceberg with my daughter, came rushing back. My heart, kickstarted by the shock of the whisper, fell back into the abnormal rhythm of last night when I had heard the same whisper.

I knew it was Grace, but I was still trapped in that strange dream. Instead of the word 'Mommy' being whispered to me, I heard 'Alison.' My name, and one Grace never called me.

'Alison …'

I bolted upright.

It must have scared Grace, as she emitted a small yelp. Seeing me move so quickly must have petrified her. My eyesight refocused, and as I looked upon the face of the most beautiful little girl in the whole world, I began to calm down. Her face was creased, and her eyes, even in the dim illumination, looked wet, like she'd been crying. Even in the fuzzy state of being rudely awakened, I didn't think her state had been caused by my shocked exit from a dream.

'Hey, baby girl,' I whispered, pulling her close, stroking her hair. She climbed into my bed, and I could feel the warmth of her little body snuggle into me. I always loved that. 'What time is it?' My voice sounded thick with sleep, even though I was fully awake.

Grace turned her head to regard the clock at the side of my bed. 'There's a three and a thirty-five,' she whispered. 'Maybe it's thirty-five past three.'

This brought a smile to my sleep-addled face. 'What are you doing, baby?' I needed to ask because, even though she was only seven, she was not in the habit of getting into my bed. She loved her bedroom far too much for that.

'I can't sleep,' she whispered as if it was a secret.

'OK, do you want to tell me about it?'

'Not really,' she replied as if that was an even bigger secret.

'Oh, go on. You can tell me everything,' I said, making it into a kind of game. I was worried about her after the episode in her room, and now this; something felt … off.

She tried to smile. I could see it in her glistening eyes, but her face didn't seem to have received the same information. The corners of her mouth were turning up but looked to have given up halfway through. 'I want to sleep, Mommy, but the little girl won't let me. She keeps saying she'd too excited about us going to Grandma's. I told her it was just me, you, and Uncle Anthony going, but she said she'll be there too.' She pulled away from me then, getting herself comfortable. I knew at that moment I would have a companion for the rest of the night. 'She said something about the Spirit of Christmas. I didn't know what she was talking about. I thought she meant Santa. Will she be coming to Grandma's with us, Mommy?'

I shook my head, not knowing what to say. Before tonight, I hadn't heard the phrase *Spirit of Christmas* for years.

'No, baby. She's not invited,' I laughed, trying to reassure her there was nothing wrong, but not entirely convincing myself.

'Can I stay with you tonight, Mommy?' It wasn't really a question, as she was already snuggled in tight.

'Of course you can,' I whispered, stroking her long blonde hair again.

She gave a tired squeak, pulled the blankets up to her chin, and turned the other way, facing the window. 'Let's not let Lisa in, Mommy, even if she asks? I think she's nice, but I want it to be just me and you.'

I stroked her head and wrapped the covers around her, keeping her warm and safe. 'There's no room in here for Lisa, honey. Just you and me,' I whispered.

Within a few minutes, she was purring, sleeping the sleep of the innocent. The light snore was both comforting and relaxing, but alas, for me, the illusive sandman refused to revisit. There was something about the experience in Grace's room and her mentioning the *Spirit of Christmas*, not once but twice, that wouldn't allow my brain to turn off.

As I eventually drifted towards sleep, I did so with a name on my lips.

Lisa!

4.

EVERYTHING WAS PACKED into the car. There were gaily wrapped packages, a cooler filled with food, bags of bedding, and suitcases of clothes. Nothing was going to be left to chance for this holiday.

'All right, Tiddles,' I shouted. Grace giggled. It was a new name I'd just made up, and she seemed to like it. 'Have you been to the bathroom? It's a four-and-a-half-hour drive, maybe more if the weather's bad.' I looked into the clear blue sky, marvelling at the contrast of it to the thick, white coating that was hugging the sidewalks and rooftops. 'I don't want to be stopping every few miles for little tinkles.'

This tickled Grace again. 'Tinkly Tiddles,' she sang as she climbed into the back seat of the SUV. She knew the drill and was old enough to strap herself into her child safety seat.

'That's right,' I laughed. 'Tinkly Tiddles. I've left my cell phone inside. I'm just going to grab it and call Uncle Ant. Hopefully, we should arrive at the same time. That would be a nice surprise for Grandma, don't you think?' I closed but didn't lock the door and went back into the house.

I could see the car from the front door, so I didn't have to worry about Grace getting out without me noticing while I talked to Anthony. 'Ant,' I gushed as he answered on the third ring. 'I'm just calling to let you know we're leaving. We should be there about …'—I looked at the time; it was ten minutes past nine— 'two, maybe three at the latest.'

'Excellent,' came his excited voice over the line. 'I'm a little delayed. I won't be leaving until at least twelve. I've got a bit I need to do here before I can get away. I should be there about five or six.'

'OK, bro. I love you. I can't wait to see you.'

'I love you too, sis, and Gracie. You drive safe, now. The weather reports are looking good along the way. You should make good time.'

'I will, and you too. See you tonight, soldier.'

I looked out towards the car, and my stomach dropped. I could still see Grace in the back seat, but she looked like she was talking to someone, someone I couldn't see. I shoved the phone into my pocket and panic-ran towards the car, ready to confront whoever was talking to my child. She was becoming more animated in her conversation, and I tried to focus, to see who had climbed into the back of my car and was conversing with my Grace.

When I got there, she was alone.

She was still talking, but as I pushed my face to the window, she stopped. I reached out and pulled at the handle to the driver's side door, yanking it open. I burst in, thrusting my head into the back seat. As a fan of scary movies, I'd seen this scenario far too many times. A bad guy hiding in the back seat, ready to jump out at the unsuspecting driver once the car was in motion. To my relief, and confusion, there was no one there. Knowing there was no room for anyone to hide in the back, I was content there were no bad guys inside and it must have just been Grace playing a game, talking to herself.

She was looking at me as if I'd gone mad. 'What are you doing, Mommy?' she asked, a chuckle in her voice.

Ignoring the question, I closed the door and got in the driver's seat. With a shaky hand, I turned the key in the ignition. The engine roared into life. I looked into the rearview mirror for anyone who shouldn't have been there. When I saw there was only my daughter, I tipped her a wink.

'Are we all set, sweetheart?' I asked, a smile pasted onto my sweat-lined face.

'Yeah, Mommy. Let's go to Grandma's,' she shouted in reply. 'You forgot to close the door, Mommy.'

I looked out of the windshield and saw the front door wide open. I chuffed and climbed back out of the car, front door keys in my hand. 'Mommy's going cray cray,' I laughed.

This made Grace laugh too.

As I pulled out of the driveway, a cold chill ran through me again. I glanced in the mirror just in time to see Grace muttering to herself again. 'Who are you talking to, baby?' I asked, not sure if I really wanted an answer.

It turned out I *didn't* want it.

'Oh, just Lisa,' she replied in a matter-of-fact tone.

'All right.' I nodded. I was trying to keep my tone as relaxed as I could, even though I could feel my stomach bubbling. 'So, what's Lisa saying, honey?' I was trying my very best to sound calm, but my hands were slipping on the wheel, they were that wet, and the cold shivers running up and down my spine wouldn't go away. The issue with the cold door handle, the talking in her sleep, and now this; it was all getting to be a little too much for me.

'Oh, she's really excited. She said she can't wait to meet me in person.'

'She can't wait to meet you in person? You were just talking to her, baby. Isn't she here now?'

'No, silly. She's already there, at Grandma's. She can talk to me even from far away. She's funny like that.'

This conversation wasn't doing me any favours. 'She sounds like lots of fun,' I lied. 'So how long have you been friends with … um, Lisa?'

'I don't know. Just a few days, maybe. She's nice, but sometimes she's sad. She said she's looking forward to this Christmas. She said there are lots of things for us to do.'

I looked at my daughter again in the rearview mirror. She was playing with the hair of her favourite doll, not looking at me. Her vivid imagination was having no effect on her at all, but I could feel goosebumps crawling all over me as I grasped the steering wheel a little tighter. 'Well, enough about Lisa for now,' I replied, trying to keep the shake out of my voice. 'Let's talk about how excited you are to see Grandma and Uncle Ant.'

'Yeah,' she yelled. 'And let's talk about Santa and Christmas. Can we put Christmas songs on the radio, Mommy? Can we?'

There was no way I could refuse such a cute request, so I slipped a Christmas CD I had brought into the player in the car's dash. 'White Christmas' came on, and all thoughts of Lisa must have vanished from her head as she swayed in time to the slow song.

'I love the old man singing!' she shouted and promptly put on a deep voice, singing along with the tune, mimicking Bing Crosby.

I sang along too. A few miles in and we had forgotten all about Lisa.

However, it seemed Lisa hadn't forgotten about us.

5.

AS I PULLED onto Mom's street, twilight was full upon us. The sparseness of streetlights added to the eerie scene as my headlights cast a yellowish, phosphorescent glow on the snow on the ground and in the branches of the trees. The white stuff had been falling, as it tends to do in Wisconsin in winter, but it was nowhere near as bad as it had been on some of the journeys I'd taken back and forth. As Anthony predicted, we had made good time, and Grace had slept for long portions of it, giving me time to reflect on what we were about to encounter.

Even though she had sounded like her old self on the phone, my mind had mapped out every disastrous and negative scenario it could muster. From her being stick thin and emaciated to her being bed-ridden and ringing a bell every fifteen minutes to empty her bedpan. Not that I would have refused to do that, she was my mother after all, but I didn't want Grace to have her last memories of Grandma as a sickly old woman.

As it turned out, my fears were completely unfounded, as when my headlights bounced over her driveway, my mother did her own bouncing, out of the house, wrapped in a thick coat, scarf, and hat. There was a huge, healthy smile on her face.

'Oh, finally, there you are,' she gushed. 'I've been waiting all day to see my two sweet girls.'

Grace had been asleep, but the slowing of the car as it bumped onto Mom's driveway roused her. It was beautiful to watch her sleepy eyes morph big and wide as she saw her grandma tapping eagerly on her window. She must have had a Santa hat in the pocket of her housecoat, as suddenly, she was wearing one, along with a huge grin.

'Grandma?' Grace asked, her voice still thick with sleep. She asked this question as if she hadn't known we were going to see her today and this was a special surprise.

I noticed her struggling with the seatbelt to get out of her booster, eager to greet her grandma with a hug and a kiss, so I reached into the back and unclicked the buckle. Once free, there was no stopping her. She flung herself at the door, opening it with such ferocity that she nearly knocked Mom back into the snow. She buried herself in her grandma's embrace, wrapping her arms around her so tightly it looked like she was attempting to absorb her.

My mother was laughing and crying at the same time. 'Oh, my sweet girls. My sweet, sweet girls. I've missed you both so much,' she sobbed.

As I kissed her on the cheek, I felt her paper-thin skin almost crinkle beneath my lips. But as she turned to look at me, I saw the ferocious fire in her eyes, the same one I had grown up with and loved so much. It twinkled and shone. There was so much life within those brown irises.

'Alli,' she gasped, wiping the tears from her eyes. 'My beautiful Alison.' She held my face with her gloved hands. The strength she held me with was so alive that I found myself second-guessing Doctor Browning's prognosis.

This woman has years left in her, I thought, falling into her embrace.

'Let's get indoors. I've got the fireplace going, and the house is cosy warm.' She laughed. The sound was so high-pitched, so child-like, that I had to double-take to see if it had been Grace who was laughing and not Mom.

I watched as my daughter took hold of my mother's hand, deserting me outside in the cold for the much better option of the promise of warmth, hot chocolate, and Grandma. I rolled my eyes and watched some light flakes of snow fall in the stark illumination of the car's headlights. Knowing how fast a flurry can become something different, something dangerous, in these parts, I opened the back and began removing the items we'd brought with us. Knowing it would be at least three trips to get everything inside, and I wouldn't be getting much help from either of them, I sighed and began my first journey, carrying the larger bags filled with bedding.

I felt the warmth of the house before I entered it.

A strong feeling of being welcomed home overpowered me, and as I put the bags down on the long couch in the living room, I inhaled. The smell hit me like a runaway truck. Cookies, cinnamon, and bread. Add coffee into that mix and they would have been all of my favourite smells in the whole world. The sensory overload transformed me into a little girl, zooming and zipping my way through this very house. Anthony chasing me, his heavy diaper dangling around his behind, squealing with joy at the high intensity of the game.

There had been so many happy times here.

There's also been unhappy times, Alison. You need to remember that too.

I didn't know where that thought came from, but the intensity of it slapped me in the face, bringing me back to Earth with a bump. I shivered as I tried to rid myself of the particularly nasty feeling. I went back out to the car to get more bags.

I walked to the end of the driveway and gazed down the long street. The twilight of the few working streetlamps coupled with the mist the falling snow was creating meant I couldn't see too far down, but I could just about make out the lights of Mr Sharpe's house in the near distance. He had once been a teacher at the high school and had always been the local boogieman. In all the time I'd lived on this street, there had never once been a single Christmas light on his property.

Today was no different.

Today was the twenty-second day of December, and on the drive through town and down the county road, we had seen many houses already decorated with colourful illuminated displays. It always gave me a funny feeling in my stomach when I saw Christmas lights, and watching the way Grace responded to them, with all her coos and ahhs, it was good to know that feeling had been passed down to her.

'Penny for them!'

The voice made me jump. I'd been so engrossed in my thoughts about the beautiful winter scene before me that I'd missed the car pulling into the street behind me. I turned, my heart thumping in my throat, and saw the third most beautiful sight I'd seen that day. Anthony was standing next to me, looking down the county road. His smile was as charming as it had ever been, although now it was nestling inside the beginnings of half-decent beard. He was wearing a red woollen hat with his collar pulled up to combat the cold.

'Ant? Oh my God, you scared the crap out of me,' I shouted, and play punched him on the shoulder before falling into his strong arms. I allowed them to wrap tight around me. 'It's so good to see you,' I sobbed into his already wet coat.

'You too, sis. You too. So, what's so interesting down there?' His neck stretched to look in the direction I'd been gazing.

'I was just thinking about when we were kids,' I said, wiping the tears from my eyes.

'Jesus, we were awful to poor old Mr Sharpe. I think it was mostly because he didn't put up any Christmas lights.'

I looked at him and pulled a wry smile. 'It wasn't *just* because of the lights, now, was it?' I asked.

'Well, it might have been because his house was haunted too,' he replied, shrugging and laughing at the same time.

I laughed, then took his hands and looked at him. My brother could always make me smile.

'How is she?' he asked finally.

I nodded and wiped at the fresh tears that were forming in my eyes. 'She great …' I said before feeling those strong arms around me again. 'She's great …' I repeated, this time in a sob.

'Come on. Let's get in and get this Christmas started.' He looked up at the house and shook his head. 'The first thing I'm going to do tomorrow is get up there and cover this house in lights from top to bottom. We're going all out this year.'

I squeezed his hand and led him inside to the screams and squeals of a loving, doting mother and a star-struck niece.

6.

'GO ON, ALLI, the dare's been set. You have to do it now.' The little boy wearing the red galoshes and dungarees was shouting from the end of the driveway. It was dark, not quite full dark, but a twilight that promised the mystery and excitement that kids on a Halloween night can't get enough of.

'I … I don't know about this,' she whispered. The eight-year-old tomboy was standing just inside the gates of the scary property, her hand gripping the rusted gate as if her very life depended on it. Her other hand rested sassily on her hips. With wide eyes, she regarded the house. There were no lights on inside. She hoped this meant that Old Man Sharpe was out. *Probably collecting kids to eat later,* she thought as a shiver rippled through her.

'You can't chicken out now Alli,' her little brother shouted from the other side of the street. Anthony was six—'Nearly seven,' he would argue with anyone who asked him—but he was already bigger than most of the other boys, the ones who were currently daring her to trick-or-treat Old Man Sharpe. She didn't want to appear to be a scaredy-cat in front of any of them, even though she knew her brother would stick up for her if they began to tease.

Old Man Sharpe had once been a teacher at the high school, but her father had told her, not long before he died, to stay as far away from him as she could. He'd been in prison, and as everyone in town put it, 'He's bad news.'

He was old, with grey hair and a big grizzly beard. Alli had seen him in town a few times. He looked scary. His eyes were wild, and his clothes were always shabby. When they saw him, her mother would pull her out of his way and walk off in the opposite direction or cross the street to avoid any contact with him. Whenever this happened, Alli would always turn to look at him. There was something strange about the way he looked at her and her mother, but especially *her*. It was different from the scowls and rude gestures he offered the other people he passed on the street. It was as if he had a special interest in them that he didn't have for anyone else.

He was known for running after kids he'd caught playing in his yard. Some of the older kids told stories of him owning something they called a 'mash-etty.' Alli didn't know what one of them was, but the stories of him running after the kids, waving it in the air, petrified her.

Others told stories of kids going into his house, usually on dares, and never being seen ever again. She'd never believed these stories and always asked what the names of the kids were but was told the families had moved out of the area to avoid the scary man. However, she'd always taken heed of her father's advice and given the strange old man a wide berth.

As stated, she never believed in any of these stories, until now, standing at the end of his yard on Halloween night. She was more than relieved that the windows were dark and her friends, including her brother, were close.

'Go on, knock on the door,' one of the older boys shouted to her. 'You have to. It's part of the dare.'

She shrugged, making it as visible as she could, as if the thought of knocking on this haunted old house was nothing to her. Deep down, though, every inch of her being was screaming at her not to do it. She cursed herself for not staying with the other girls from school, instead opting to go trick-or-treating with the boys. She looked at Anthony, and there was fear in his eyes, but there was something else too. *Is it pride?* she thought. *Is my little brother proud of me?* She thought it was, and that was enough to spur her on to complete the dare.

She pried her gloved fingers from the gate post and pulled up her jeans underneath the makeshift witch costume she was wearing. She took in a slow, deep breath and set herself on the path to be the bravest kid in town. *Maybe even the bravest girl in the state*, she thought. Her mind was filled with the accolades she would receive when the mayor handed over the big money prize and the huge golden key to the city for being the bravest person in Wisconsin. Her mind had been so filled with this silly fantasy that she failed to notice the light flicking on in the hallway.

~~~~

Everyone else noticed it, and every one of them scarpered. Anthony, to his credit, lingered longer than the rest. He tried calling out to his sister but only with a whispered shout that he hoped beyond all hope she might hear, and the monstrous Old Man Sharpe wouldn't. It was to no avail. She looked as if she were in her own little world, and no amount of whisper-shouting would get through to her. He hesitated for another moment, looking longingly towards the bushes where his friends had scattered and then anxiously back to Alli, heading blindly into the lure of whatever Old Man Sharpe had in mind for eight-year-old girls. He dropped his head, exhaled, and ran over the road, towards the yard from Hell.

'Alli … Alli,' he whisper-shouted again. 'Alli, look out. He's in.'

Still, she made her way towards the door, lost in her own dream world. A silhouette that was very possibly Old Man Sharpe was looming through the window. Anthony knew if she knocked, she'd have no time whatsoever before the door would be answered and she would be caught, out of his grasp and at the mercy of the town's very own lunatic. He was just about to yell again, to warn her of the impending doom residing mere inches from her, when something caught his eye.

Someone, or something, was hiding in the bushes of the yard. Whoever, or whatever, it was made him stop mid-shout. He felt the words die in his mouth, slipping back down his throat like a thick loogie he couldn't get rid of. His mouth was suddenly dry, and all the wind in his lungs was gone.

He stared at the figure.

It looked like a person, but the way the shadows that enveloped it shimmered, he couldn't tell for sure. Something about it told him it was female.

He'd never been so scared in his almost seven years.

His feet were lead weights, far too heavy to move, as he watched the shimmer of a girl reach an arm out towards his sister. Alison was at least ten feet away from her, but her arm somehow extended—or unfolded, as he would think later when he had time to ponder on what had happened—to touch his sister's hair.

His bladder was heavy, heavier than when he was in bed and either too cold or too scared to go down the hallway to the bathroom to pee. He had visions of his pants turning a darker beige at the front and that darkness spreading down his legs. He knew if that happened, he would never, ever live it down. He'd have to move schools, towns, even, *maybe states,* he thought.

He watched as the apparition moved towards his sister's head. He wanted to scream, to run to her, to save her from the ghastly thing, but he couldn't. His feet were stuck to the floor, rooting him to the spot as if he'd been standing in Crazy Glue and hadn't noticed. All he could do was watch helplessly as the thing continued to stretch, inching closer to his sister. He couldn't even close his eyes. He needed to see, to witness what was about to happen; he had to. If something terrible happened here, then at least he would be able to tell the tale of Alli.

Long, spindly fingers unfurled from the unnaturally protracted arm. In his young head, he could hear bones snapping and clicking as the ghastly appendage edged ever closer to her.

Then it touched her.

He could feel the scream. He could hear the shout, the yell. He could feel himself running, waving his arms in the air, warning Alli away from the terrible thing touching her.

However, it was all in his mind.

As the impossible fingers caressed Alli's cheek, she turned. The touch seemed to snap her out of whatever dream she'd been in. He watched as she shook her head just as the front door of the old house opened. He held his breath as she ducked into the covers of a nearby bush, out of sight of the dishevelled man poking his head outside, just in time.

'You,' the gravelled voice of Old Man Sharpe shouted as his eyes fell on Anthony standing just inside the overgrown path of the yard. 'What are you doing here? Get off my property, right now, before I call the police.'

Anthony's six-year-old brain interpreted this shout as: 'You, boy! Get over here now. I'm going to skin you alive and put you in my Halloween pot.'

Once more, he was rooted to the spot, trapped in a true dichotomy. He wanted so much to help his sister, to get her out of the yard and away from the evils lurking in this property, but he also wanted to get himself away from them too. He wanted to run and run and never, ever go back anywhere near this place. His eyes absorbed the huge, lumbering figure that was struggling, in its haste, to get out of the door and down the path, no doubt to swoop him into his huge arms and tear him to pieces right there. It wasn't until he felt the warmth beginning to spread down his leg that his paralysing fear broke and he was able to turn and bolt towards the gate, the one that looked like it was more than a hundred miles away.

Being six, nearly seven, he hadn't had a chance to develop a true sense of guilt, but he did have a strong sense of loyalty. As he ran, the loyal brother felt terrible about deserting his sister in the garden of death. As he reached the tree line and the path that took him to the back of their home, he stopped and turned. 'Alli!' he shouted. 'Get out of there. Get out now!'

The shambling man heard this shout and turned his attentions towards the location he was shouting at.

Anthony could see his sister trembling in the bushes, trying to make herself as small and invisible as she could. It was too late for her now, and he cursed himself for being so stupid. He'd given the bad man the exact location of his prey. His dichotomy was complete as he watched Old Man Sharpe lumbering towards her. He wanted to help her so much, but he was scared and embarrassed about the wet patch at the front of his trousers. *Don't forget freaked out about the strange girl too,* he finished in his head.

He spun full circle. He didn't know what he could do or what he should do. He looked towards the backyard, where he could just make out a large tree in the centre of it.

The tree looked like it was glowing.

In the centre of the eerie light was a girl. For some reason, he thought it was the same girl he'd seen reaching towards Alli.

Impossibly, he felt his bladder release for the second time.

The girl put her finger to her lips as if to shush him.

'Go and tell ...'

The words were in his head, but they didn't sound like his. They sounded like ... hers.

He was about to finish her sentence for her with the word *Dad* but had to stop himself at the very last minute. Their father had died earlier that year. Their mom had told them it was due to complications of something called pneumonia. Apparently, he'd caught a bad chill a few years earlier and had never really recovered. He'd been sad that he would never see him again, but he'd been too young to completely understand what it really meant to lose a parent.

'Mom,' he finished.

The glow from the tree diminished, and the little girl disappeared.

Offering one last glance towards the man looming over Alli, he sped off as fast as his little legs could carry him.

It took him almost five minutes, at the full sprint that only seasoned athletes or adventurous six-year-old boys with pee all over the front of their trousers can maintain, to get home. As he got there, his mother was on the front porch, wrapped in a thick coat with a bowl filled with candy on her knee, waiting for the trick-or-treaters, as she did every year.

'Mom … Mom, he's got her … he's got her. The b-b-boogieman! He's got Alli!' he shouted, his voice coming in fits and bursts, stealing all his breath and preventing him from forming full words while still running full pelt towards the safety of his mother.

~~~~

Delores turned towards the small boy speeding through the twilight towards her. As a mother, she instinctively knew the sound of her own distraught child.

Her heart pounded as she dropped the bowl of candy, spilling tiny bars of chocolate and packets of candy corn everywhere. She threw herself up and ran towards her son, slipping on the discarded treats on the porch. She was trying to form words, but nothing wanted to come. Only thoughts moulded. Horrible, nasty thoughts. *Not again. Please, Lord, not again.*

'Mom. Old Man Sharpe,' her son panted as he continued his sprint towards her. 'Old Man …'

Her mind raced at the mention of that name.

Please, Lord, no.

Time stood still for her then. An age passed before her boy was within talking range of her. All she could do was reach out and grab him by the shoulders. He was hot, sweaty, covered in pee, and scared half to death.

'Anthony, what is it? What about Mr Sharpe?'

'He's got her. He's got Alli.' He gulped as he talked. 'He said something about putting her in a Halloween pot … and boiling her up. Honest, Mom … I'm telling the …' He gulped before continuing. '… truth. We need to call …'

He never finished his sentence before Delores grabbed his hand and dragged him back the same way he had just come. She dragged him almost as fast as he had run. 'Now you tell me where you saw her. You tell me right now, son, or you're in for a whipping.'

'No, Mom, honest. He had her. There was a little girl with weird arms. She was grabbing at Alli, then Old Man … I mean Mr Sharpe came. He's got her, I'm telling you.'

It took a few minutes of almost silent travelling to get to the gate to Mr Sharpe's overgrown yard.

'Alli, are you in here? Alli, where are you?' she shouted as Anthony broke free of her grip and ran towards the gate.

'Alli, are you there?' Anthony screamed, leaning on the wire fence, not quite daring to enter. 'What's Old Man Sharpe done to you?'

'I'm here,' the quiet voice came from behind them.

As a single unit, both mother and son turned.

Delores, her hand clutched to her chest, ran towards her confused daughter.

'What do you want?' Alli asked, looking from one to the other.

'We came to rescue you from Old Man Sharpe and the strange girl,' Anthony gushed.

'From Mr Sharpe?' Alli replied, squinting as if she didn't have a clue what her brother was talking about.

'I saw him. I saw him grabbing you after the little girl poked you.'

'Ant, what are you talking about? I did the dare. I thought I saw something in the bushes, then Mr Sharpe came out and asked me to leave. He was very nice about it.'

'He didn't …' Delores paused for a moment before continuing her line of enquiry. She knew this was going to be a tough question, and she wasn't entirely sure she wanted to know the answer, but she knew she needed to ask. '… didn't touch you, did he?'

Alli looked at her mother with the same expression she'd given her brother. 'Yes, Mom, he did.'

Delores felt something inside her die, and her knees began to buckle.

'He helped me out of the bushes. I think I've got some splinters,' she explained.

'The girl is fine.' The deep male voice came from somewhere behind them, within the yard. 'She'll have a few scratches, but—'

'You stay away from my children,' Delores spat, grabbing hold of both brother and sister and dragging them close. 'You just stay away from them, and me. Do you hear? Far away!' As she ranted at the man, she was checking Alli's face and arms. 'Come on, we're going home,' she snapped at the siblings, pulling them away, almost yanking their arms from their sockets in the process.

When they were a good distance from the house and from Mr Sharpe, Delores pulled her daughter closer to her. 'What were you doing in that man's yard?' she scolded in a whisper that wasn't really a whisper.

'It was a dare,' Alli replied. 'All the boys dared me to trick-or-treat him.'

'And if all the boys dared you to put your finger in the fire, would you do that too?'

Alli fell silent as her mother pushed her onwards and out of the way of the prying eyes of Mr Sharpe, who was standing at his gate, watching the family hurry away from him.

Alli turned to look at him just once as they were ushered off toward the safety of home.

7.

I WAS SITTING at the dining table, Anthony was opposite me, and plates of long-forgotten fruits that had been dessert languished between us. I was caressing my half-full long-stemmed wine glass while basking in the dim glow of the roaring fireplace.

'I'm sure that was the first time we saw her,' Anthony said as he swirled the claret liquid around his glass.

'Not for me. I didn't see her that day. I remember you telling me about her, though. It sounded pretty horrific.' I laughed, taking another sip of my drink, although I could feel the crawl of goosebumps itching my flesh.

Anthony chuffed as he sat back and stretched. He shook his head. 'I can still see her to this day. She was in the bushes, and her arm …'—he shook his head, a little more vigorously this time—'it *was* horrific. It kind of … unfolded,' he reminisced, doing the actions of waving his arm in the air. 'I honestly thought she was trying to grab you. Oh, I don't know.' He laughed a little. 'It was all so long ago. Maybe I didn't see anything but a branch.'

I shivered again and held my glass closer. 'Don't. The thought of it still freaks me out, even today.' I put my glass down on the table and took stock of my family. Grace was asleep on the couch, and Mom had gone to bed, blaming the excitement of the day leaving her bones weary. My brother was facing me, grinning like a Cheshire Cat, as we talked. 'That was a strange year. Do you remember Mom telling us about the Spirit of Christmas?'

He nodded slowly. 'I remember. She told us Santa might not be able to make it that year because he was busy with the poor boys and girls of the world, but the Spirit of Christmas wouldn't let us down.' As he mused, his grin turned into a small pout.

'When I think back about that, it still makes me want to cry. Can you imagine what she was going through? Dad hadn't been dead long, and there was next to no money coming in. Only what she could get for taking in washing and ironing.'

Anthony's grin widened, almost impossibly. 'But she still managed to bring up two amazing kids who've both grown into well-balanced and well-to-do adults,' he said, raising his glass over the table towards me.

I responded by chinking mine against his. 'She really did,' I replied, hoping the rogue tear in my eye wasn't going to ruin a beautiful night.

'All right, I think I'm going to hit the hay. Big day tomorrow, putting the Christmas decorations up. You think Gracie will help?'

My brows came together. 'Are you kidding? You just try to keep her away. Any chance she's going to get Uncle Anthony all to herself, she'll grab with both hands. You're her hero, you know.'

He smiled as he stood and finished off the last of his wine. He offered me a wink. 'Do you want me to carry her up?' he whispered.

I drained my own glass and began to gather the rest of the dishes from the table. 'Do you mind? I'm going to clean up here and give the kitchen a quick wipe. I don't want Mom to wake up to a mess in the morning.'

'Not at all,' he replied, making his way into the living room, where Grace lay cuddling a teddy bear, covered by a blanket on the couch before the fire.

I watched him pick her up and carry her up the stairs, my heart bursting with love.

'Night, sis. See you in the morning.'

I sighed, looked at my empty glass, and entered the kitchen.

I was instantly struck by how cold it was in there. The sight of my breath misting shocked me more than the bites on my exposed skin. I placed my glass on the countertop. I was shivering, my teeth chattering together making a fie rhythm in my mouth. *If the heating is on, then why is it so cold in here?* Turning the gas rings on the stove on, I hovered my hands over them, welcoming the warmth.

After a few moments, I felt warm enough to move away from the blue flames, and I turned on the hot water tap, leaving it to run for a small while to allow warm water to run through. I accidently touched the metal of the faucet and the sting of it forced me to step back. At first, I thought it had been too hot to touch, but then I noticed the frost on the underside. A funny thought ran through my head of Anthony as a child with his tongue stuck to one of the lampposts by the school. Shaking my head, I chuffed as the bowl began to fill. By the time I'd found and squirted the liquid soap, a satisfying steam was rising as the hot water mixed with the cold air.

Grabbing the dishes I'd brought into the kitchen, my heart almost missed a beat as I caught the silhouette of a young girl standing in the doorway, watching me. 'Oh Jesus, honey,' I stuttered, turning back to my chore. 'You scared the life out of me. Did Uncle Anthony wake you?'

As I plunged my hands into the sink, I splashed my top a little with the sudsy water. Tutting, I stepped back and grabbed the towel hanging from the cupboard door beneath the sink. 'I suppose you think that's …' I never finished my sentence as I turned around, expecting Grace to be in the doorway watching me, holding her teddy bear, and laughing as I swilled myself with dishwater, an event she never failed to greet with hilarity.

The doorway was empty.

I stood for a moment looking for any sign of my daughter. Shrugging, I turned back to the sink, thinking she must have gone back upstairs to bed, maybe led by her favourite uncle. *Looks like you get storytelling duties tonight.* I scoffed, getting back to the dishes.

Ten minutes and a quick wipe of the countertops later, and the room had warmed up, probably from the exertion of my tasks. Either way, I ached for my bed. The long drive, the emotion of being with Mom and Anthony, plus the bottle of red wine, had all collaborated to take their toll. I dried my hands, dumping the towel on the table, and left the kitchen, turning the lights off as I went. As I made it to the living room, the cold had begun to creep back. I rubbed my hands together as I leant over the open fire, making sure nothing could fall out of the grate overnight and burn the house, with all of us still in it, to the ground. I'd seen my mother do this ever since I could remember.

The giggle from behind me sounded like Gracie playing a game. I closed my eyes and turned, tutting, ready to scold her before chasing her back upstairs and back to bed. *Where's my brother when I need him?* I fussed as I scanned the empty room.

I saw the back of Grace's head and the swoop of her black dress as she ran up the stairs. She was still giggling. I couldn't stay mad at her because she was obviously excited about being in Grandma's house for Christmas, so I followed her, ready to swoop her up and carry her off to bed. *If Ant can't do it, then I might as well do it myself.*

Suddenly, the laughter stopped.

I stopped at the same time.

Mist was once again pluming from my mouth, giving the perfect illusion of smoking a cigarette. *What was she wearing?* I thought. Her dress had been dark and flowing, almost as if she had been wearing an old-fashioned overcoat. I knew she'd fallen asleep wearing her unicorn pyjamas. Ant had gifted them earlier this evening, and she'd insisted on wearing them right away.

I looked up the stairs, but all I could see was darkness. A chill—no, it was more than that—it was a deep frost that seeped through my clothes. It bit into my skin. For the third time that day, I felt goosebumps rising, tightening my skin, making me want to rub my arms. I needed to follow Grace up those stairs, but something about what I'd seen was urging me not to. *A black coat can't be mistaken for pink unicorn pyjamas, can it?*

Forcing myself to sound more confident than I felt, I cried out into the darkness above me: 'Gracie, if you're not in bed and asleep by the time I get up there, then there's going to be big trouble.' The sound of my own voice buoyed me, and I decided to make my way up the stairs. As I placed my foot on the first step, the temperature in the room plummeted.

I imagined I could hear the carpet crunching beneath my feet as if I were walking in snow. My vision began to blur. It started with a dizzy, drunken feeling but soon evolved. A mist descended, reminding me of when my sunglasses would steam up when I entered a warm car. I reached out, searching for the banister to guide me up the stairs.

I couldn't believe my senses.

The room felt bigger somehow, and the air had a different feel about it. I could smell evergreen pines and feel the sting of snow in the air. I looked around, expecting to see the kitchen door blown open, allowing the cold and the snow inside, but that was not the case. The door hadn't blown open; it had disappeared completely. The kitchen I had been standing in just moments ago had ceased to be. The doorways to the living room and the hall were gone too. I was outdoors, in the woods, surrounded by trees that were covered in snow.

A panic washed over me, taking my breath away as it descended. The cold caught in my chest, and I struggled to breathe. I turned, taking a three-hundred-and-sixty-degree view of my new surroundings. All I could see through the snowy twilight were trees, snow, and mist. The furniture, the walls, the house, they were all gone. What short breath I could exhale blew out of me in a physical vapour that rose into the night air, clouding around me.

'Gracie,' I tried to shout, not knowing what else to do.

Thoughts of a book I had once loved raced through my head as I remembered the little girl passing through a wardrobe into a snowy landscape. That book was fiction, a Christian allegory;

besides, I hadn't travelled through any wardrobes, or closets, or secret portals to get here. This was real. As real as anything else in my life.

'Gracie,' I croaked again, noticing my faint voice was muffled by the trees and the thick snow piled on their branches.

'Alli? Are you OK?'

The voice sounded normal. Like an oasis of rationality in a desert of frozen madness.

'Alison, what's up?' the voice asked again.

I felt hands, strong hands, grabbing me by my shoulders. The touch had a grounding effect, and everything, the whole maddening scene before me, narrowed before blinking out of existence.

I was back in the hallway of my mother's house. The cold of the woods was gone, along with the trees, the snow, and my clouding breath. It took me a moment to realise that the person standing before me, holding me, was Anthony.

'Alli, are you OK? You look—'

'Grace! Where's Grace?' I spluttered, pushing past my brother in an attempt to get up the stairs.

'Alli, she's asleep. I just left her. She's fast asleep in your bed. I carried her up. She didn't even wake, just wrapped her arms around me.'

'Why isn't she wearing the pyjamas you bought her? Why was she wearing a coat?'

Ant looked at me, his expression one of wonder, as if this was the first time he'd ever seen me in his life. 'What coat?' he asked. 'She's got her unicorn pj's on.'

I whipped my head around so fast I felt my neck crick, but I ignored it. The confusion inside my brain was overpowering. It felt like I was in a rock concert, and someone had gone overboard with the fog machine. 'If she's wearing her pj's, then who's the little girl in the black coat?'

'Alli, you're scaring me. What are you talking about? What black coat?'

I grasped my brother's arms. I must have gripped him too hard, as he winced, just a little. 'Ant, I just saw Grace run up these stairs. She was wearing a long black coat. I swear it. The room was freezing. I saw her, and then I …'

'You what?' Ant was now at the base of the stairs looking into the darkness beyond. Before he began to climb, he looked at me. 'You what? You were pretty spaced-out, there. What did you see?'

I shook my head and put my hand to my temple. 'Nothing, it … it doesn't matter.' I pushed past him and ran up the steps, taking two at a time. Anthony was close behind.

I burst into my bedroom and was just about to flick on the lights when Anthony's hand stopped me. 'Don't,' he whispered. 'You'll wake her, look.' He pointed towards the large bed, where Grace was lying, the covers kicked off her. She was fast asleep wearing her brand-new unicorn pyjamas and hugging her favourite teddy bear.

'See?' he whispered. 'Unicorns.'

We backed out of the room, closing the door behind us. 'What did you see, Alli?' Ant's intense eyes were burrowing into mine. I could feel the scrutiny in them.

'I don't know.' I turned away from him, not liking the way he was looking at me. 'I'm sure it was Grace. I'm telling you. She ran up the stairs, giggling, and then everything changed. I … I was outside, in the woods. I could see my breath.'

'Alli, it's been a long day. Between Mom's sickness and the drive, I think you're exhausted.'

I rested my head on the wooden door behind me and exhaled a long, shaky breath. 'Maybe you're right.' I laughed. 'I think I'm done for the day.' I turned back to my brother and offered him a small smile. There was precious little humour in it. 'I think I'll turn in. You don't mind, do you?'

Anthony offered me a small, lopsided grin. 'Mind?' he asked. 'I'm relieved. I'm done in myself. I was hoping you wouldn't ask me to stay up drinking with you some more. Because, you know, I can never refuse my big sister.'

'You want to know something?' I asked, looking at him, really looking deep inside of him, seeing the strong man he was. 'You're the best little brother anyone could ask for.'

'I know,' he laughed before kissing me on my forehead and entering his own room.

As I watched his door close, the smile on my lips was warmer, and it felt genuine.

8.

HER BEDROOM WAS chilly, but that was to be expected due to the inclement weather outside and the old windows. Anthony had spent some time a couple of years ago making sure all the windows were well insulated, but she had steadfastly refused his offer of getting new ones put in. She had gone on about keeping the character of the house intact.

I was used to the cold anyway, having grown up in this climate before moving on to another cold one, so it didn't bother me in the least.

Grace was snoring gently, and the soft purr issuing from her comforted me. To say that my nerves were more than a little on edge from the scare I'd just had in the hallway would be doing them an injustice. I knew Anthony was right. It was just everything getting on top of me, and I needed to relax, to unwind. I'd expected to find Mom in worse health than she was, and after all the worry, it had been a pleasant surprise to see her so animated. Although as the evening had worn on, she *had* begun to wane. I knew she wouldn't have wanted to, what with the family milling about the house, but I could see the relief in her face when I suggested maybe she should go and lie down.

Her face had brightened at the suggestion. Although I could see she was disappointed, the constant attention from Grace and the excitement of the day had physically taken all it could from her, for now.

I'd walked her up to her bedroom and stayed with her for a moment until she fell asleep. It was a beautiful mother and daughter moment, reminiscent of the many we'd had over the years, only with the roles reversed. The instant she closed her eyes, she began to snore lightly.

I mused on how that snore was almost identical to the sounds Grace was making now.

As I slipped into my nightgown, my skin once again told me how cold it really was. I released a drawn-out sigh. *It's been a long day,* I told myself. *Too long.*

As I lay in my old but still familiar bed, a small noise disturbed me. It was tiny, but it cut through Grace's purring. It sounded far away, yet it was as clear as day.

It was a little girl's voice.

She was singing.

'*Do you believe in Christmas magic?*'

There was a dreamy, phasing-in-and-out feel to it, but it was consistent. '*It sings to us this day ...*'

I opened my eyes. As I did, the singing stopped.

I looked into the darkness and held my breath. My eyes searched the shadows, looking for something I knew shouldn't be there, something wrong. Nothing was forthcoming. Even in the deepest, darkest shadows where the light couldn't penetrate, everything looked normal. Finally, I allowed myself to exhale, most of the air coming through my nose. *Come on, Alli, it's your imagination.* I closed my eyes as I shook my head, resting it on the pillow.

~~~~

It was moments later that sleep found Alison.

She fell so fast and so deep that she didn't notice the temperature in the room dropping at least ten degrees and the breath of the two girls in the bed shrouding over them in the crisp of the frigid night air.

Neither mother nor daughter saw the little girl's face appear within that breath. They missed the droplets of mist merging together to form a silhouette. The apparition's hair was plastered to her face, and icicles hung from the strands. Her skin was as white as the snow that had fallen in the fields outside and, unbeknown to the sleeping Alison and Grace, on the floor around the bed.

'*It beats in time with our childlike hearts ...*' the girl whispered as she reached out and touched Grace's cheek.

The sleeping child flinched at the caress. She murmured something before a smile stretched across her face. 'Lisa?' she said in a slow, sleepy voice.

The apparition blinked, her dark eyes turning a deeper obsidian, darker than any of the shadows within the room. Small pinpricks of white formed in their centre. '*Childlike hearts ...*' she whispered again in the same tune as the popular Christmas carol she favoured. She then turned her attention to the larger of the two in the bed. She reached out and stroked Alison's face too.

Alison jerked at the touch, although the small, sudden movement did not bother the ethereal child.

Alison brought the thick blanket closer to her face and turned the other way.

'*Love never goes away ...*' the girl continued to sing as she removed her hand from the older woman's face.

Then she was gone. The room temperature rose again, returning to the ambient temperature it had been before her arrival. The snow that had gathered around the floor of the bedroom, creating small drifts against the legs of the bed and the chest of drawers, disappeared too. It didn't so much melt as it just vanished.

In another room, Delores stirred in her sleep.

'Lisa,' she mumbled before relaxing back into her pillows.

9.

THE YEARS REWOUND like an old video recording.

It was Christmas again. The snow was thick on the ground and hanging heavy in the branches of the trees. The fields and forest that Alli and Anthony called their playgrounds were transformed into winter wonderlands during the day and beautiful, picturesque Christmas card scenes during the night.

The beautiful twilight scenes belied the dangers within them, as when the temperatures dropped, they could fall to well below freezing, and being caught outside for very long could be deadly.

It had been snowing heavily all morning, and the weatherman had informed everyone that it was probably not going to stop for a while, so the school had decided to close down early for the day. As it was the last day of the semester, it was deemed that the students wouldn't miss anything important.

Anthony and Alli were laughing as they made their way home. It was a mile-and-a-half trek from the school to their house, and due to the heavy snowfall, the school buses hadn't been able to get out of the garage to give the children their usual lifts home. The parents had been informed, and alternative arrangements had been made for most of them. However, for Alli and Anthony this gave them the opportunity to walk home, cutting through the fields. There would be plenty of time for snowball fights and possibly to build a snowman or two. Maybe just a couple of hours for them to be children together before they got home and had to start whatever homework they had been given and the chores their mother had in store for them.

It shouldn't have been a problem for either of them, as it was a path they'd trod many times before. However, today, it was proving difficult, mainly due to the cold and the deep drifts.

'I'm telling you,' Anthony berated his sister. 'I know what I saw. It was a little girl. She was in the bushes, and she was reaching out to get you.'

Alli shook her head. 'Ant, give me a break. You're only scaring yourself. Besides, it was almost two months ago. All you saw was Old Man Sharpe coming down the walk. If I hadn't jumped into the bushes, then I'm sure he would've gotten me and done whatever he wanted with me. Eaten me, probably.'

Ant shook his head as he struggled to catch up to his big sister, jumping in her footsteps so as not to make his own. 'I'm not kidding around, Alli. There was a scary little girl. She reached out to you, and I thought she was going to get you. When Old Man Sharpe came out, she disappeared.'

Alli shook her head. As she did, her damp hair whipped across her pink, wind-burnt face. 'Little girls don't just disappear,' she shouted over the rising wind.

'But this one did.' He shrugged. 'One minute she was there; the next, she wasn't.'

Alli laughed despite the snow and wind in her face. She turned around to check on her brother's progress, saw that he was directly behind her, and continued on her way. 'You were too busy getting in the Halloween spirit,' she chided. 'I reckon at that point, with all the sugar you'd eaten, you would have seen ghosts and boogiemen everywhere.'

'That's not true. I did see her. I'm telling you, and she was going to get you,' he shouted as he slapped her on her well-padded behind before running off into the snowstorm, laughing as he did.

'Come back here, you,' Alli shouted as she watched her brother disappear into the whiteout. She could hear him laughing from somewhere within the mists of the storm, but even though he was wearing a bright-red coat, he was already lost to her.

'Anthony! Don't run off into the storm. Come back here right now. Mom will kill us if we're late.'

She stopped shouting, waiting for his reply.

There wasn't one.

She covered one ear, trying to block the noise of the storm so she could hear his laughing over the howling wind. There was no high-pitched, shrill laugh to be heard, only the wail of the cutting icy gusts. 'Anthony!' she shouted again. She could feel the fear in her stomach, knitting her innards into tight knots. 'Anthony, come on, this isn't funny. Where are you?' She stopped in her tracks and turned, performing a complete circle, her eyes scanning everywhere, but all she could see was more and more snow blowing into her face.

'ANTHONY!' she screamed.

She was answered only by the wind picking up. The moan sounded, to her petrified senses, like a ghoul groaning as it clambered out of its stinking grave, seeking the human flesh it required to continue its tragic survival. This thought sent a real shiver up her spine, and she whipped herself around again, checking there was no monster creeping up on her. *Or Old Man Sharpe, for that matter,* she thought.

It was the thought of Mr Sharpe that scared her more than anything.

After their last encounter, they had told the other kids in school what had happened. They in turn told Alli and Anthony all about him and why he'd been in prison. They told them that a few years back, a little girl had gone missing, and Mr Sharpe, who had been the teacher at the high school at the time, had been arrested for something called abduction and had been charged with something called molestation. They had to release him due to lack of evidence, as no one never found the girl's body. But, they continued, everyone knew he was guilty and that he was a dirty, rotten pervert, whatever that was, and deserved to rot in hell for what he'd done.

All the tales the kids told her came back at once. Stories of how he'd eaten the little girl, boiling her bones to make soup. Another story told of how he had kept her alive for years, cutting away her skin every year to make himself an Easter hat.

That one had made her laugh when she'd first heard it, but now, in the dimming light of the day and in the face of the storm, all alone in the snow, she hoped it *had* just been a tale. She wanted to call out to Anthony again, to find out where he was, to grab him and run all the way home, but she was too scared. *What if Old Man Sharpe has him? What if he's out there right now looking for me, and the only way he can find me is by my voice?* If she hadn't been so cold, there would have been tears pouring down her cheeks, but the wind ripped them away the moment they formed.

Suddenly, exhaustion overcame her, and she felt her legs begin to buckle. Even the cold of the snow beneath her and the freezing damp seeping into her clothing couldn't rouse her from this overwhelming fatigue. The wind whistled around her ears, numbing her to the plummeting temperatures. She felt herself slipping into a strange, fuzzy warmth.

The darkening landscape began to filter into a lifeless grey as her eyelids felt like they had one-hundred-pound weights attached to them. The white blanket beneath her suddenly seemed so inviting, so comfortable, as she drifted off into the howling wind.

Then everything changed.

The wind died.

It was an eerie feeling. She could hear the sway of the trees, but the cruel wind was no longer lashing at her face. The rustle of the branches became rhythmic.

Then the music began.

It was faint at first, nothing but a distant tingle in the air. It sounded like there might be a band playing a mile or so away, and their noise was carrying on the breeze of the warm, balmy night, floating on the eddies of the summer wind.

In her confused mind, the music began to make sense.

There was a brass section—she thought it could be a trumpet, but there was no way to be sure. It complemented the pulsing rhythm of the beat and the vocal chanting beneath it.

Then came the lyrics.

'Do you believe the magic?'

'Do you believe the magic?'

The line was repeated, as if by multiple voices.

'That's in the air tonight ...'

It was muffled, confused. She couldn't tell if it was being sung by a little girl or by a full choir.

'It illuminates our hearts and minds ...'

'Hearts and minds ...'

Until that point, she hadn't noticed she was shaking, but the voice and the sway of the music, with the rising, marching drumbeat, soothed her mind and body. Her tremors began to subside, and she could feel her temperature rise. She opened her eyes, expecting to see the trees dancing in the wicked wind of moments ago, but she wasn't overly surprised to see them standing still. The dark of the coming night had enveloped her, except for a strange glow that was coming from somewhere behind her. It looked like the coming of the dawn, but she knew it couldn't be; it was far too early for it. It hadn't even been night yet.

'A bright and blinding light?'

The song continued. This time, she was sure it was a little girl singing.

'Do you believe in Christmas magic?'

'Do you believe in Christmas magic?'

It was a choir following the little girl's lead. She was convinced the voice was coming from behind her, from the same direction as the warm glow. Slowly, she turned. This wasn't an easy manoeuvre, as her clothes snapped and cracked as the snow that covered them fell. It didn't bother her. She was only interested in the source of the light and the song that came with it.

The radiance was bright, almost too bright. She held her hand to her face, attempting to filter out the glare, attempting to see who, or what, was in the centre, making that sweet music.

After a moment, the dark, fuzzy shape in the centre began to focus. As it did, the music became less fuzzy too. It became louder and faster. The rhythm gained momentum as the chorus became rousing, morphing from a light carol into a stirring anthem.

'*That sings to us this day!*'

Alli could hear it was a single person singing the song. Although she wasn't sure if it was her mind playing tricks on her.

'*It beats in time with our childlike hearts …*'

It was a little girl.

'*Our childlike hearts …*' the unseen backing choir echoed.

The apparition's blonde hair was tied in pigtails. She was dressed in a long dark coat, but underneath, flapping in some unseen wind, was a nightgown. It, too, was long and flowing, and it looked old-fashioned. It also looked wet and dirty as it stuck to her little legs. Her face was familiar, although at the same time, she could swear she'd never seen her before.

The girl's mouth broke into a smile.

Her wet face began to beam with a radiance that challenged the very light emanating from behind her. She held out a hand towards her. Alli, her arms acting independently from her brain, reached her own hand out to take the girl's offered one.

They were maybe less than an inch from each other when something happened.

The music stopped … suddenly.

The drums, the brass accompaniment, the singing, everything.

The silence felt heavy, almost laboured.

The girl's smile faded as she looked towards the tree line behind Alli.

Alli thought about turning. She wanted to see what had gotten the little girl's attention, but what was happening *to* the girl had captured all of her attention. Her beautiful face was turning pale. Her healthy pink glow was fading, as was the bright glow of her eyes. They darkened, almost to the point where Alli could no longer see them. They became nothing more than dark holes within a willowing face. Her skin began to wrinkle, and the corners of her mouth creased and cracked.

Her former radiant smile disappeared as the little girl aged, maybe a hundred years, in the wink of an eye.

Alli tried to scuttle away, but her feet couldn't find the purchase they needed in the snow-lined ground, and she slipped in her rush to put the horrifying vision behind her. The vicious wind returned with gusto. It lashed at her face with wicked fingers, stinging her exposed skin, bringing icy tears to her eyes that the hungry wind whipped away. Her damp hair, collaborating with the rancorous wind, flayed her face. The winter's frozen twines penetrated her clothes, stinging and soaking her undergarments. The light dissolved, leaving behind nothing but a withered, dizzying vision of the little girl, who was disappearing into the mist of the blizzard raging around her.

The girl once more looked past her, at something behind Alli, before disappearing completely into the dark and the whiteness of the storm.

~~~~

I jolted bolt upright in bed.

I was covered in sweat. Where the warmth of my exposed flesh met the cold air of the room, goosebumps ruled the landscape. *It was a dream,* I thought. *Just a dream.* Although, deep down, I knew it wasn't. It couldn't have been. It was more than that.

It was a memory!

It was the time when Mr Sharpe had found me in the snow, half-conscious, shivering, frozen through and through.

Nearly frozen to death.

The memory came flooding back.

Anthony had realised he'd run too far and could no longer see me. He'd then reluctantly ran off to find help. The only person he could find was Mr Sharpe, who had been outside going for firewood. He told me about how they'd returned to find a bundle of pink rags half covered in snow on the ground. He told me about a bright light he'd seen; told me he thought it was a fire and that he was scared.

I closed my eyes, sinking back into the warmth of the bed, allowing the cool air of the night to soothe me. My heartbeat, the same one that had been thrashing against my chest only moments prior, was slowing as my body eventually concluded I wasn't caught in a blizzard in the woods but safe and warm in my old bed, in my old room, with my daughter asleep next to me.

Still feeling shaky, I turned to Grace, making sure my dream, nightmare, memory, or whatever it had been, hadn't disturber her. I reached out to put my hand on her forehead. My body tensed, and my already tested heart felt like it missed a beat. All the breath I had in my body was taken in that single moment, and I couldn't breathe.

Her side of the bed was empty.

Grace was not there.

In a blur of movement, I flung off the covers and jumped out of the bed. My body recognised the shock of the cold, wet carpet but didn't register it. It didn't allow my head to ask the question of how it could have gotten wet. Right then, it didn't matter. All I needed was to know where Grace could be.

If she'd needed to go to the bathroom or to get a drink in the middle of the night, she was the kind of girl who would have woken me rather than go wandering around a strange house in the dark.

I kept slippers by the side of the bed, as Mom's stairs and landings were wood and tended to be cold if *I* needed to go wandering in the middle of the night. I slipped my wet feet into them, picked up the robe that was hanging on a chair, and wrapped it around myself, cutting out the night chills, before making it out of the dark room.

'Grace,' I half-whispered as I exited onto the landing. 'Gracie, are you out here, honey?'

There was no answer.

The only sound I could hear in the house was a slow *tick tock* of the large clock Mom kept in the living room. It had echoed around this house for as long as I could remember. There were no creaks or cracks from the house settling, and stranger still, there were no sounds of the whistling wind outside.

There was nothing but an eerie silence.

'Gracie, where are you? Answer me right now, honey.'

My head was spinning. All the memories of my dream came flooding back. Wandering in the snow, the wind howling around me, my breath lost in the cold of the storm. I wrapped the robe a little tighter in a weak attempt to combat the feeling of dread I was succumbing to. The music, the song, the glowing light—everything was rushing back to me. I was beginning to get annoyed with the feeling of my skin prickling.

'Gracie, answer me. Right NOW!' I snapped, frowning down into the abyss that was the ground floor of the house.

'What's going on?' The deep but sleepy voice from behind made me jump. I breathed a sigh of relief when I saw Anthony tying his robe around himself, his dark face alert.

'Oh, thank God!' I exclaimed, my hand instinctively going to my mouth. 'Ant, it's Grace. I've just had the worst dream ever, and then I woke up and—and …'

'Where is she?' he asked, looking past me, back into my bedroom.

All I could do was shake my head. I couldn't form the words I needed to tell him that I didn't know where she was.

He pushed past me and darted down the stairs. As I watched him go, a noise caught my attention. Hoping it was Gracie coming out of the bathroom, I looked up just in time to see Mom's bedroom door open. She peeped her head around the door and regarded me with red, tired eyes. For the first time since we'd arrived, I gazed upon her as a sick woman. Her neck was stick thin, and the skin hanging off it looked yellow and sallow in the dim light.

'What's all the fuss?' she whispered, her voice croaky as if it hurt to talk.

'Grace is missing.' It was all I could manage. Pesky words were still eluding me.

I watched as her rheumy eyes widened, and she tightened the collar of her nightgown around her neck. 'The spirit,' she whispered.

'What? What spirit?' I asked. The image of the little girl in my dream came back, and whoever I'd seen earlier in the black coat. I shivered again.

That Christmas, I did an awful lot of shivering.

'The Spirit of Christmas,' she whispered.

As I looked away, I did a double take because I thought I saw my mother cross herself like a gypsy woman warding off a curse. *Mom's never been religious,* I thought as she retreated back into her bedroom.

I stared at her closed door for a few moments before continuing down the stairs to help Anthony search for my six-year-old daughter.

'Did you leave a radio on when you came up?' he asked as I joined him in the hallway.

'No! Why?'

'Can you hear that music?' he asked, holding his hand out towards me.

I shook my head, although I knew what he was talking about; I'd heard it earlier.

He put his finger to his mouth. I listened.

Finally, I could hear it, instantly wishing I couldn't.

'*Do you believe in Christmas magic?*' was quickly followed by the echo, '*Do you believe in Christmas magic?*'

Everything about my dream came rushing back. 'Turn it off,' I snapped.

Anthony looked at me. 'What?' he asked.

'I said turn that fucking song off. It gives me the creeps.'

'I don't know where it's coming from,' he replied, poking his head into the living room. When he was inside, he flicked on the light switch, and the music stopped. He turned to look at me. It was the worst look I'd ever seen from him, even as a child. It unnerved me more than I already was.

He was scared. If Anthony was scared, I knew I was in trouble.

'It's freezing in here,' he whispered.

I watched his breath spread out like mist over a lake. I cocked my head and watched the phenomenon. It wasn't *that* cold in the hallway; how could there be such a difference in temperature between rooms?

Following him into the living room, I felt like I'd passed through an ice curtain. It was as cold as a walk-in freezer in there. 'Jesus Christ.' I gulped as the cold infiltrated my chest, dragging at even the smallest bits of exposed skin.

A creaking on the stairs alerted us. With my heart pounding in my throat, I turned to see what it was. I reached out and grabbed my brother's hand. He gave me a little squeeze, silently informing me that he was just as scared as I was but was ready to do whatever was needed of him. This movement, this tiny gesture, gave me all the reassurance I needed. My brother, although scared, was there for me, right now and forever!

It was all I needed to know.

He stepped forward, towards the hallway and the stairwell. I could see hesitation in his advance, and I felt for him. I knew it wasn't physical contact with someone he feared, Anthony was a match for any man in a fight, but I could tell it was due to the house feeling so creepy right now. Even through the stress of the situation, I had to hold in a laugh at the thought of my big, strapping brother being scared of ghosts.

The mood was lifted when Mom appeared at the bottom of the stairs wearing a thick robe, looking a little more like the fearless, strong woman we knew she was.

Or had been, I thought with a sad smile.

'Mom, is there anywhere you can think of where Grace could be hiding?' I asked, the panic in my voice evident not only by the high pitch I was whispering in but by the way Anthony and Mom looked at me.

'This'll be the spirit's doing,' Mom whispered. Her voice was low, but what she said and how she said it was enough to cut through the atmosphere and the cold. It was like a statement from a revered sage in a horror movie.

Anthony and I both looked at her. She held on to the neck of her robe, pulling the ends together.

'What are you talking about?' Anthony asked, shaking his head, dismissing her words.

'The Spirit of Christmas,' Mom replied. 'It's about that time for her.'

I sighed and put my arm around her, pulling her away from the cold of the living room, into the relative warmth of the hallway.

As my arm reached around her shoulders, I was shocked by how thin she was beneath the robe with only a nightgown beneath. 'Come on, Mom. Let's get you over here in the kitchen while me and Anthony look for her. She won't have gone far. She's scared of her own shadow sometimes.'

'She told me about her friend,' my mother confessed as she allowed herself to be led.

It was crazy how much warmer it was in the other room. *How can that be?* I thought. *There's no physical barrier between them.* Another shiver ran through me as I thought about how cold I had been in my dream.

I thought about the freezing wetness all around my bed.

'Did you hear the music?' she asked as she sat at the table.

The question caused me to stop what I was doing, going out of my mind worrying about Grace. 'What music, Mom?' I asked, knowing exactly what she was talking about.

She shared a sad smile. '*Do you believe the magic?*' she began to sing, swaying her head slowly.

A cold splinter entered my heart. My knees weakened as the words left her lips.

'Was that the song you heard?' she asked, her voice nothing but a rasp.

I sat at the table, doing my best to pretend it wasn't because I felt like I was about to fall down.

'It's her favourite.'

'Whose favourite?' I asked.

'The spirit's. She always sings it, every time she comes.' As my mother looked at me, her face changed. Suddenly, she was a child, one who had said too much and realised she might be in trouble. Her old eyes still held a youngster's spirit within them.

'When who comes, Mother? Who?' I could feel myself slipping into something like madness or anger then. I couldn't deal with my daughter being missing and my mother losing her marbles, not all in the same night.

She looked away from me. Her shifting eyes exposed her embarrassment and more than a little fear. 'The spirit,' she said eventually, lifting her eyebrows.

'Oh my God …' Anthony's cry interrupted this intense conversation, coming from the living room.

I jumped up in an instant. Once again, my breath was pushed from my stomach as I rushed from the table into the living room, barely noticing the temperature change. It had gone from the piercing cold of moments ago to a more ambient level.

'What are you doing in there, little lady?' Anthony asked as I made it just in time to watch him climb into a small cabinet behind the couch. 'Come on out of there,' he continued, reaching in. 'You'll catch your death.'

I watched as my hero pulled my little girl from the space. My champion of many an encounter was a star once again. He stood, holding Grace in his arms, both wearing huge grins.

'Mommy,' Grace shouted and held her hands out towards me.

My heart felt like it was melting as warmth spread through me. The shaking that had been a constant companion since finding Grace missing subsided.

'Wow, baby, you're freezing,' was all I could say as I accepted the offer of her embrace.

'You're so warm, though, Mommy,' she said with a giggle as she snuggled into my neck.

'Why were you hiding in there?' I asked, wracking my brain trying to think of a fun way of asking this so it didn't sound like I was angry or scared out of my wits, even though I was both of these things. I thought the simple route may have been the best.

'I was hiding with Lisa,' she answered, her sweet breath warming my face. 'She wanted to play, so I held her hand, and we played.'

'You held her hand?' I asked, cocking my head. I'd never heard of anyone having physical contact with an imaginary friend before, not ever.

Grace lifted her head from my shoulder and looked between me and Anthony. Her face reminded me of my mother's moments ago, like she was in trouble and didn't know what to say next. 'Erm, yes, Mommy,' she stuttered. 'She came into our room and took my hand. She told me she wanted to tell me a secret. A secret that no one else knew.'

I put her down on the floor and looked at her. 'What was the secret, baby?' I asked, trying to keep my tone light. I could feel Anthony's concern as he looked at her. 'What did your friend tell you?'

'I can't tell you, Mommy,' she replied, shaking her head and rolling her eyes. 'It wouldn't be a secret then, would it? But she did say that when I know what it is, I can tell Grandma.'

I blinked and shook my head. 'You can tell Grandma? Who said you can tell Grandma?'

'Lisa,' she replied matter-of-factly. 'She told me I was only supposed to tell Grandma.'

'Well,' I said, real anger building inside me. I didn't like where this *Lisa* thing was going. It was one thing to have an imaginary friend; it was quite another when they took your hand, led you off to hide, and told you secrets. 'You do know that secrets aren't very nice, don't you?' I asked. 'They can be rude or even mean sometimes.'

Grace's face fell, and her eyes looked like they were about to cry. 'She told me this secret was mean,' she whispered. 'So mean that Grandma was the only one I could tell.'

I looked back into the kitchen and could see my mother sitting at the table, nodding her head as if she were falling asleep and jerking herself back awake again. If I hadn't known she was sick, that scene would have been a lot funnier than it was. As I did know, it broke my heart. 'I'm not too sure Grandma is up for secrets right now, baby. I think she's tired. Will it be OK to wait until the morning to tell her?'

Grace's face brightened. 'Oh yeah. Lisa said she doesn't need to know until Christmas Eve anyway. That's the day after tomorrow.'

Anthony reached out and stroked her face, and she curled her head into the caress. 'OK, then,' he said, his voice deep and authoritative. 'But you do know that technically its Christmas Eve tomorrow as it's already half-past three. I say we all go back to bed and get our beauty sleep, and we can talk about this in the morning. Agreed?'

'You don't need beauty sleep, Uncle Ant; you're a boy,' Grace said shyly, moving back towards my embrace.

'Oh, you cheeky monkey,' he said, wiggling his fingers at her as if tickling was in the cards. She squealed and snuggled into me a little tighter.

'OK, Uncle Anthony. Let's not get her even more hyped up than she already is.' I scowled a little playfully, but there was enough serious Alison for him to take note.

He did. He offered me a wink, understanding and accepting the scolding. 'Well, I'll get Mom back to bed, then, and I'll see you two in the morning.' He leaned in and gave Grace a kiss, and then me. 'Goodnight, my little Christmas berries,' he whispered before leaving the living room and going into the kitchen to help Mom upstairs.

'And you, little lady. Do you want to tell me why you'd think it was a good idea to run off and hide in a little cabinet like that at stupid o'clock in the morning?' I scolded her as she rested against my hip.

She laughed at my *stupid o'clock* reference. 'I told you,' she continued when the laugh had died down. 'Lisa told me to.'

'So, if this Lisa told you to jump off a cliff, would you do that too?'

Grace laughed; it was a girlish giggle. I knew she was testing the water to see if she was really in trouble. 'Of course not, Mommy. I'd come and ask you about it first.'

'Well, I'm glad to hear that. So come on, let's get back to bed. And no more shenanigans, OK?'

'OK, Mommy. I love you,' she said, kissing the side of my head.

'I love you too, baby,' I replied, putting her down on the bottom step. 'Now get up those stairs without another peep. Otherwise, Santa won't be making any stops here for a certain young Gracie.'

Her eyes widened with a sharp intake of breath before she zoomed up the stairs. 'Grandma said that Santa doesn't come to this house,' she said as she reached the top.

'Oh, did she, now?' I replied with a frown, wondering what my mom had promised her in return. *There must be something,* I thought. *There's no way we're getting away with it that easily.*

'She said when you and Uncle Ant were my age, you were too poor for Santa Claus, and the Spirit of Christmas used to come instead. She said that if we were all very good between now and Christmas Eve, then the Spirit of Christmas would look after us too!'

I smiled as I made my way up the stairs behind her.

As we got into the bedroom, Grace ran towards the bed. Just before she jumped on it, she stopped dead and turned back to look at me, her mouth pouting and her brow furled into a frown.

My stomach turned. *What now?* I thought.

'Mommy,' my little girl whispered. 'Why is the carpet wet?' She began to hop from one foot to the next. Her frown was gone and had been replaced by a smile.

'I don't know, sweet pea. It was like that when I woke up.'

She accepted this explanation without any further cross examination and clambered onto the bed. 'Lisa was wet when I took her hand,' she said, climbing under the blankets and pulling them up to her chin.

'Was she, now?' I asked. 'Well, no more talk about Lisa tonight. I think there's been a bit too much excitement for one night.'

'Fine with me,' Grace said as she snuggled into the blankets. 'She told me that she wanted to speak to you herself anyway.' Grace put her head on the pillow, turned around, and pulled the blankets all the way over her head, leaving me staring at her.

I wanted to shake her, to ask her what she meant by that, but I'd already said there was to be no more Lisa talk. I couldn't go back on that. I got into the bed and stroked my daughter's hair for a few moments until I felt the small vibrations of little snores escaping her. I lay back on the bed and closed my eyes. I thought sleep would be the unattainable dream after the night's excitement and after what Grace had just told me about Lisa being wet, but I was wrong.

10.

THE SENSATION OF being carried overwhelmed her. Her head bounced in rhythm with every step taken. She was aware of the cold, the lashings of the icy wind stinging her face, but there was a warmth around her that she couldn't fathom. She had no idea where it could be coming from.

A voice cut through the wind. It was a child's voice. There was a high-pitched element to it, but it was most definitely male. *Please let that be Ant,* she thought, not daring to open her eyes to see for herself. She didn't want to know who, or what, was carrying her, but she was eternally grateful for the warmth.

'Mr Sharpe, where are we going?' the young voice asked.

She knew now that it was Ant, but by his pitch, she could sense he was scared. *Mr Sharpe?* she thought. Her eyes shot open. She was expecting the glare she'd seen from the young girl to blind her, but as she opened them, there was very little to differentiate between them being closed. It was an almost complete absence of light, just glimpses here and there. Moving only her eyes, not wanting to give away the fact she was awake, she scanned her immediate environment, hoping to identify landmarks or anything that might give a clue to where they were going.

She moved her head slightly, hoping it would look like a natural movement, and gazed behind them. She'd been right; Ant was trailing them. He was silhouetted in the dying glow of the setting sun. These woods always had an odd feel to them at this time of the year. In front of you, it could be pitch black, while behind, there would be a glorious sunset. The young boy in this sunset looked like he'd been crying, and she could see he was exhausted, far too tired to keep up the pace that her abductor was leading.

'Mr Sharpe, where are you taking Alli?' he cried.

'Home,' was the only word she heard. She felt it rumble in the man's chest as his strong arms held her tight.

They continued to trudge on through the snow.

Initially, the word gave her hope, a slim hope, but hope, nonetheless. As she looked at the pained face of her brother behind them, that slim gleam of optimism began to dim. *Did he mean my home ... or his?* she thought. This horrible idea was given credence by the sobs from the trailing Ant.

'Please don't kill her. She's my sister. I ... I need her.'

Even within the deep fear of what, maybe, was about to happen, her heart reached out to her brother. She already knew he was loyal and brave; his actions now were proving that to her. *It's a shame I won't be around to see him grow into a fine man,* she thought as he continued to lag behind them.

All Mr Sharpe did was grunt and keep on trudging onward through the snow.

She counted the crunches under his feet as his heavy boots broke the virgin snow. She thought about trying to wriggle free. If she bucked hard enough, he was bound to drop her, but her body was aching, and she was too stiff to even twitch her leg. All she could do was lay back and succumb to his will ... *whatever that might be,* she thought.

They walked on for a while further. She didn't know if they had walked far or if the debris left behind by the snowstorm, which had since diminished, had made the walking conditions hazardous. She was praying for the latter. All she could do was check back every now and then and thank God, or her father, or whoever it was who had given Anthony the tenacity to not give up. She could just about see him maybe ten feet behind, on the fringes of her vision, in the strange twilight of the winter wonderland, or nightmare, that the snowy woods had become. He looked older somehow, like he was a grown man and not a six-year-old boy—or nearly seven, as he would vehemently snap at anyone who made that mistake. *Am I seeing him as he will be? Because I'll never see him again?* This thought made her want to cry. She didn't want to resign herself to death, but the fact she couldn't move any of her limbs to save herself and was relying on a—no matter how obstinate he was—six-year-old boy didn't give her much hope.

The tears refused to come. She made a decision that no matter how hot the pot Mr Sharpe put her in was, she wouldn't scream or cry. *I won't give him the satisfaction.*

From out of the darkness, a voice called out.

It snapped Alli from her reverie, and she moved her head, ever so slightly, in the direction the voice had come from.

'ALISON … ANTHONY …' the voice called again.

This time, she recognised it, but there was something about it she didn't like.

Her abductor stopped. She didn't know if it was because of the shouting or if it was the moving of her head alerting him to her wakefulness, but either way, she was glad. Whoever owned the voice may well be her and her brother's salvation.

'WHAT ARE YOU DOING WITH HER?' the voice shouted again, and Alison was able to identify two things about it. The first was that it was her mother's voice; the second was she sounded scared out of her wits. The sound of the voice had a duplicitous effect on her. Within the same breath, it reassured her that her mother would surely save her from this vile monster, but it scared her by how terrified she was.

'Put her down. Now. Put her down and walk away, or I'll call the police,' her mother shouted. 'Don't you dare test me!'

Alli still couldn't see her, but she guessed she was near. Mr Sharpe had turned, and as she craned her neck, she could see Anthony had stopped too. She sensed Mr Sharpe was in two minds about something. *Is he thinking of killing my mom and Anthony too?* she thought, wishing her brain and inner monologue would just go away. *Please don't kill my mother and brother,* she cried in her head.

For a few moments that felt like hours, Mr Sharpe stood still. She could feel his arms trembling as he held her dead weight, and she prayed again. Prayed he would put her down, that he would go away, and they would never, ever have to see him again.

Two of her prayers were answered.

She felt herself being lowered onto the snow. Her body relaxed as the cold and damp of the ground seeped into her already damp clothing.

'I didn't …' was all he said as he stepped away from the bundle of shuddering rags.

'I don't care what you did or didn't do. You need to stay away from my family.'

Alli managed to look up from her prone position. She could see her mother. She looked like a superhero wearing a long, thick coat, buttoned all the way up to her neck. Behind her was a strange light. It looked like car headlights, but Alli knew they were too far from the road for any cars to be able to be there.

Delores raised a finger, and her face creased. Alli could see water dripping from her pink digit. 'You stay away from me and my family; do you hear me? Don't you think you've caused enough trouble?' she hissed over the howling wind.

Alli squinted. She wanted to see the light behind her mother a little better. There was something about it, something she remembered.

'I didn't want …'

Alli assumed it was Mr Sharpe talking, as there wasn't anyone else around with such a deep voice. *Not unless the vision I had of Ant has come true,* she thought.

'I found her in the snow. The boy, he was running …'

A figure stepped out of the strange light behind her mother. It was a little girl. She was wearing a black coat that looked heavy. Her blonde hair was dark and wet, and her dripping pigtails hung limply down the sides of her face. It was obvious Delores hadn't seen her, as she showed no indication she was there. All her attention was between Alison lying in the snow and Mr Sharpe.

'Stay away from her, and stay away from him, you pervert,' her mother hissed.

Later, Alli and Anthony would have lengthy conversations about what the word *pervert* meant. This conversation would continue on for the months to come.

In one motion, Alli felt herself swamped by hands. Loving, strong hands. As Ant's arms enveloped her, relief washed over her like a wave cresting before it smothered the sand of the beach. The warmth of him covering her was the best feeling she had felt in all of her short life. His face was raining kisses over her cheeks and forehead. 'Alli ... Alli, I'm so sorry. I'll never run away from you again. It was just a joke. I swear. I didn't mean to lose you.'

'Ant, can you see her?' Alli whispered, keeping her voice low so her mother, who was still standing defiantly between her and the looming Mr Sharpe, couldn't hear her. 'Can you see the little girl?'

The boy turned to look where his sister was indicating. In the yellowing, waxy light of the moon, she saw his eyes shift between the light and their mother. 'Yes,' he whispered. 'It's how I found you. I followed that light.'

With that, the odd illumination winked out of existence, as did Mr Sharpe.

Alli turned to watch his large frame slip into the darkness of the snow-laden trees. Then she felt her mother smothering her in similar hugs to her brother's.

'Alison. Oh, Alison! Don't you ever scare me like that again. Or you, Anthony. I've lost too much in this life already. I won't lose you two as well.'

Alison had expected their mother to be upset, maybe even angry, but his reaction confused her.

However, she accepted the offered hugs gladly.

As the moonlight cast its silvery glow, Alli noted they were not too far from home. All three of them clung to each other, happy to be reunited and safe.

~~~~

From deep in the trees, unbeknownst and unseen by anyone, Mr Sharpe watched.

He watched as they hugged.

He watched as, eventually, they got themselves up from the snow and began to make their way home.

He watched as they walked off, the three of them, hand in hand, into the night.

When they were gone, he headed back towards his own home. As he walked, he hummed the tune that had been stuck in his head for the last few days. It was a Christmas song that had been a hit some years back. One that seemed to haunt him each Christmas.

'*Do you believe in Christmas magic?*' he whispered as he trudged home. His feet crunching in the freshly fallen snow was the only accompaniment to his song.

11.

THE WIND WAS whistling through the eaves and sleet, and snow battered the windows. Slowly, I opened my eyes to the dim light of the new day. The warmth of the blankets, combined with the comfortable familiarity of the mattress, combated the protestations of the weather outside. I took a few moments to relish the luxury of the bed before even beginning to think about getting up and facing whatever challenges today might bring.

It was the day before Christmas Eve, and Mom still didn't have a tree or any of her decorations up. I also knew there wouldn't be much in the way of food in the house for a traditional Christmas dinner. A small smile broke on my face. This was my kind of situation. I loved Christmas shopping. Whether it was for presents, or food, or even decorations, I always found it enjoyable. This year, I was determined to stretch it out, to savour every moment with Mom. *Because this will be her last,* the ominous voice of Dr Browning echoed through my head. I gave my brain a mental shuffle, hoping to kick the negativity out of it. Today was going to be a fantastic day, as the rest of the week would be.

With a yawn, I stretched, filling my lungs with the fresh air the storm had brought with it. I always loved being inside during a storm. Watching everything Mother Nature could throw at us from the safety and security of a large glass window.

That was when I noticed the space next to me, the space that should have been occupied by Grace, was once again empty.

Not again! I thought, rolling my eyes. Grace had always been an early riser, but she would normally let me know she was getting up, even if I wasn't in her early morning plans.

Throwing the covers back, I jumped out of the bed. I noticed, only in my peripheral thoughts, that the carpet was dry. Grabbing the robe that was hanging on the door hook, I wrapped myself into the warmth of the fleece. As I exited the room, the heat of the house hit me like a wall. A smell, one that had time-travelled all the way from my childhood, wafted towards me. It was the aroma of freshly cut firewood burning on an open fire. It conflicted my memories, bringing back some beautiful reminiscences of this house when we were children, and it made me think about my father. I don't have many memories of him, I was only eight when he died, but the smell of wood burning always made me think of him. I smiled. It was a bitter-sweet moment, but I knew I couldn't linger here. After the events of last night, I needed to find Grace.

Anthony was shuffling around downstairs; no doubt he was the founder of the warmth. 'Grace … are you down here?' I shouted, hoping that she, after all the excitement of last night, had gotten up early and decided her mother needed at least another hour in bed. 'Ant, is she down there with you?'

Anthony popped his head around the stairwell. He was wearing a thick red coat, and his hair had the look of someone who had recently been wearing a hat. His face was ruddy, as if he had been out in the cold.

'Who? Mom?' he asked.

My stomach dropped again, and the hackles on the back of my neck stood up. It was a feeling I probably should have been used to, at least over the last few days, but I knew I never would be.

'No, Grace,' I replied, finding it difficult to form the words in my mouth.

Anthony's shoulders fell as his eyes drew closer. 'Again?' he asked.

I shrugged.

He sighed. 'I'll check the cabinet.'

I bounded down the stairs and into the living room, a room that was dominated by the roaring fire and an impressive stack of firewood next to it, drying out. Anthony's head was already deep inside the cabinet. There was nowhere to hide inside it; it was far too small. I instantly began to shake.

'Ant,' I sobbed, feeling as if I was overreacting but couldn't help myself. 'Why does this keep happening?' The tremor in my voice gave away the fact that my whole body was trembling.

'She has to be here somewhere. Go and look in the kitchen,' he ordered.

I had an inkling he was trying to get me out of the way as he searched the rest of the house. There were fewer places to hide in the kitchen.

'Shit,' Anthony shouted from the other room.

I lifted my head from beneath the table and looked towards the living room. I ran in, hoping beyond hope it wasn't bad news. *How can it be good news with a 'shit' at the start of the sentence?* 'What?' I demanded, bumping into him in the hallway.

He was looking at the coat rack. There were two coats hanging from it. One short blue one, and one long grey one that belonged to our mother.

'Where's Grace's?' I almost shouted. 'Where the hell is Grace's coat?'

Without another word, Anthony reached up and flung the blue one my way as he zipped up the red one he was already wearing.

'Why would she have gone outside? There's a storm blowing out there,' I hissed as I struggled into my coat. I could feel that the colour had drained from my face, as I suddenly felt clammy, dizzy, and unsteady on my feet as the room began to spin.

'Maybe the same reason why she hid in that cabinet last night.' Anthony's reply did absolutely nothing to reassure me. 'Come on, we need to get out there and find her. That storm is coming in fast,' he finished.

I looked at what I had on, pyjamas, a robe, and my thick outdoor coat. I was no way equipped for an expedition, not with a storm brewing. What good would I be to Grace if I was caught in the snow with no protective clothing? Without another word, I thundered up the stairs and quickly changed into cold weather clothing. Within less than three minutes, I was ready to search for my missing child for the second time.

~~~~

Anthony was already outside. As I stepped out into the stormy morning, an ugly feeling of diminished hope, of not finding her alive out here, overwhelmed me.

'Grace!' I shouted over the howling wind. 'Grace, are you out here?' The storm stole most of my voice the moment it left my lips. It also filled my mouth full of snow and wind. Breathing and shouting at the same time was a struggle.

'Grace ... Grace ...' Anthony's voice was cutting through the storm much better than mine. 'Grace, can you hear me?' he shouted as I watched his red coat disappear into the mists of the storm.

A brief flashback of the dream/memory I'd had last night came flooding back. It was so strong that I felt I had to physically shake it off before concentrating on the job at hand. Fortunately for Grace, I had drummed it into her from a small child that if she was ever caught outside during a storm, she was to find the nearest shelter and sit it out. I hoped she'd taken heed of my words and wouldn't be stupid enough to walk around in it. But still, the thought of my daughter, my seven-year-old Grace, out here on her own was making me sick to my stomach.

Without thinking too much more about it, I headed towards Old Man Sharpe's place. The wind was blowing the snow hard into my face, making it almost impossible to see where I was going, and the thickness of the snow on the ground was making walking difficult, but the determination in my heart and my maternal instincts to protect my child were overwhelming. The dense clouds were too thick for the sun to break through, causing a premature dusk in what should have been a bright part of the day.

Visibility was almost zero.

That was when I saw the glow.

It took me a moment to register it was there, as it was something that shouldn't have been. It was an alien glare, and I think my brain didn't want to acknowledge it.

It was coming from up ahead, not too far away. Through the mist, the storm, and the trees, it was almost impossible to gauge distance. It looked like someone could have been standing in the trees holding a bright lantern.

My first thought was *Old Man Sharpe.*

However, there was something about the light, something oddly familiar. I knew it from my dream, but as usually happens to dreams in the cold light of day, it had become fuzzy and protracted. But there was *something* about it.

'Hey …' I shouted, not knowing if my weakened voice would even carry through the whistle of the wind. 'Can you help me?'

Whoever it was holding the light must have either heard my shout or seen my plight, as the illumination flickered for a moment. I could only hope the bearer had heard me and was coming to help. To my relief, the light began to draw closer. I struggled on, hoping I wouldn't trip and snap my ankle or worse. 'Have you seen my little girl?' I panted, my voice breathless, close to breaking. 'Have you seen my Grace? Please … help me … she's lost in the snow.'

With the words out of my mouth and not able to take them back, my fear intensified, and my foot *did* become entangled in something beneath the snow. Before I knew what was happening, I was face-down in the cold, spitting out mouthfuls of melting slush. Once the surprise of the fall and the sudden numbness of my face subsided, I looked up towards the light. It was still there, but it hadn't gotten any closer. I would have expected whoever was holding the lantern to have come to help. I checked my leg, hoping there wasn't any damage. I was relieved to find there wasn't, except for a small tear in the fabric of my pants.

'A little help here,' I shouted, but the light didn't move.

Even more determined to get the attention of the light-bearer, I struggled to my feet. Dusting the powder-like snow off my clothing, I began to scramble towards the light. As I drew closer, I felt sure, but couldn't be certain, that the light was moving farther away. 'Wait! Stop! Help me!' I screamed, or at least I thought it was a scream. I was almost certain it was moving away, through the trees, retreating into the mists of the prematurely dark morning.

It was getting closer to Mr Sharpe's house. It was the last place I wanted to be, and the very last place I wanted Grace to be.

Certain boogiemen stayed with you, no matter how old you grew or how stupid it was that you were afraid of them in the first place.

Mr Sharpe was *that* boogieman.

My mother had always told us never, under any circumstances, to play in or near his yard or house. Her foreboding words flooded back to me now, and other than one silly incident on Halloween, we had always heeded that warning. So as the light began to move closer to the old house, the trepidation of my mission grew. Finding Grace was my only priority. My petty fears and childhood prejudices would need to be pushed to the back of my mind for now. I closed my eyes, wishing Anthony was with me right now. The only redeeming quality was that the wind had died somewhat, taking most of the storm's bluster and anger with it. It was still too misty to see through the trees properly, but it was suddenly easier going. Crying out to whoever it was creating the light had proven useless, so I decided to save my breath and just follow it as fast as I could.

Since the wind had died, the only sounds I could hear were my own breathing and the crunching of the snow beneath my feet. But as I got closer to the house, this was broken by the eerie sound of what I thought was a child's laughter.

I turned my head and removed my hood, exposing my ears to the icy air, to get a better idea of what I was hearing. My heart was pounding, not only from the physical exertion of the morning but with the hope the sound I could hear was Grace and she was not stuck somewhere, freezing cold and soaking wet, but safe, and alive, and … laughing at the trick she had pulled on us.

It seemed unlikely, but it was a hope, and I was going to cling to it for dear life.

I didn't know if my mind was playing tricks on me, but I thought I could see footprints. Well, calling them footprints might have been a stretch, as they were merely imprints that were being filled rapidly by drifting snow. But I needed to think of them as prints, a child's prints. I decided to follow them, no matter where they led, because they were the only lead I had.

The wind was screaming around my head again like a hungry banshee determined to collect its souls, but I was determined too. I measured the distance between the indents in the snow with my own stride, concluding they *had* been made by a child. They took a path that skirted along the line of the snow-covered foliage, making their way either to or from Mr Sharpe's house, which was now nothing but a dark shadow looming not too distant. If I was to follow the tracks, I needed to up my pace; otherwise, there wouldn't be anything left to follow.

'Grace,' I shouted again through the storm. 'Can you hear me? Answer me. I'll come to you.'

The only answer I received was the shriek of the wind.

Lowering my head against the wind and snow, I continued following the rapidly disappearing prints. They were almost gone now. I was making prints of my own and hoping I'd be able to follow them home again when I found her safe and well—*and alive,* I added, although I really didn't want to acknowledge that thought.

In-between the howls of the wind and the creaking of the trees, another sound was cutting through. It was the child laughing again. It might have been the same child I heard before, it certainly sounded like it, only this time she seemed closer.

After a few more steps, pushing everything I had against the storm, the tracks disappeared. Panicking, I turned and looked behind me, hoping to see where, or if, I'd veered away from them. The eerie glow I'd seen before was back, pulsing a dim yellow, illuminating the tracks I'd just made. I saw that I'd deviated from the path of the original prints a little. *No wonder they disappeared,* I thought. *I'm heading in the wrong direction.* I'd assumed they were heading towards the old house, but I could see now they weren't. They were heading towards the backyard. I turned, retracing my steps, heading towards the strange, warm-looking light. Towards the sound of the mysterious laughing child.

My progress was slightly quicker using my footprints as a guide. I was exhausted, out of breath, and conscious that I was out here on my own now too. I hadn't seen or heard anything from Anthony since we'd left the house. I assumed he'd gone the other way rather than towards Old Man Sharpe's house.

Wow, I haven't thought of him as Old Man Sharpe for what? Thirty years?

The child's laughter continued, making me conscious that every moment it took to find her could be a moment closer to Gracie … *Don't you dare say dying,* I scolded myself. The laughing was now cutting through the wind. There was something odd, maybe artificial about it, like it had been recorded on a different track and someone with bad skills had attempted to mix it in louder than the rest of the recording.

I had an idea it was coming from wherever that light was coming from. The thought that someone could be out here in this storm messing with me, messing with the rescue attempt of my daughter, scared me more than the fact that I was now skulking around the one house that still gave me occasional nightmares. I hoped whoever it was would make themselves known, and soon.

'Who are you? Do you have Grace?' I screamed into the grey abyss, but again, I might as well have been shouting into a real one. There was no discernible answer, just a chuckle that sounded ghoulish, and maybe even a little nasty, rather than the light, playful laugh I'd heard earlier. The devilish quality might have been my imagination, or at least I *hoped* it was my imagination.

The illumination continued to move further away, fading into the darkness of the morning.

'Come back!' I cried as I tried to move faster, retracing my earlier steps.

That was when it winked out.

My stomach dropped with its disappearance. All the hope of finding Grace alive died with that illumination. I looked up, my vision impaired by the storm and the tears forming in my eyes, and I was ready to give up. I was ready to slump down into the snow and let the storm's icy fingers embrace me, let them take me, envelop me, carry me to my sweet Grace.

A small, very small but obvious flicker in the darkness caught my eye. My despair waned, and a fresh glimmer hope sparked within me once again. The light hadn't died; it had just disappeared around a large bush as it headed into Mr Sharpe's yard. Even with my renewed vigour and hope, I was more than a little hesitant to follow. I had spent my whole life being told never to go in there. That level of influence from an early age can and did have a lasting effect, but I knew if there was any way, any hope of whoever this person was helping Grace, then I was going grasp at it with clawed hands.

The light disappeared again, and I saw the day as it was, almost as dark as night. My eyes took a moment to get used to the lack of illumination, and the shadows became recognisable objects again. I looked around. It took another moment for me to grasp that I was in a place I had never been before. Although it was covered in thick snow, I could see that the yard I was standing in had been well tended. The almost impenetrable bushes around its perimeter were manicured and cultured on this side, and I could tell by the even surface of the snow that it had fallen on a well-maintained and cared for lawn. The flatness was broken by a huge tree. It was a gnarly old oak. The trunk was thick, twisted, and tall. I looked up, noticing it was probably about the same hight as the house itself. Its branches were empty of leaves but heavily laden with snow.

The strange glow was back, just as bright and pulsing as it had been outside the yard, only now it was closer. It was coming from the other side of the tree.

The trunk bisected the light down the middle, hiding whoever, or whatever, was causing it. The wind had died down some again, and the snow falling from the moody sky was now just fat flakes. The wind's eerie howls had died too, which was a relief, though I had a feeling the reprieve might not last long.

It had been replaced with delicate music, a song I knew. I'd heard Mom whistle it many times during my childhood, usually when she was washing the dishes or doing something that didn't require her full attention. There was always a vacant look on her face, almost dream-like, whenever she whistled or hummed or sometimes sang this tune. Of course, I'd also heard it many times on the radio or on compilation CDs released at Christmastime. To hear this song now, outside, in the snow, unnerved me, especially since it wasn't the first time I'd heard it since arriving back at Mom's house.

The thick tenor of Johnny Plaid seemed as alien in this environment as the warm, golden glow that was pulsing in perfect time with the rousing, marching drumbeat.

'*Here it comes again ...*'

The echo of the backup singers was eerier than the main voice.

'*Here it comes again ...*'

With my pulse throbbing in my throat, a tremor that rattled my bones, and the cold that was penetrating all my layers, including my torn pants, I approached the tree and the strange glow behind it. The closer I got, the dimmer the light became. When I was close enough to touch the trunk, the light was barely there, and the dullness of the ugly morning had been restored. I reached out a shaking hand to touch the trunk, and the instant my hand touched the rough bark, the light blinked out completely.

It was gone, along with the music.

Suddenly, Grace came into my vision. She was standing before me, motionless. She was wearing her thick winter coat and was looking up into the tree, her face pink, wind ravaged yet filled with wonder.

My breath was lost again, but I managed to fling myself at my child, my arms wrapping around her the instant I touched her. She snapped out of whatever dream she was in, her focus moving from the tree to the madwoman in the blue coat attacking her. She stepped back, her eyes not recognising me for a moment. Then a wide grin spread on her ruddy face, and she allowed my arms to take her in whole before she hugged me back.

'Grace, what are you doing out here?' I gasped, still struggling to form words. I should have been angry with her, but the relief of finding her alive and well was overwhelming me. I could feel sobs heaving in my chest before I could hear them. 'We've been out of our minds with worry. What possessed you to venture out here in a storm? Haven't I told you how dangerous the snowstorms are around here?'

She turned away from me and looked back up into the tree. Confused, I followed her gaze and noticed she was looking at the remains of an old tree house. 'Lisa brought me here,' she said, as if it was the most normal thing in the world.

It wasn't the answer I wanted. 'Come on,' I snapped, taking her hand in mine. 'We'll talk about this later. We need to get you back to the house before we all catch our death out here. Didn't you hear me shouting?'

She shook her head. 'No, Mommy. Lisa was singing, and it was all I could hear.'

'Singing?' The conversation had taken an interesting turn. 'What song?' I asked.

'A Christmas one. I think it's a little bit spooky, but it's her favourite. It was asking questions about believing in magic. I'm not too sure if I liked it.'

My blood froze in my already freezing veins. I felt as if my insides were now the same temperature as the air around me. '*Do you believe the magic*?' I asked, not knowing if I wanted an answer.

I got one anyway.

'Yeah, that's the one. She was singing it, and it was all I could hear. She brought me out here to show me something, but she disappeared before she got the chance.'

I tried to shake off the nasty feeling growing inside. I held Grace by the arm, pulling her way from the tree. 'Come on, we need to get back inside before the storm blows up again. Uncle Ant is out looking for you too. You can't just leave the house, Grace, especially when there's a storm outside.'

'She kept me out of the storm, Mommy. She told me I was safe. She had a strange light, and it kept me warm. It kept the snow and wind off me.'

I could understand what she was saying, even though I didn't want to. It brought up too many questions that I didn't want but did need answering. However, one look skywards told me the questions were going to have to wait. The clouds looked pregnant, and the strong wind was threatening again. 'We'll talk when we get home. Come on, before that comes again.'

~~~

As we arrived home, soaking wet and freezing, the look on Anthony's face as he arrived, almost at the same time, was uplifting. He'd removed his hood, and his hair was plastered to his head, but the warmth of the smile breaking through his icy features not only thawed his face but warmed me too. As he approached, he attempted to run towards us, but the depths of some of the snow drifts in his path prevented him from even getting started. I watched his struggle and signalled for him to slow down.

He complied.

In a short while, the three of us were hugging on the patio. Me and Anthony in relief and happiness, Grace in confusion.

'Grace, you can't keep doing this,' he tried to scold her, squeezing her tight to his chest at the same time. She returned the hug with the same ferocity as I held back, but only slightly. 'Where was she?' he asked as the hug came to a natural conclusion.

'In the backyard of Old Man Sharpe's house.'

Anthony's face fell at the mention of Old Man Sharpe. It took a moment for him to compose himself. 'How did she get so far in this storm?' he asked as we entered the warmth and safety of the house, shedding our wet layers and muddy boots at the doorway.

'Lisa took me,' Grace said as she sat pulling at the boots she had put on all by herself. 'She told me I needed to wear these boots and my thick coat. She said she *needed* to show me something.'

I was pulling at the leg of my own ripped waterproof pants after already removing my boots. 'We need to talk about Lisa, honey. We can't have you just walking out into a storm on the say-so of an imaginary friend.'

'She's not imaginary, though, Mommy. She's real, and she looks just like me.'

Anthony, stripped down now to his thermal underwear, was handing out towels. I took one and rubbed Grace's head with it. 'Enough of this now, Grace. What you did this morning was silly, not to mention dangerous. Me and your uncle could have gotten lost in that blizzard. Something bad could have happened to all of us.'

'But Lisa said ...' Grace began to protest at the scolding she was getting.

I was adamant I wasn't going to let her off with this one. 'I don't care what Lisa did or didn't say, Grace. This is serious. You could have died out there today. Me or Anthony could have died looking for you. No more Lisa. If I hear one more thing about this imaginary friend, then you're going to be in some serious trouble. I might even have to speak to the Spirit of Christmas, to tell them not to come.'

'But, Mommy ...'

'No more,' I snapped, surprising myself at the anger in my voice.

Grace looked at me, and there were tears welling in her eyes that looked just about fat enough to burst their confinement. She turned away from me and ran up the stairs. I heard our bedroom door slam. I was angry and upset, and not to mention exhausted.

I started to go after her, but Anthony held me back. 'Don't,' he said, putting his hand on my shoulder. In truth, I didn't need too much encouragement. I was upset, and I might have said some things I'd regret later. 'Leave her be. She needs to think about her actions, and their consequences. She'll come around.' He was nodding and smiling.

I could feel the tears in my own eyes already falling. 'I know, but—'

'But nothing,' he replied.

I knew he was right, but I'd never, not even once, had a falling out with my daughter before. I wasn't entirely sure how to handle the situation.

'What's all this noise?' Delores asked as she made her way down the stairs, tying the belt of her robe around her as she did.

Both of us looked up towards her.

Her hair had been combed, and there was a brightness about her that had been noticeably absent last night during Grace's first little adventure. I wiped the tears from my cheeks—my mother didn't need to see me crying, not on the day before Christmas Eve. I breathed a small, shaky sigh of relief at seeing the old woman. Since last night, I'd been dreading seeing her, as she'd been so tired, so drawn. This morning, however, she was her old self again.

I smiled. 'Oh, we've had some early morning drama,' I explained.

'Grace decided to go AWOL again,' Anthony added, making light of the situation.

'She disappeared again. Out into the storm this time,' I said, walking over to greet her with a hug. I was happy to note that she hugged me back with real strength.

'She went outside? In this weather?' Mom asked after the hug ended.

I nodded. 'Don't worry about it. We found her. I just don't want her to think she can get away with this kind of stupid behaviour.'

'Did she come back on her own?'

'No, we had to go out and look for her.'

Delores's face fell. 'You both went out to look for her?'

The look of horror that had dawned on her face concerned me. I stepped backwards; I wanted to look at her. 'Yes, of course we did. We weren't going to leave her out there all on her own.'

'No, no, of course not. It's just …'

'Just what, Mom?' I asked.

Anthony returned to the hallway after hanging the coats in the kitchen to dry. 'I've just put some coffee on. I think we could all do with a nice cup of …' He stopped halfway through his announcement as he looked at us.

Mom looked around the room, obviously searching for somewhere to sit down. I guided her into the kitchen and sat her at the table we'd sat around last night. All the colour I was marvelling at moments before had drained from her face, taking the brightness with it.

'What's wrong, Mom? Are you OK?' I asked, sitting opposite her. I leaned in and grasped her hand, disliking the frail feel of it in mine. It was too thin, too bony; it was also far too cold for the warmth in the room. 'Come on, Mom, you're scaring me. What's the matter?'

'It's nothing, really. It's just …' She took a moment to compose herself. Her eyes were dark as she sniffed before looking back up at me and Anthony. 'It's just … that's how your father died.'

I watched her swallow after she managed to expel these words. The dry click it produced was followed by a frown. I squeezed her hand a little tighter, and she smiled.

Anthony sat down next to me. His eyes were intense, and I could see the hundred or so questions he had. They were written all over his face.

'He went out into a storm. He had to go to find … someone,' she continued.

I glanced back at Anthony, who was still looking at Mom. She had never, ever, talked about how Dad had died. Anthony had been too young to really know him, and it was a subject that was seldom brought up. It had always felt too raw a subject, even now, after all these years. I'd always had a sense it was too painful for her, too taboo to even think about, never mind talk about.

'He did?' I asked, nervous talking about this with her.

She nodded. It was her turn to tighten the grip of our hands, only for a moment. I thought that was going to be the end of it, and I went to release her hand, to stand up and give Anthony a hand in getting the coffee that would warm us all up after our excitement of the morning. But she had other ideas. She strengthened her grip on my hand again and looked at me with eyes that pleaded to be heard. There was nothing else I could do but lightly return the squeeze and settle back down into the chair.

'It was Christmas Eve,' she continued after taking a deep breath. I could feel her shaking through our connection. 'He went out'—she swallowed, and another painfully dry click ensued—'looking for a little girl who had gotten herself lost in the heavy storm that was blowing. A few of the men in the town did. Only, in his haste to get out there, your father took the wrong coat. It wasn't as thick as it should have been. Hours later—and I mean hours; he wasn't the kind to give up easily—he had caught a chill. This chill got into his lungs. He caught pneumonia, and he was sick for months.' She paused again; this tale was taking its toll on her. 'He never really recovered from it. He went back to work too soon, as his sick time was running out. That's what eventually …' She paused again, longer this time, taking a moment to wipe the tears from her distant eyes. I leaned in and took her into my arms. 'Took him from us,' she finished.

I released her from the hug but didn't sit back down. 'It's OK, Mom, we're all here now. We're all safe. We made it home OK,' I whispered. 'We all had the correct clothing on. Even Grace had dressed herself correctly.' I stroked my mother's head and pressed it lightly to my chest. A small laugh escaped me as I held her. 'She told me Lisa showed her what clothes to wear. She said the little girl had something to show her.'

Delores stiffened in my embrace. She pulled away and looked at me. The first thing I noted was how much of the colour had come back into her face. She was looking more like her old self again and less like the old woman who had replaced her for the duration of the story. 'She said *Lisa* told her?'

'I'm just going to go and check on Grace,' Anthony announced, standing up with a comforting hand on my shoulder. As he exited the room, I could see his eyes were wet and pink, and I squeezed his hand, letting him know it was OK for him to go.

As my attentions returned to our mother, I chuffed. It was a small, humourless laugh. 'Yeah. She's becoming obsessed with this imaginary friend of hers. I'm going to have to have a serious talk with her about it, though. I think it's because she's a little isolated out here that she's brought this friend with her.'

'Has she had this friend long?' Mom's pupils grew wide as she asked the question.

I shook my head. 'No. She only turned up a few days before we came out here. I'm not going to allow her to use this as an excuse for acting up. Twice, she's misbehaved and blamed it on Lisa.'

Mom smiled; it looked wistful.

My eyes narrowed, and I cocked my head. It was a small, almost humourless smile, and there was something about it that I didn't like, not one bit.

'You need to keep her away from Lisa,' she said as she looked towards the window. The snow was falling, and the day was once again as dark as night outside. She pulled her robe closer around her neck as if stifling a chill I couldn't feel. 'Lisa's not good for her,' she continued. Her voice was monotone, slow, and quiet.

I was not enjoying this talk.

'What do you mean?' I asked, leaning towards her, reaching out for her hands again.

Mom's eyes moved away from whatever was holding her attention outside and caught mine in their wake. 'I mean you need to keep her away from Lisa. She can't be good for the child.'

My brow furrowed as questions flashed through my mind. Before they could make the long journey from my brain to my mouth, something unexpected happened.

Mom began to cry.

The questions melted away as I wrapped my arms around the weeping woman, once again wincing at how thin she was. 'Hey, hey, come on,' I soothed as she began to openly sob. 'Come on now. What's the matter?'

As I held her tighter, I could tell she was trying to speak, but the sobs were taking her breath away, and her words were going with them.

Anthony came back into the kitchen, wiping his brow and smiling. 'Well, she's asleep now, but I'm thinking we're going to need to keep an eye on ...' He stopped mid-sentence as he saw us embracing. I caught his eye and shook my head, taking a long blink. He took the hint and left the room, nodding, leaving me and Mother to our moment together.

'Do you remember growing up here?' Delores asked when she'd finally composed herself and the sobs had receded, giving her enough breath to talk.

I wiped the tears from her cheeks and cupped her face in my hand as I looked at her. 'Of course I do. We had such special times. I know it was sad after Dad ...'

'Do you remember the Spirit of Christmas?'

As the words left her lips, a moment of clarity flashed through my memories. It was of the three of us, me, Mother, and Anthony as a child, sitting in the living room, drinking hot cocoa, and wearing our new Christmas clothes. Well, they were new to us, but we kind of realised, as we got older, that most of our clothes had come from the Goodwill stores after Dad died. Money really was that tight. A smile broke on my face as I remembered our Christmas clothes always consisted of at least *one* new item. It was usually a knitted sweater or something of that ilk.

We had never been what you might consider rich, and we never really expected Santa to bring us much on Christmas morning, but Mom never let us down. However, after Dad died, things were a little different. She told us about the Spirit of Christmas, and every Christmas morning, Anthony and I would wake to a small toy or gift. She never, ever let us go without.

So, the Spirit of Christmas meant a lot to us, both of us.

'Well, the spirit is real. There really was … is a Spirit of Christmas. I think she's back, and I think she's somehow attached herself to Grace.' She was speaking slowly, whispering, as if trying to keep what she was saying a secret from the rest of the room.

I was shaking my head, worried that the cancer had gotten to her brain and she was losing her grip on reality somehow. 'What do you mean the spirit is real? Mom, this is a serious situation here. I know it's normal for children to have imaginary friends, but Grace is living in a delusional state. She's gone missing twice, and one time nearly got herself killed. I'm not in the mood to talk about spirits.'

'You need to keep her safe,' Mom burst, lunging forward, grabbing hold of my hand again.

I stepped backwards, away from the unexpected embrace.

'Keep her safe. I can't lose anyone else. Alison, I nearly lost you, and I did lose *her* all those years ago. Keep her safe. Please!'

'Who did you lose, Mom?' I asked, holding her hand again. 'When did you nearly lose me?' I was staring at her, real confusion and more than a smattering of anger creeping over my face.

Anthony walked back into the room. 'Hey, what's all the shouting about? Are you two fighting?'

We both looked up at him. The older face was wild and scared, the younger one tired and irksome.

'We're not fighting,' I soothed, shaking my head. 'We're just talking about the Spirit of Christmas. Why don't you join us?'

He smiled; obvious relief washed over his features. 'I will, but I just need to call Richard first. I need to know how the system upgrade is going. After that, I'm all yours.'

I nodded as he turned and left the room, leaving me alone with our mother, who was still on the verge of tears.

'I don't know if you remember the year you were eight?' she asked after Anthony left.

I took hold of her hand and squeezed it gently. 'Of course I remember. I'm not going to forget the year Dad died.'

'Well,' she continued, 'that was the year the Spirit of Christmas came into our lives. We were so poor after your father died.'

'I remember,' I whispered.

'That was the year I told you the truth about Santa Claus.' She was shaking her head slowly. The tears that had been threatening were now streaming down her face, making little runs along the wrinkles of her aged skin.

I smiled. There was real melancholy in it. 'You asked me not to tell Anthony. You told me I had to be a big girl and look after my brother.' Tears were trickling down my face too.

'And you were. But that was the year you started to see things. Do you remember? It began around Halloween. You were caught in the yard of that awful Mr Sharpe?'

'I remember. I remember you saved me. You and Anthony.'

Delores was nodding. 'That's right, and later on in the year, you were caught in a storm coming home from school. That was when I thought I'd really lost you.'

I held on to my mother's hand. I didn't want to squeeze it any tighter than I already was, as it already felt like her fingers might snap in my embrace. 'But you didn't. I'm still here. We're all still here.'

She smiled, but I could see sadness in her eyes. 'Where was Grace found this morning?' she asked. I noted her eyes were not looking at me anymore; they were fixed on the window, where I noted the snow had almost stopped.

'By a big tree in Mr Sharpe's yard. She was sheltering in it. I think it's what saved her life. If she'd been caught—'

'Was there a light?' Delores interrupted.

Still holding her hand, I sat back in my chair and regarded her through tight eyes. It was a moment or two before I could answer. 'Yes,' I said finally, nodding a little. 'I thought it was the sun poking through the clouds, reflecting off the snow, or something like that.'

The look my mother shot me surprised me. Her eyes were all business now; they were done shedding tears. 'Go and look outside that window, child. Tell me if you see any break in those clouds.'

I looked towards the window, then gazed at the clock. It was not even eleven yet, and it was almost full dark outside.

'Do you see any sun poking through those clouds?'

I breathed out of my nose, a short, sharp breath.

'It's happening again,' she said, still nodding. 'I know it is. Grace is about the same age now that you were then. The same age when the Spirit of Christmas came and I nearly lost you so many times.' Tears began falling down her wrinkled face again. 'Has Grace been hearing the noises? The click-clacking?'

I squinted again. 'Click-clacking?'

'Please tell me she hasn't heard it,' Delores pleaded.

'No. Well, she hasn't mentioned anything to me about any noises. You're scaring me now, Mom. What are the noises?'

Mom smiled; it was same sadness-tinged smile that broke moments ago. She let go of my hand and tapped it. 'Thank God,' she whispered, standing up. It took her a few moments to get out of the chair, and I had to help her in the end.

'Mom, you're really scaring me about these noises. What are they? Why are you saying the Spirit of Christmas is real?'

She was holding the small of her back when she turned to face me. 'I have to go and lie down. Will you wake me in an hour for me to take my pills? My head and back are throbbing.'

'Of course,' I agreed, checking the time. When I looked back, Mom was already on the stairs, making slow progress up them. More questions ran amok through my mind. There *were* answers, and I needed them, but watching her climb slowly up the stairs, I knew I couldn't badger a sick woman for them, not now.

~~~~

I searched the house for Anthony, eventually finding him in the utility room, just off the kitchen. His mobile phone was to his ear, and the finger of his free hand was in his other. It looked like things at the software upgrade weren't going to plan. He didn't even acknowledge I'd entered the room.

'I don't care what they say. We signed the papers, and they are legally binding. Go and tell her that we need to …'

I was already bored with this one-sided conversation. I'd never had a head for business, so I returned to the kitchen, putting the stove on to make myself a cup of hot-milk coffee. A couple of minutes later, I was sitting at the kitchen table with two steaming mugs. Anthony loved sweet hot-milk coffee just as much as I did, and I thought it might help him wind down after his stressful conversation. I sat and listened to the sounds of the house. I could still hear Anthony arguing in the utility room, his tones unusually hushed for him, but then I supposed he didn't want to be yelling while Mom was sick and Grace was sleeping. Filtering my brother out, I sat back, hot mug in my hand, and relaxed.

The wind was still blowing outside. It was nowhere near as bad as it had been, but it was still banging something gently against the side of the house. It was a pleasant sound. *Christmassy,* I thought.

Then it changed.

It sounded like the banging was coming from somewhere *inside* the house.

Taking a sip of my coffee, I continued to listen, surmising it couldn't have been anything to do with the storm or the wind, as there was a rhythm to it. It was too regimented for it to be a noise created by the randomness of the wind.

There was something else about it.

Click …

It sounded like someone banging a wooden stick …
Clack …
Against another wooden stick.
Click …
In rhythm.
Clack …
Keeping time.
I shook my head and took another sip of coffee.
Click … Clack … Click … Clack …

The sound was real; there was no denying it. *Alison,* I scolded myself. *You're listening to your mother's stories too much.*
Click … Clack … Click … Clack …

That's not my imagination, I thought, looking around the room. *It's coming from* this *room.* I stood up. My old friends the goosebumps were back covering my skin. I could still hear Anthony arguing on the phone, but his voice sounded like it was hundreds of miles away.
Click … Clack …

It was clearer now, and the rhythm was defined. Whatever was causing it was human. Someone knew what they were doing.
Click …

It was coming from *in* the living room.
Clack …

A cold wind tickled me, and I shivered. I picked up my coffee, hoping the warmth of the cup would ground me, but it was stone cold. I looked at the thick skin floating on the top of the liquid, confused. It was as if the drink had been standing for hours rather than minutes.
Click …

The sound was close.

I spun around the kitchen. I must have looked like a madwoman trying to shoo a fly or a wasp with my hands.
Clack …

'Who's there?' I asked, surprised by my shaking voice.

As if triggered by my voice, the noise stopped. The room suddenly felt empty, hollow. Somewhere in the distance, Anthony's reassuring voice, still shouting in a whisper, kept me anchored as, slowly, the noise returned.

Click ... Clack ...

It was laboured now, as if the person making the sounds didn't want anyone to hear them. My heart was pounding as I scanned the room, searching for what could be making the disturbing noises. *Why did Mom put this stupid sound in my head?*

Then I saw it. The source, the location from where the noise was emanating.

Click ... Clack ... Click ...

It was the small cabinet, the very same one Grace had been hiding in last night. With sweat-lined palms, I looked longingly out of the kitchen, towards the utility room, where Anthony was still talking.

Click ... Clack ... Click ... Clack ...

The noise was speeding up.

Click ...

I swallowed. I hadn't realised that my throat was so dry.

Clack ...

I couldn't tell if the last noise had come from the cabinet, like the others, or if it was the sound of me attempting to swallow. Either way, I didn't care for any of it.

I entered the living room. I moved the couch away and looked at the small cabinet door.

Click...

Feeling like a third party, I watched a shaky arm reach out towards the door. The fingers on the hand feeling around for the metal handle of the cabinet, the same one my daughter had been hiding in, playing with *Lisa,* last night.

Clack ...

The sudden drop in temperature bit into my skin, entering my bones. Somehow, I knew, no matter how many layers of clothing I could put on, nothing could keep that cold from sinking deeper.

Snowflakes fell around my head. It was impossible. I was inside, and there were no windows or doors open to allow the storm to enter the room, but they were there. If I stuck out my tongue like we used to do as children, I would feel their icy sting as they landed on the warmth of it.

My eyes fixated on the small door.

Click ...

It was louder now. The sound *was* coming from the small cabinet. There was something in there, something *or someone.*

Clack ...

As my hand touched the handle, the cold of the metal stung my skin. The disembodiment of the arm disappeared, and I knew the limb I was seeing was my own. They were my fingers touching the metal. I wanted to jerk my hand back, to put it into the warm safety of my mouth. But something wouldn't allow me to do that.

Something was compelling me onwards.

Click ...

I turned the latch.

Clack ...

12.

CLICK ...

'Can you hear that noise?' Alli had tiptoed her way into Ant's room. The whole house was dark. It always seemed so much darker since their father had died, and she was already beginning to dread Christmas Day, just two days away. Mom had made an effort to put up a tree and hang decorations around the living room, and as always, there was a big angel on the top of it, but to Alli, it felt hollow, like they were just going through the motions. Nothing was helping her get into the spirit of things, not since the talk with her mother.

The talk had been about money, presents, and Santa Claus.

It hadn't been a fun talk for either of them. She wasn't aware of it at the time, but she'd done a lot of growing up during that talk. She'd promised not to say anything about it to her little brother. She'd agreed to this readily, as she wanted Ant to have the best Christmas he could, given their circumstances.

Deep down in her eight-year-old heart, the selfish part that was still a child, she hated that she'd just had Christmas torn away from her. All the magic in the world was now gone, it had been since Daddy died, but Ant still got to carry on believing. It wasn't fair, but as Mom had pointed out, she was now her partner, her rock, and she needed her more than she had ever needed anyone else in her entire life. This meant looking after Anthony.

Clack ...

'Ant … can you hear it?' she whispered. 'It's keeping me awake. I could hear it all last night too.' She crept up to his bed and sat on the edge of it. 'Ant … are you awake?'

A slight snore and a mutter told her everything she needed to know. Ant was in that special place, the one she was having trouble getting to.

Click …

Alli, eight years old, who would turn nine in less than one month, was now a lot older than her years. Daddy had been sickly for a long time. He had caught a really bad cold one night and had never gotten over it. There had always been something sad about him too. Whenever she entered the room, he never once failed to have big, bright, beaming smiles for her, but sometimes she caught him *just before the smile.* That bit had no beams, only deep thoughtfulness and, sometimes, tears and sadness too.

Clack …

'I really miss him, you know?' she whispered to her sleeping brother. 'Dad, I'm talking about,' she explained, even though another look towards him told her she didn't have to. It felt easier talking while he was asleep. Anthony was just a little too young to understand the magnitude of the loss. He knew Daddy was no longer there, but he didn't know why. 'I miss the way he used to sit me on his knee and tell me things about how the world worked. He used to tell me that I, I mean we …' she added, touching the mound of bedclothes that covered her brother, 'had our very own guardian angel. That she was the brightest star in Heaven, and she looked down only on us two.' Heavy tears began to fill her eyes.

Click …

'He used to tell me that, when he got better, he was going to take us all on a long vacation, somewhere warm, somewhere we can see and smell the ocean.' Her head bent low, and two fat tears dripped from her chin onto the thick blanket before seeping into the stitching.

Clack …

'That noise,' she said, looking towards the door. She wiped her eyes and sniffed. 'I need to know where it's coming from.' She got off the bed and looked back at her sleeping brother. 'Thanks for the talk, Ant.' There was a little humour in her whisper, but mostly, she meant it. She'd needed someone to help her get things off her chest. Ant had been that someone.

Click ...

Her attention was back on the door now, and the infernal sound that was coming from ... somewhere else in the house, keeping her awake.

~~~~

The house was in darkness. The lack of moonlight from outside, due to the thick cloud covering, made sure no excess light streamed through the windows. She knew the house like the back of her hand and had no trouble finding her way in the dark. The *click-clack* sound was coming from somewhere downstairs. Originally, she'd thought it was coming from inside her bedroom. When she finally found the courage to search the room and found nothing, her curiosity compelled her to extend her investigation. It then sounded like it was coming from Ant's room, but once she entered, the noise moved. Now feeling her way along the dark landing, she thought it was coming from downstairs.

As she creeped down the steps, dressed only in her nightgown and a robe, she could feel the air around her getting colder. She tightened the robe, wanting to stave the sudden chill. As her other hand touched the wooden banister to help guide her through the darkness, she recoiled. The cold of the wood had burnt her hand. 'Jesus!' she cursed, looking around in the dark just to make sure that her mother wasn't around to chastise her.

As the cold become more intense, the strange sound became louder.

Click ... Clack ... Click ... Clack ...

Whoever it was, it sounded like they were banging sticks together at a rapid rate. 'Hello?' she called in a forced whisper down the stairs. She hoped it would be her mother, knitting away in the living room, although something told her there was no way her mother would be working in the dark, in this cold.

'Hello?' she shouted again, marvelling at how dense her breath was as it plumed before her on the cold, dark staircase. She was not expecting an answer. In fact, she hoped there wouldn't be one. For if there was, then she'd know there was an intruder.

The click-clacking stopped.

'*Alli* …' a strange voice whispered through the darkness. It sounded as if it had been recorded on two different tracks and she was listening to it through earphones, rising and fading in each ear separately. Even though the room and the stairs were cold, the voice chilled her more than anything else.

'Who's there?' she stuttered. Her teeth were chattering, both from the powerful cold and from fear of the ghostly voice.

'*Alli* …' it whispered again.

The cowardly side of her wanted to run back upstairs, to wake her mother and her brother and urge them all to leave this house and never, ever come back again, but she felt obligated to find out what the noise could be.

The further down the stairs she got, the colder it became.

Something brushed past her ear. She lifted her hand to shoo whatever it was away, but it had been joined by something else. Something cold and wet. Another one brushed her cheek, melting as it made contact with the warmth of her skin.

She was shocked to see that these irritations were snowflakes.

It was snowing inside the house!

She looked down at the rest of the stairs and was surprised to see them covered in a thin white sheen. The impossible snow was falling hard and sticking to the hardwood floors. She lifted the collar of her robe around her cheeks and continued into the improbable winter wonderland of the hallway.

'*Alli* …' the voice whispered again.

The first two times, she might have dismissed it as a figment of her imagination, but that third time, with the snow all around her and the temperature dropping rapidly, she couldn't ignore the reality, albeit warped, of the situation.

Her thin slippers were saturated, and her feet were on the verge of turning numb. The cold was clawing up her legs, towards her already cold body. No matter how tightly she pulled the robe around her, it was useless against the freezing room.

'*Alli ... help me!*' the voice whispered.

The hallway was a haze of movement. The heavy snowfall restricted her vision, playing tricks with her eyes. She envisioned a legion of ghosts hiding in the storm, all of them hungry, all of them waiting to ensnare a little girl into their lair, where they would hold her, tormenting her for all eternity. She took another step down and felt the temperature drop again as a hard, cutting wind attacked her.

There were only two more steps, and she would be in the hall, a hall that was rapidly disappearing into a blizzard. The walls were no longer made from smooth plasterboards but looked to have thick foliage growing from them. There were no longer kitchen or living room doorways. Snow had piled thick on the floor, and drifts had begun to emerge against what used to be walls and what she assumed had been furniture.

She was soaked through. Her robe and nightgown clung to her freezing body. Her hair felt like icicles, and if she reached up, she would be able to take her strands and snap them off. *That would save Mom money on haircuts,* she thought, a sad one for an eight-year-old girl.

Unperturbed, she continued down the remaining steps.

As she hit the bottom, the snow was deep. It was past her ankles, and the hardwood floor that she expected to feel beneath her was nothing but sludge, cold, wet mud. *How can this be?* she asked herself, taking another, tentative step into the mid-winter scene.

The *click ... clack ...* began again.

'H-h-who's there?' she stuttered. Her teeth chattered as she took another step into the hallway.

Just in front of where the kitchen should have been stood a large, gnarly old tree. Its trunk was thick and twisted, and its empty branches looked like snow-laden fingers pointing wickedly and accusingly at her.

The iced tongue of the wind was lapping at her, stabbing her, and no amount of wrapping her arms around herself or hopping from one leg to another could keep that dagger from penetrating her. She spun around and around, disorientated, until she was dizzy. The house was no longer there. It had been replaced with snow-laden hedges, foliage, and trees. The ground was spotlessly white. The only break in the pristine blanket was the tree where the kitchen should have stood.

It seemed to be the centre of everything.

Everything in this forest of madness revolved around the tree.

She felt her knees weakening beneath her, but she didn't care. The whipping wind was cutting her, stealing her breath, her feelings, all her cares and worries. It was carrying them away with it like a thief in the night. The numbness that began in her legs was spreading out from her centre, travelling to her head, into her brain. Even though she was a healthy, strong-willed eight-year-old, very nearly nine, she wanted to give up.

She fell onto the soft ground, her body no longer caring that it was cold and wet—it had moved on from such trivialities. Absolute nothingness occupied her brain.

Nothing except the bright light shining from behind the tree.

The illumination was warm and inviting.

She'd heard Heaven was a bright, warm, inviting light. She'd heard stories of people who, when dying, had seen and reached out to similar lights. With nothing else to occupy her, she reached out a heavy arm. The frozen fabric of her nightgown popped and snapped in protest to her movements.

A silhouette appeared within the light.

It took what little breath she had left away, and her vision began to waver.

Am I dying? It was a horrible thought for a young girl, but it was one that occupied her whole brain.

Then the vision of a little girl stepped out of the light.

It was the same girl she'd seen before, when she'd been lost in the storm and Mr Sharpe and Ant had found her. She was wearing a black coat, but she didn't look cold, and she wasn't even a little bit wet.

A goofy smile spread across Alli's face as the ghost regarded her. She saw the little girl wasn't smiling.

It was far from a smile.

Her eyes were wide, and her mouth was pulled back, revealing her teeth. Alli didn't know if the girl was in pain or if something was scaring her. Either way, she didn't like it. The spectre's mouth opened wide. It looked to Alli like she might have been screaming, but either no sound came from her or the whistle of the sharp wind carried it away. The silence of the apparition scared Alli more than the fact she was currently freezing to death beneath a large tree that had somehow grown in her own house.

Then she saw something else. Or *someone* else.

The large, unmistakable frame of a man appeared in the light coming from behind the tree. At first, Alli couldn't see who it was. All she could see was a dark outline.

Then he stepped out of the light.

She sucked in a deep breath. She felt the ice in the air stab at her throat and her passageways as iced breath attempted to travel through her body. She didn't know if she would be able to scream, but she knew she was going to try.

The man, Mr Sharpe, was holding his hands out before him. He was looking directly at her. His eyes shifted between his hands and the small girl before him. There was something dark covering his hands, something wet and dripping. They were covered in blood. The dark crimson clashed with the stark white of the snow and the dull greys of the forest mists before her. It was dripping and melting in the snow beneath them.

Alli looked at the little girl again.

At first, her brain didn't or wouldn't register the change. All it registered was the little girl falling forwards onto all fours, the deep drift of the snow almost covering her face. She wanted to help her. She wanted to get up from the cold, wet ground and help the little stranger.

It was a while before she noticed the blood on Mr Sharpe's hands originated from the little girl. Initially, she thought the blood on the little girl had been drips from his hands, but she saw there was too much of it. As her eyes focused, she could see the blood was pulsing from a deep wound in the girl's neck. There was so much more of it than there should have been.

She watched Mr Sharpe as his focus shifted from his hands to the little girl, then back to his hands again. Then he looked up and saw Alli. At first, it looked like he didn't know what it was he was seeing. Then recognition dawned. His eyes widened, and his lips pulled back into a snarl.

That was when Alli's breath returned, and she screamed …

~~~~

'Alli … Alli, wake up. You're screaming.'

Rough hands were shaking her.

She covered her face with her hands, trying to block out the large man with the blood on his hands, the little girl's blood. 'Go away! Go away! Leave me alone!' she screamed.

'Alli, it's me. It's Mom. You need to wake up.'

Her eyes opened. Instead of the expected winter scene and the warm illumination of the light coming from the tree, the room was dark. 'Am I dead?' she asked in a thin, shaky voice that was more a croak than anything else.

'What?' the voice that had identified itself as her mother but she thought was more likely that of St Peter at the gates of Heaven asked.

'Did Mr Sharpe get me? Did he do to me what he did to that little girl?'

115

'Alli, wake up.'

The voice was female. As her senses began to wave around her, zoning in and out of the darkness, she recognised it. She could still feel the wet of the snow round her, but the temperature had risen. Compared to what it had been moments ago, it was positively balmy. She blinked hard, and the world began to swim into place. The bushes at the edges of the forest were now walls, complete with wallpaper and panels. The floor, although still wet, was now hard. The owner of the voice was leaning over her with her hair tied back. There was a warm, comforting hand stroking her face.

'Mom?' she asked, trying to sit up.

Delores stopped her. 'Shhh, child. You were having a nightmare. You were sleepwalking.'

Her eyes scanned the room wildly. 'Where am I? Where's the tree? The snow?'

Her mother shushed her again. 'Don't get too excited, honey,' her voice soothed. 'You're downstairs in the hallway. I think you've had an accident.'

Alli's eyes opened wide as she remembered the little girl falling onto all fours. The thick, stark red pouring from the wound in her neck, discolouring and melting the snow. The man's, Mr Sharpe's, face watching her, laughing, enjoying what he was seeing.

'Is it bad?' she asked, her voice now a little girl's, not one who would be nine years old by the middle of next month.

'Is what bad?' her mother asked, her eyes shifting quizzically.

'My accident? Am I going to die? Am I bleeding like the little girl?'

Her mother chuckled. Alli could feel anger building deep inside her. She felt like a bottle of soda that had been shaken violently. She was ready to burst. *How can she laugh?* she thought.

'You're not hurt, silly.'

'But you said I've had an accident,' she argued.

As her mother's face moved towards hers, Alli could smell toothpaste on her breath.

'You've wet yourself,' she whispered conspiratorially.

She felt around the hardwood floor, her fingers splashing in the cooling liquid that was pooled around her. She then felt her nightgown and realised that it was wet in the areas where she would have expected it to be with the nature of her *accident*.

She sat up a little too quickly, and her head wavered. She looked at her mother, looked deep into her face for a few moments, before tears began to fall. She wrapped her wet arms around her.

Her mother, despite the cooling urine on her daughter, hugged her back.

~~~~

Ten minutes later, with a wash, a change of clothing, and a steaming cup of hot chocolate before her, Alli had calmed down. She was glad her brother hadn't seen her lying on the floor covered in her own pee. She would *never* have lived that down.

'It was so real, Mom. The snow and the tree.' She took a swig of the hot, sweet liquid and licked her lips. She relished the warmth of the drink travelling through her tubes, a feeling she adored, be it hot or cold. 'And Mr Sharpe,' she finished, putting the cup on the table and looking up shyly.

'Mr Sharpe was in your dream?' her mother asked, her attention becoming real. 'Why was he there?'

'It began with a *click-clacking* noise. I thought it was real, but thinking about it now, it couldn't have been, could it?' She looked at her mother, whose features had narrowed, and eyes had become sharp. 'I mean, I could hear it all the way from in my bedroom, and then down here in the hallway. It sounded like—'

'Someone knitting?' her mother finished for her.

Alli looked at her. It was her turn to narrow her features. 'Yes. Knitting. How did you know I was going to say that?'

Her mother smiled. It was the strangest smile Alli had ever seen her make. It was warm but also sad. 'That's the Spirit of Christmas,' she replied in a hushed tone. 'She comes every year.'

'The Spirit of Christmas?'

'Your father had been sick for a while. His wages were the only thing keeping us in this house. Doctor Browning's medicines were not free either. Times were tough, how do you think we could afford to buy you all those lovely gifts from Santa? It was The Spirit of Christmas who brought you them, every year.'

Alli pulled a face that only eight-year-olds who had been forced to grow up far too soon can pull. 'Mom, you already told me about Santa Claus. You can't go back on that now and tell me a different story about a Spirit of Christmas.'

Delores closed her eyes and shook her head. She looked tired, worn out. 'It's a tale for another time. Tell me about Mr Sharpe.'

'Mr Sharpe?' Alli had almost forgotten about her vision. 'Oh, him.' She adjusted herself in the chair and took another swig of the cooling chocolate. She inhaled a deep breath and steadied herself. 'I was coming down the stairs to find out what the noise that had been keeping me awake was. I went in to see if Ant had heard it, but he was asleep. When I got down here, it was full of snow. There was a tree, and Mr Sharpe was hiding behind it. A little girl was also behind it, but she was bleeding.' Alli stopped for a moment, catching her breath. As she drew in deep, it came in stages. Tears were forming and falling from her eyes. She wrapped her arms around herself as if staving off the cold she was reliving. 'He was behind the tree. Why would he be hiding behind a tree?'

Delores leaned in and took her daughter in her arms, holding her tight. 'Never you mind anything about that nasty old man. You stay just as far away from him as you can.'

'Is he a bad man?' she asked. 'Like … like a stranger?'

Delores held her daughter close. A tear formed in her eyes as the eight year old girl, the one she should have *always* been, returned. She nodded, unable to answer in fear of giving way to the sob forming in her chest.

Click … Clack … Click … Clack …

Delores's eyes wandered, looking for the source of the sound.

13.

MY FINGERS GRIPPED the cold metal of the latch to the small door. The noises were coming from inside; I was sure of it.

Click, clack, click, clack …

It was faster now, as if whoever was making them knew they'd been found out and wanted to get as much of what they were doing done in the small amount of time they had left. Anthony was still arguing on the phone, but it felt like he was a hundred, maybe a thousand, miles away. I felt as if I was the only person left on Earth.

Me and whoever was in this cabinet making these sounds.

Without even thinking about it, I turned the latch.

Click …

I pulled the door open …

Clack …

My heart was thrashing so hard, I marvelled at how much abuse the organ could take. I also worried a little about it too. I realised my eyes were closed, as if I didn't want to see who it was making the sounds. Eventually, I persuaded myself to open them, to look into Grace's hiding space, to see who was there.

The cabinet was empty, as I kind of knew it would be.

The noise had stopped too.

I crouched down onto my hands and knees, putting my head inside as far as I could, which wasn't very far, as the space was not overly large.

The noise did *come from in here, I'm sure of it,* I told myself so as not to feel stupid poking about in a tiny cabinet, looking for a silly noise that may or may not be in my imagination. I stood up, wincing at the pops and cracks of my knees, and slammed the little door closed. It wasn't until it clicked that I realised the room was no longer cold. *What is happening here?* I thought. There was an anger in my inner voice, one that I don't think I'd ever heard before.

Am I going mad?

I looked over, out of the living room and into the kitchen, where Anthony was finishing his lengthy conversation on the telephone. I wanted him to come to me, to wrap his protective arms around me, to tell me that everything was going to be all right.

He entered the room, putting his phone back into his pocket. 'Fucking idiots,' he mumbled before noticing me. He jumped as if he'd seen a ghost. 'I didn't see you there,' he said putting his hand to his heaving chest. He looked shocked, and also a little sheepish. 'What are you doing, creeping around?'

'Did you hear a noise?' I asked, ignoring his question.

'A noise? What noise?'

'A click-clacking noise.'

His eyes narrowed on me. 'A click-clacking noise? Like the one you used to hear when we were kids?'

I didn't want to look at him. I was embarrassed, and I was scared, but I was adamant I'd heard the noise. 'Yes,' I declared, enforcing the word, hoping he would notice how important this was to me. 'That same fucking noise I heard when we were kids.'

He must have picked up on my anxiety, as his face fell from the mocking smile it had been wearing. He shook his head. 'No. I didn't hear anything. I've been on the phone with Richard—'

'It was coming from this cabinet,' I said.

'In here?' he asked, bending down to look inside.

'Yeah, in there. It's gone now, but it was definitely coming from inside.'

'Well,' Anthony's voice strained as he opened the door and looked inside. 'There's nothing in here now. Maybe it's coming from behind the walls or something,' he mused rapping his knuckles on each wall.

I could gauge the solidness of the structure from the dullness of the knocks; there were no rats in this building. I already knew it hadn't been rats making the sound I'd been hearing.

'Alli, are you OK? You look like you could do with some rest.'

'Remember Old Man Sharpe?'

The question took him by surprise. 'Of course I remember him. It's difficult not to.'

'I remembered something about him today. The noise I heard, *I've* heard it before. You heard it too. It sounded like someone knitting. It only ever happened around Christmastime.'

Anthony looked confused. 'I heard it too?' he asked.

'Yeah. Years ago. I'd had that dream, the one I told you about, where I saw Old Man Sharpe covered in blood?'

A thoughtful smile broke on his face. 'Was that the dream where Mom found you covered in pee on the hallway floor?'

I laughed and slapped his hand. 'Yes.' I blushed. 'That was the dream where I first heard the click-clacking sound. Do you remember? You have to.'

Anthony was still shaking his head. 'I remember you talking about it, but I don't recall ever hearing it myself.'

'Remember what we used to get for Christmas every year? Dad had died, and Mom was living on welfare and food stamps, taking in washing and ironing and stuff.'

As he exhaled, his nostrils flared. Then he nodded. 'I remember that. We mainly used to get clothes, usually from the Goodwill, sweaters, cardigans, stuff like that. I remember we used to get knitted toys too.'

I was nodding. 'Did you ever see Mom knitting?' I asked. My face had fallen, and I could imagine my lips were just a tight, white line across the bottom of my face.

'Not really, once or twice maybe.'

'So where do you think she got those gifts from?'

Anthony shrugged. 'I don't know. I never really thought about it. She could have knitted when we were in bed. To make sure the gifts were a surprise.'

I shook my head. 'I don't *ever* remember Mom knitting. When we were older, do you ever remember getting anything knitted for Christmas?'

Anthony shrugged. 'I …'

'We didn't. I remember Mom telling me something that year. Something that's just come back to me. She told me that the Spirit of Christmas … You do remember the Spirit of Christmas?'

'No Santa Claus for us,' Anthony recalled with a chuff.

I nodded, my eyes wide in excitement. 'Mom told me that night, after my dream, that the Spirit of Christmas was real.' As I walked into the kitchen, I sat down hard on one of the chairs at the table and lifted my head towards the ceiling, letting out a huge sigh. *What the Hell have I just told him?*

'Alli, come on. You've had a stressful morning. Don't let any of the old bullshit get to you.'

'I'm telling you, Ant, Mom was serious.'

He sat forward, resting his arms on the table. As he looked at me, I could see the ghost of a patronising smile forming on his lips. I hated him for that. 'Alli, you were eight. It was our first Christmas without Dad, and Mom had just told you there was no such thing as Santa because we were too poor. She was feeling guilty, and, I don't know, maybe she was overcompensating.'

'That was the day she told me to stay away from Old Man Sharpe. I remember my dream now. There was a little girl, and blood, a lot of blood. Some of it was on his hands, but most of it was coming from a wound on the little girl's neck.'

'He saved you that day in the snow, Alison. If he hadn't found you and carried you home, you'd have died.'

'How do we know that he didn't have other plans? Plans like he had for the girl in the dream?' I snapped. I was feeling defensive, angry, and trying to take it all out on my brother.

'I was there, Alli. I saw him running to you when you fell. He's just a sad, lonely old man. You've got the wrong idea about him. Shit, we all probably had the wrong idea about the poor bastard.'

'OK, then why is it that Mom still has those same ideas about him? Why is it that people in town used to talk about him?' I was shaking my head. There was more to this; I was adamant. 'No, Ant. There's something about him. Something wrong. I hate the fact that Grace was over there this morning. Who knows what could have happened if we hadn't gotten there in time?'

Anthony shook his head, smiled, and leaned back, his body language diffusing the whole situation. 'Listen. The storm has passed. Why don't we all go into town, buy a truck load of Christmas decorations. Let's get this place festive, eh? It's Christmas Eve tomorrow, and'—he lowered his voice—'it could be Mom's last. So let's make it as special as we can. What do you say?'

I closed my eyes. This was why I loved my brother so much. He could always soothe my anger. I smiled and nodded, wanting that shopping trip more than anything else. I was getting myself far too worked up over silly daydreams and nightmares from decades ago.

It was agreed. We were going on a family trip into town.

~~~~

Within the hour, me, Anthony, Mom, and Grace were dressed and in the car, ready for an afternoon of shopping in town. 'You're going to love what they've done to downtown,' Delores said between a spate of coughs.

Anthony and I exchanged looks. We were both on the same page.

'The mall's finished now, and there are some lovely restaurants,' she continued.

'Can we go for a burger, Mommy?' Grace asked, listening to her grandmother. 'Lisa's hungry,' she concluded.

Delores looked at the little girl, offering her the kind of look you give to someone you don't know, who you find in your living room. 'Who?' she asked. Her voice was croaky, and I didn't know if it was because of what Grace had said or her coughing fit.

'Lisa,' Grace replied with a grin. 'She's my friend.'

'Honey, we talked about this, didn't we?' I half scolded her.

She dropped her head and began stroking the hair of the doll she had in her arms. It was a habit of hers that she'd fallen into when she'd been caught doing something she wasn't supposed to be doing. 'I know, Mommy,' she whispered. 'But she's right there.' Her head indicated towards the trunk of the car.

'Who is this Lisa?' Delores asked, facing me in the passenger seat.

'I told you the other night, Mom. She's her imaginary friend. It's all OK.'

'She's not imaginary,' Grace shouted, her anger surprising everyone—most of all, me. 'She's real. Aren't you, Lisa?'

'You told me about her dreams and hearing things, but you never told me it was *Lisa* who was her imaginary friend.'

There was an emphasis on the word *Lisa* that I didn't like. I also didn't like the fact that we *had* been speaking about her and how she'd told me to keep Grace away from her but had obviously forgotten. 'I did tell you that, Mom. Yesterday, you told me to keep her away from Lisa.'

'Keep me away from Lisa?' Grace shouted. 'Why? She's my friend.'

'What's the problem with Lisa, Mom?' I asked, ignoring Grace's protests. Knowing Mom, I wasn't expecting a straight answer. She had always been the type to zip up tight and keep everything inside, to just shake her head and purse her lips. This time, however, I was shocked to see tears welling in her eyes. 'What is it, Mom?' I asked, nudging Anthony. He turned too, careful not to take his eyes off the road for too long.

'Nothing,' she sniffed. 'It's just the …'

'Why do I need to keep away from Lisa? She's my friend,' Grace was asking.

'Oh SHIT!' Anthony shouted as he turned his attention back to the road, pulling on the steering wheel. Everyone in the car stopped what they were doing and grabbed on to something. When the car came to a shuddering stop, Anthony pressed the horn in the centre of the steering wheel, lowering the window. He leaned out and shouted something I hoped Grace wouldn't understand before the car in front started up and drove off. 'Is everyone OK?' he asked, turning to check on everyone. 'Mom, are you OK?'

Delores, the tears already gone from her eyes, smiled and nodded. 'Yes, son. We're OK back here,' she said, checking on Grace, who was still looking shocked.

'OK, then,' he sighed, grasping the steering wheel and turning the key to the stalled vehicle. 'Let's get to that mall!'

I don't know if my brother had slammed on the brakes on purpose, just to stop the rousing arguments. If he did, he was a genius, because it had worked great.

~~~~

It took Anthony over ten minutes to find a parking space, and when he did, it was an unofficial one. 'Come on, everyone out,' he ordered. I could tell he was trying to sound chirpy because it was Christmas, but it was not coming across at all.

Mom was right; downtown had certainly changed. The last time I'd been here, less than a year ago, there had been a lot of construction work happening, and now I knew why. The mall was huge. Much larger than a small town like Kitchowa needed, but when I saw how busy it was, granted that it was the day before Christmas Eve, I realised it was bringing some much-needed business, life even, from all over the state. It was obvious people had driven some distances to peruse the wonders its marble walkways had to offer.

'We need decorations, a tree, and loads of goodies and treats.' I listed as we passed through the large automatic doors. The moment I was inside, I was already too hot in my winter wear. The temperature must have been at least twenty-five degrees warmer than it was outside. 'Ant, can you take Mom and get the decorations? Me and Grace will go and look for the treats,' I announced as I began unravelling my scarf and unzipping the thick winter jacket I was wearing.

'I saw a tree lot just around the corner before we parked,' Delores said as she, too, began to undo her jacket. I watched with a tinge of sorrow her hands shaking as she unzipped the zipper. I was about to help her when it caught, and she successfully completed her task.

I smiled.

'I'll check that out,' Anthony said as he fished his vibrating phone out of his pocket. He looked at it and walked off. 'I just have to take this. One moment!' He walked a little distance away, holding the phone to his ear with the customary finger in his other ear, posing the exact same stance as he had during his stressful conversation in the house earlier.

'Are we getting presents, Mommy?' Grace asked as she tugged eagerly on my arm, snapping my attention away from my brother. I nodded and smiled at her, rubbing her hair. 'Are you OK, Mom?' I asked.

Delores was looking just a little flushed. She nodded and flapped her hand at me in a parody of shooing me away. 'Oh yes. It's just warm in here; that's all. You two go on. I'll wait here for Anthony. I think he's talking to Richard again. I hope they're not fighting.'

I squinted a little. 'Probably just missing each other. It is Christmas, after all.'

Delores was watching her son pacing back and forth as she nodded. 'Yeah, that's it. Just missing each other.'

'We'll meet up in an hour and a half in the food court. OK?' I shouted as an excited Grace pulled me along.

'See you then,' Mom shouted back, finishing the sentence in a fit of coughing.

How long has she got left?

The thought surprised me as I watched her sit down on a bench next to a marble fountain.

'Come on, Mommy, we need to get treats. Christmas treats. I need to get stuff, so Santa knows I'm here and not at home.' Grace had run off ahead, into a small crowd. For a moment or two, I couldn't see her, and a small, now familiar, panic rose in my stomach. It bubbled like acidic bile before she came back into view, looking in the window of a large toy store.

Relief washed over me, flushing the bitter bile back where it belonged. I rushed to see what it was she was looking at. It was a large doll, standing up on its own. I stood next to her, looking in the window too. A secret smile broke out beneath my stoic exterior, and I made a mental note of the shop name.

'Come on, honey. We need to make a start on those treats.' I removed my phone and texted the shop name and the doll's description to Ant. As we moved away, I received a thumbs-up emoji.

That's the Spirit of Christmas taken care of, I thought as I began to look for something for Anthony and Mom.

~~~~~

Almost two hours later, we were all sitting at a round table in the food court. Drink cups and burgers in foil wrappers sat before us. There were quite a few bags, some large, stuffed under and spilling out around the table. Christmas music was playing over the PA system, and the temperature had been set to sweltering. Everyone in the mall had removed their coats, hoodies, scarfs, and gloves, and were all looking as flushed as I felt.

I was sitting back trying to suck soda out of a floppy paper straw that was protruding from my cup, fighting with it as the liquid swamped it, making it pretty useless. One part of the march on global warming and the use of disposable plastics I was going to miss was straws, but if it helped save the planet, it was a small price to pay. *First world problems,* I thought to myself with a grin.

I was watching the others. Anthony was texting on his phone, looking more distracted and possibly a little angry—I didn't like that. Grace was having a conversation, and what looked like a tea party, with someone I couldn't see. *You know her name, though,* I thought. Delores was sitting fidgeting with her food, trying to make it look like she was eating when I could clearly see she wasn't.

'OK, then,' I announced. 'What do we say to another hour of walking around, just to see what we can see, then we get home for hot chocolate and a Christmas movie?'

Everyone agreed, and the mood at the table brightened.

I gathered up all the trash and left-over food, noting that Mom's was mostly untouched, and sorted it into recycled and non-recycled waste, ready to dispose of everything. Anthony helped Mom with her coat.

As I got up from the table, the song over the PA system changed. The tinkle of a guitar with a slow clarinet accompanying it announced the first chords of the song that had been plaguing me for the last few days. '*Do you believe the magic?*' soothed out of hidden speakers. The song probably went unheard by ninety-nine percent of shoppers and diners alike, but not me. I looked up to where I guessed the music was being piped from and shook my head, overtly aware of the goosebumps that had returned on my arms.

Grace had helped me carry the trash to the cans, tagging behind like the little shadow she sometimes was, especially in crowded places. I looked at her as she sang along with the tune.

How does she know these words? I wondered absently.

'Oh, I'm so sorry,' I mumbled.

As I was concentrating on Grace, I hadn't been looking where I was going and had bumped into someone.

'That's perfectly all right, ma'am,' the man replied.

His voice was deep and rich; it was also familiar.

I looked up and was horrified to see the face, albeit aged, of Old Man Sharpe. His once dark beard was now entirely grey, and his haunted eyes were rheumy, but they still had an edge to them.

We stared at each other, shock registering on both our faces.

I gasped. Even though I hadn't seen him for years, the old, familiar fear rose within me the moment I recognised him. 'M-Mr Sharpe?' I stuttered.

A ghost of a smile broke on his face as recognition and recollection lit in his eyes. 'Alison? Alison Wynne. Is that you?' the last words were whispered as if the man was in shocked amazement.

I didn't know where to look. All my old fears of this man came rushing back. Panicking, with my already sweaty forehead getting wetter, I turned to where my mother was being helped up from the table by Anthony, hoping one of them would see me and spring to my rescue from the man who I'd grown up thinking was the boogieman.

'I, erm … yes,' I stuttered. Balancing the tray of trash in one hand, I began to fidget with my hair, attempting to put an imaginary rogue strand back behind my ear. I looked at him, feigning self-confidence that I was sorely lacking. 'Yes.' I beamed, holding my hand out to him. 'Alison Wynne, even though I flirted with the name Dickinson for a small while, I'm still a Wynne.' *Shut up,* I scolded myself. *He doesn't need to know everything about you.* 'And you're Mr Sharpe, if I haven't forgotten.'

Old Man Sharpe put his hand out to accept my offered one when he spied the little girl hiding behind me, pulling at my shirt, peering up at him. 'Oh, and this little one?' He smiled. 'What's her name?' he asked, leaning to one side to get a better look as she tried her best to become invisible behind me.

I silently cursed and closed my eyes. 'Oh, this little one is…'

I didn't get to finish my sentence, as Grace popped her head out from behind me and smiled shyly. 'I'm Grace,' she said, barely above a whisper.

Mr Sharpe's face fell. The genial look of his features melted as his eyes narrowed on the small figure of my daughter. I watched as he forgot to breathe. The colour in his face drained as if someone had unplugged a sink, allowing all the healthy pink to flow down the drain.

'I … I …' He gulped and swallowed. 'I'm … pleased to make your acquaintance, erm … Grace,' he stuttered. An odd, false smile cracked his lips as he looked around the crowded food court as if searching for someone, or something, anything other than to talk to me and my daughter. 'I—I have to go,' he said with a smile, although it was obvious that his eyes hadn't received the same memo from his brain. 'I have to, erm, meet someone.'

It was an obvious lie.

'I'm afraid I'm running a little late.' He took another quick look at Grace and swallowed again.

He looked nervous, jittery, scared, even.

'Oh, OK, then. It was n—' I was about to lie and say *nice seeing you,* but I never got the chance, as he was suddenly gone, mingling with the other shoppers in the crowded mall. I watched as he turned back, just once, to look at me and then Grace before scurrying off in the opposite direction.

A hand touched me on the shoulder, and I jumped. Anthony was behind me. 'Are you OK?' his face looked worried.

I turned to Grace, who was still standing behind me, holding on to my leg. 'Has the man gone?' she asked.

'What man?' Anthony asked.

'Yes, baby, he's gone. He won't worry us anymore.'

'Worry you? Who was it?' Anthony asked, his brows coming together as he looked into the crowd of people.

'Aw, that's a shame. I think Lisa wanted to meet him.'

'Alli, who was it?' Anthony asked, his voice concerned, defensive.

'It was—'

'Mr Sharpe. He said his name was Mr Sharpe,' Grace chirped.

'Old Man Sharpe? He was here?' Anthony asked, looking back into the crowd. His concern had turned to anger and wonder. 'Which way did he go?'

I shook my head. 'I—I don't know. He looked kind of shocked to see me, then when he saw Grace, his face changed, he became flustered, then he left.'

'Well, he's gone now. It's a good thing Mom didn't see him.'

I shook my head. 'I never understood that. I only remember him turning up when I got lost in the snow, and the time he caught us in his yard.'

'I think, before our time,' Anthony explained, 'there was some talk about him in town. He used to be a teacher at one of the schools, but there was a scandal or something, and he went to jail. I don't know if it was for something little, or if he had been proven innocent, or what, but he wasn't in for long. When he got back to town, they gave him his job back, but I think he was shunned by most of the town. Once a small town thinks you're guilty, that's it, even if you're proven innocent.'

'I just remember Mom and Dad telling us to stay away from him,' I said as I finally disposed of our trash.

'Well, he's gone now. Come on, let's get this shopping finished so we can get back home, start on the decorations, and enjoy Christmas.'

I took another look into the throng of shoppers moving through the mall, looking for a glimpse of the old man I'd just bumped into, but he was nowhere to be seen.

14.

THEY WERE JAM-PACKED into the car. The presents, decorations, and treats had been stowed in the trunk, and a large fir tree had been strapped to the roof. A festive, excited atmosphere was growing inside. Delores was in good spirits, and when Grace insisted they listen to the radio station that played all the Christmas songs, she seconded the motion. Everyone sang along to 'White Christmas,' with Anthony providing the baritone. Grace surprised everyone by knowing all the words to 'All I Want for Christmas Is You,' and Delores provided the biggest surprise of all when 'The Little Drummer Boy' came on and she announced that she had seen David Bowie in concert many times in her youth, even meeting him on one or two occasions.

It wasn't until 'Do You Believe?' by Johnny Plaid came on that the atmosphere dipped. 'Let's turn this one off,' I said as the song kicked in.

'Hey,' Grace shouted from the back as the radio went off. 'That's Lisa's favourite!'

Delores turned to look at the little girl, who had crossed her arms in protest. 'Honey?' she asked. 'What does Lisa look like?'

'Well, she's got long hair like me and Mommy, and it's the same colour too. She loves to wear the same long black coat. I've never seen her without it.' Grace squinted before continuing. 'It looks like she might have a nightgown on underneath it.' The last sentence was whispered in the little-girl whisper that was just as loud as their normal voices but, to them, seemed like the quietest, most secretive voice ever.

As I listened to this exchange, I noticed Mom's face had lost a little of the shine it had during the singing a few moments earlier.

'Does she look like you?' Delores asked. It was a strange question to ask a child, and by the way Grace's expression changed towards her grandmother, it seemed like she thought so too.

'Well, she's a little bit like me. I think we're the same age, only I think Lisa might be from a different when.'

'A different when?' Delores asked.

'Yeah,' Grace said, losing interest in the conversation.

'What do you mean by that?' Delores pressed, adjusting her sitting position.

'From a different time or something. I don't know what I mean exactly.' She shrugged. 'Just a different … when.'

Delores looked like she was about to ask another question when I interceded. 'Should we put the music back on? I liked it better with that Christmas music.' I twiddled the knob in the centre of the car's dashboard, and Bruce Springsteen, blasting 'Santa Claus is Coming to Town,' roared out of the car's speaker system.

'I love this one!' Grace announced to the whole car and proceeded to sing the second verse at the top of her voice.

I turned around, pulling a face at her, but she ignored me and continued to sing, albeit with a chuckle in her voice. I noted Mom had readjusted her position back to face the windshield. She was smiling and tapping along with the beat, but I could see her eyes were somewhere else.

~~~~

The rest of the journey was uneventful. The good feeling returned, and when Anthony pulled the car into the driveway, the already dull sky was nearly dark. 'All right, then, let's get all this stuff inside and get the hot chocolate going. This house isn't going to decorate itself, now, is it?' He was laughing as he alighted the car, running through the snow towards the house with his keys in his hands. Everyone stayed inside until he was back. He leaned in with a huge, goofy grin. 'Well, come on. Christmas will be over by the time you guys have gotten yourselves in gear.'

Grace was struggling with the latch to her door, having already unbuckled her booster seat. 'I want to put the tree up first,' she shouted diving out into the snow.

When I was alone with Mom, I turned towards her and smiled. 'Are you OK?' I asked.

She looked at me as if realising for the first time that I was still in the car. 'What? Me? Oh yes, I'm fine. Just a little tired is all. These couple of days have been the most fun I've had for a long while.' She grinned.

My eyebrows drew together as her smile softened. 'Are you OK with Grace's invisible friend? It's just that you seem a little—'

Delores leaned forward and patted my hand that was sticking through the gap between the seats. 'I'm fine, darlin',' she interrupted. 'I'm just tired and looking forward to Christmas with my family. That's all it is. Now, let's get in and decorate my house, shall we?'

My genuine smile returned. 'Yeah. Come on, let's do it.'

As I helped her out, we were both laughing and joking about skating on the driveway at our ages. I thought this could very well be the best Christmas I'd ever had.

The only thing was Christmas hadn't really started yet.

15.

CHRISTMAS EVE MORNING came around, and even though we were tired from all the Christmas preparations we'd done the night before, we were all up early. There was still so much to do before the big day tomorrow. The tree was up, coffee and hot chocolate were on a constant rotation, and we had all watched as many Christmas specials as we could fit in between decorating, 'Rudolph the Red-Nosed Reindeer' and 'A Charlie Brown Christmas' being the highlights—for me, anyway. However, Grace wasn't overly impressed with the old-fashioned animation and wanted to watch something called the 'iCarly Christmas Special.' I'd never heard of it.

A few hours later and everything was done. Decorations were hanging from the walls and ceilings. The windows were adorned with winter and Christmas scenes and the words HAPPY HOLIDAYS spelled out in bright jelly-like letters that stuck to the glass. Anthony had spent an hour or so, dressed in his thick winter coat and hat, putting lights up around the outside of the house that flashed red, green, and blue. But best of all for Grace was the tree. It was standing proud in the hallway, wrapped in tinsel garland and dripping in ornaments and lights. There was a great big golden star on the top of it. She hadn't taken her eyes off it for at least ten minutes. The way the lights were blinking and reflecting off the ornaments looked to be mesmerising her. She'd asked if there might be any critters hiding within the branches, as she'd recently seen a cartoon where two chipmunks had been living in a Christmas tree and causing all kinds of mischief with the dog who lived in the house it had been brought into. It was one of her favourites, but she didn't like the fact that the dog kept getting the blame for everything that went wrong.

I was in the kitchen, and Grace was sitting in the living room, looking out at the tree in the hall. I turned as I heard her speaking, thinking she was talking to me.

She wasn't.

'Can you see anything in the branches, Lisa?' she asked.

My stomach dropped again at the mention of that name.

Grace smiled and shook her head as if who she was talking to was doing something funny. 'No, although I think it would be funny if there was. I saw a cartoon once …'

'Who are you talking to, honey?' Uncle Anthony asked as he entered the room.

'Oh, no one,' she replied. 'Just Lisa.'

'Oh, OK. Is she here right now?' he asked, raising his eyebrows.

Grace looked around before shaking her head. 'Nope. I think she's gone home.'

Anthony sat down on the floor next to her and looked at the tree. 'Do you think we did a good job?'

Her eyes widened as she nodded.

'So, where does she live? Your little friend,' he asked, remembering my instructions to get as much information about Lisa as he could without really pressing her.

'She lives in the tree,' she replied, not looking at him.

'In the tree? Wow, there can't be much room in there for a little girl to live.'

Grace rolled her eyes and chuckled. 'Not in this tree. She lives in a big one. It has an old tree house in it.'

~~~~

Grace dragged her eyes away from the brightness of the Christmas tree and looked away, towards the windows. It was dark outside, and the lights inside almost turned the frosted panes into perfect mirrors, but only almost. She could just about see out of them. Lisa was outside, looking in. The cold weather never seemed to bother her, and none of the falling snow landed on her, or even settled in her hair. She smiled, and her face lit up just like the Christmas tree had when Uncle Anthony had plugged it in. She waved. Grace just had time to wave back before Lisa disappeared into the night.

16.

THE REST OF the day was fantastic. As a family we cleaned the kitchen in preparation for cooking the big dinner the next day. Everyone helped to peel vegetables, even Grace, who threw away more carrot than she peeled, and what she did peel, she mostly ate. I washed the turkey and peeled potatoes.

Christmas and rock music blared through the house well into the evening, when the party games, including charades and the yes/no game, began.

Everyone was having a wonderful Christmas Eve. Delores took a couple of naps, and there were a few times when Anthony had to take phone calls, but nothing disturbed or disrupted the flow of the magical day. As the evening drew to a close, Delores was visibly tiring, and I could see her draining the later it got.

'Well, why don't we all look at getting ourselves to bed?' I announced, stretching rather theatrically for Grace and Delores's benefit. 'Big day tomorrow, what with it being Christmas Day and all.'

'Do we have to go to bed?' Grace whined as she flopped back on the couch. Her little face looked half asleep as the familiar vacant look of a too-tired little girl descended on her.

'Yes, you do.'

'But I'm not even tired,' she protested, her nodding head giving away the lie of her statement.

I smiled at my brother, who raised his eyebrows. 'Well, I'm going to wash these dishes, then I'm hitting the sack myself.' He got up and made his way to the kitchen, and I noted Grace's eyes followed him. I also noticed them closing over as they did.

Delores was already up and making her way towards the stairs. 'I need to take my pills, and then I'm going to bed too. Got to be a good girl or the Spirit of Christmas won't bring me anything nice tonight.'

Grace's eyes widened. 'The Spirit of Christmas!' she declared, as if she had only just remembered it.

Delores turned and winked at me before passing her gaze onto Grace. 'Oh yeah, the Spirit of Christmas is always watching. She knows everything you do. She's the one who tells Santa when you're asleep and if you've been naughty or nice.'

'Really?' Grace asked, her eyes drifting between her grandma, her mother, and sleep. 'Is the Spirit of Christmas an Elf? Does she really do that, Mommy?'

'Of course, baby. She watches everything you do and reports it all back to Santa. She tells him where you are and what you've been doing. Then she recommends what list you go on,' I explained.

'What list am I on, Mommy?' she asked, and the look of worry in her tired eyes almost broke my heart.

'What list do you think you're on?' I countered.

Grace dropped her head—I thought there might be tears welling up in her eyes. 'I don't know. Not after what happened yesterday!'

My heart did break then, or at least it bent a good bit. 'Come here, baby. Stop crying,' I soothed, wrapping my arms around her. 'What happened was nothing more than a silly incident that we've all learned something from. Nothing more.'

'But it wasn't, was it?' she sobbed. 'Lisa told me to go out. She told me where to go. I didn't want to go into the yard, Mommy, honest, I didn't. She only had her black coat on, but she made sure I wore my thickest, warmest coat. She said she doesn't feel the cold.'

'Well, next time Lisa tells you to do something silly, you come and tell me or your Uncle Anthony, OK?'

'I will, Mommy,' she replied, getting up off the couch. 'Are you coming to bed too?' she asked, taking hold of her grandmother's hand, who was standing a little unsteadily at the bottom of the stairs, waiting for her.

'I'll be right up, honey. I'm just going to help Uncle Anthony in the kitchen. You run along … and don't forget to brush your teeth,' I added.

'I won't,' she answered, following Delores up the stairs. As I watched them go, a strange melancholy settled over me as they disappeared into the darkness.

'Hey, a little help in here?' Anthony called from inside the kitchen.

'Coming,' I replied, tearing my eyes away from the now deserted stairwell.

~~~~

'What a day,' Anthony sighed as he poured a large serving of red wine into a fishbowl glass and handed it to me.

I closed my eyes and accepted this gift as if it had come from the gods themselves. 'You read my mind,' I said, taking a long sniff of the dark, red liquid. The spices coupled with the alcohol mingled to make an aroma that my body and my brain craved. My mouth watered in anticipation of the drink. 'What a day,' I mimicked, offering my glass to Ant, who dutifully tipped his against it.

The resounding *ching* was delightful.

'Amen to that, sister,' he replied with a grin.

'So,' I continued. 'What's been going on with you? You've been on your phone all day. Well, ever since we got here, really. Heated conversations with Richard. There's more happening than a software audit. Spill, bro.' I laughed, hoping it wasn't bad news.

Anthony looked at me over his own large glass. He pouted a little before taking a sip and relishing the taste in his mouth. He swallowed and placed the glass on the table before him, then looked up at me—my heart couldn't take the anticipation. He smiled then, heralding a definitive change in his attitude. 'Well, there is some news. I was going to wait until Christmas morning to tell everyone, but I don't think I can keep it from *you* any longer.'

I was feeling the familiar thump in my chest as my body began to get excited by Anthony's news. 'Come on, don't leave a girl hanging.' I took a sip, then put the glass on the table.

'So, there's not really an IT audit happening.'

'I kind of guessed that, going by how intense your phone calls have been.' I smiled, wondering what the surprise could be.

He grinned. His face was filled with joy, and if he hadn't had been so tired, I would have said he was beaming right then. 'On December twenty-sixth, me and Richard are going to be ...'—he paused for dramatic effect, and I was hating him for it—'fathers!' he concluded eventually.

I felt my chin hit my chest. 'What? You're shitting me!' I replied. The grin spreading across my face was in real danger of splitting my head in two.

'Yup, a little baby girl.'

'A girl?' I flung myself at him, nearly knocking the wine glasses over in my excitement.

He was laughing as he steadied himself on the stool, wrestling his over-eager sister. 'Yeah, a girl. Her name is Rosie. She's six months old. Her mother was an alcoholic, but they think she might have escaped the long-term effects of foetal alcohol syndrome.' He held up his crossed fingers. 'We hope,' he finished. 'They think that physically, she's great, but we'll need to monitor her emotional and cognitive growth.' His grin was back, bigger and better than the last one. 'That's a challenge we're more than willing to take on.' He watched as I wiped away my tears through his own moistening eyes. 'I can't wait for you to meet her.'

Eventually, I controlled myself and sat back on my own stool. 'Do you have any photos?' I gushed.

He shot me a look as he shook his head. 'What do you think?' he asked, fumbling in his pocket, attempting to retrieve his phone. 'I've been wanting to show you these ever since you told me about

Mom, but we decided to wait until it was all legit and complete. Oh, and by the way, you're fine drinking more wine, you know. You're far from being an alcoholic.'

I sniffed and wiped the tears from my eyes and cheeks. Ant took my mostly empty glass away and threw the rest of it down the sink. 'We can drink the rest of that stuff later, after we're drunk from drinking this,' he said, opening the refrigerator. He pulled out a green bottle that was wrapped with a golden label across the body and a gold foil at the top.

I raised my eyebrows as I looked at the bottle. 'Wow, the good stuff? Shouldn't we wait until Mom's here before we drink that?'

Anthony wrinkled his nose and moved towards the cupboard for the nice glasses. 'It's OK. I've got a crate of the stuff in the car. I wanted to share this first one with my sister and best friend.'

'Well, in that case, I approve.' I giggled, holding my hand out for the glass. 'So, when was all this decided?'

'Well,' he replied unwrapping the foil of the bottle, 'we've been talking about it for ages, and since Canada has more relaxed laws on same sex partnerships adopting, it was just the right time.'

The cork popped right in time with the end of his sentence, and a small gush of foam spilled from the neck.

'Whoa … don't let that get away. That's precious stuff,' I laughed, leaning forward, glass in hand, attempting to catch the flow.

'We thought it was time to take the plunge. Neither of us are getting any younger. So Richard stayed home to deal with the paperwork and the meetings. We made them aware of the situation here, and they were fine with it.'

'To Anthony, the daddy.' I giggled again, feeling giddy even before I'd taken a sip. I leaned forward, offering my glass to him again. He touched it with his, both of us relishing the sweet *ting* before taking sips. 'To Anthony, the grandest daddy of them all,' I mused, sitting back, grinning like the ginger cat in the cartoon film.

He was sitting back on the kitchen stool and smiling as he looked at his phone. I couldn't remember a time when I'd seen him so happy in my entire life. I was ecstatic for him and honoured I was here to share the moment. I sipped the fizzy wine, relishing the bubbles travelling up my nose.

'Well,' I said with a serious face. 'I hope you're ready for the onslaught of'—I raised my fingers to emphasise my next words—'big cousin Gracie!' I laughed.

Anthony's shoulders slumped as he looked at me, and he harrumphed. 'Oh shit, I never thought of that,' he laughed.

~~~~

As her mom and Uncle Anthony laughed and joked downstairs, an overly excited Grace lay in her bed, wide awake. Just like in the story of the *Night Before Christmas* that she loved so much, she was nestled warmly in her bed as visions of sugar plums danced through her head. Only her visions were coming while she was still awake.

'Are you still awake?' said the voice from the darkness, the one she could hear over the light sound of Grandma snoring in another room. It was Lisa. Her smile beamed.

'Yes,' she whispered her reply.

'Good. I need you to help me with something. Are you up for another adventure?'

This troubled Grace. She had very nearly gotten into serious trouble on the last two adventures Lisa had taken her on. She didn't want to get on Santa's, or even the Spirit of Christmas's, naughty list.

'I don't know …' she replied.

'You have to help me with this. You won't get into trouble, I promise.'

'You promise?' Grace asked, her heart hoping that her friend was telling her the truth.

'I promise,' Lisa replied, holding her hand in the air, crossing her fingers.

She sighed and sat up in the bed, then cocked her head and listened for any movement from outside her room.

'Will I be back for the Spirit of Christmas?'

Lisa nodded, her smile spreading wide across her face.

'Where are we going?'

'We have to go and see Mr Sharpe.'

'Mr Sharpe? Why?' she asked, getting some of her waterproof clothing out of her closet. 'He lives miles away. That's where you got me into trouble last time.'

'There's something important I *have* to do. I really need you there with me to help do it.'

'Is it that important?' Grace asked, not fully trusting her friend right now, not when she was talking about going to Mr Sharpe's house.

'It's the most important thing I've had to do in, like, forever and ever,' Lisa replied, her brow furrowing, offering Grace a secret look that promised more adventure than she was used to … or comfortable with.

Grace thought about it for a small while. Eventually, she pulled her lips into a pout, then smiled. 'Well, as long as I don't miss Santa, or the Spirit of Christmas, or whoever it is coming to see me tonight.'

Lisa smiled again as she held her hand out for Grace to accept. 'I promise, you won't!'

The two girls left the safety of the bedroom, hand in hand as they ventured down the stairs, offering just a small glimpse of the adults in the living room before crossing the hallway and slipping out of the front door, into the freezing cold Christmas Eve night.

~~~~

Within an hour, the bottle had been finished, and we were back onto the red wine we'd been drinking earlier. Both of us were—if not already—very close to being drunk. We'd retired to the living room, where Anthony stoked the fire, making the room cosy and warm.

'What do you think about Mom?' he asked during a lull in the conversation.

I took a deep breath, shook my head, and spun my eyes in their sockets. 'What?' I asked, lifting my hand to my mouth, quelling a spill of red liquid that was dribbling from my chin.

'Mom? What do you think?' he asked again, indicating out of the room with his glass. He took in his own deep breath and held it for a while. He shook his head. 'She's getting frailer every day.'

I lowered my eyes, contemplating my drink. 'I can see that too. Although I think she enjoyed today.' I managed a smile as I thought about the day we'd had.

He nodded as he looked at the picture of the chubby, smiling little girl on his phone again. 'We were supposed to pick her up on Christmas Eve. Richard was going to drive up and surprise everyone with her, but there's been a mess-up with the registrar. You might have heard my disappointment, if not my frustration at the situation,' he laughed.

I nodded and raised my glass.

'So, Richard is getting her on the twenty-sixth. Then he's packing everything we need into the car and driving—carefully— here. I don't think I could live with myself if she never got to meet her grandma.'

I felt my whole body soften at the thought of having a niece on my knee the day after Christmas. 'That's a fantastic idea.' I slurred a little as I took another sip of my wine. 'We had some great times in this old house, didn't we?'

'We did. Christmas was always a great time, even through the bad times. Who would have thought we'd have ended up back here on Christmas Eve all these years later?'

My face straightened, and I leaned in a little closer. 'Do you remember the ghosts?' I asked, feeling like I was sobering up slightly.

'Ghosts?'

'Yeah. That time back when we were kids. You were about six, and I was eight.' I pouted a little at the passage of time. 'About the same age as Grace is now, come to think of it.'

'I don't remember any ghosts. I do remember you going off on adventures in the snow. If it wasn't for your little brother, you'd still be an Alison-shaped icicle, even now.' He laughed.

'You remember the click-clack noise? Right?' I asked, my face straightening.

Anthony squinted.

'It was Christmas Eve, the same Christmas after our little adventure in the snow. We were kind of grounded after that incident, even though Mom was more relieved than angry. The noise was coming from everywhere. Every time there was a lull in anything we were doing, it was there in the background. Click-clack … click-clack!'

'It's coming back to me now.' His face fell from the playful smirk he was wearing to his eyes narrowing and the lines around his mouth drooping. 'I remember … blood?' His lips pouted as the memory obviously drew closer. 'There was a lot of blood.'

I was nodding. 'Yeah, and Old Man Sharpe too!'

17.

'WILL YOU QUIT with that noise, Alli? It's driving me crazy,' Ant spat as he threw his latest comic onto the floor.

Alli looked at him, dragging her eyes away from the old TV screen. *A Charlie Brown Christmas*, her all-time favourite Christmas tradition, was playing. 'I'm not doing anything. I thought it was you. Quit messing around.'

'I'm not going to be making a clacking noise while reading a comic, am I?' he growled, pulling a face at his sister.

They were both in the living room. It had been their domain for the last few days, ever since school let out for Christmas, partly due to the weather and partly due to the incident where Alli had gotten lost in the snow and Old Man Sharpe had found her. The four walls were beginning to grate on them, and the cold fingers of boredom, not to mention cabin fever, were in the process of tickling them. It was the first Christmas they were about to embark on without their father, who had died a few months before.

It was taking its toll on all of them.

'Well, if you're not doing it, then it must be Mom, because it isn't me!' Alli snapped as Ant picked his comic book back up. She stuck her tongue out at him, grimaced, then went back to watching the TV. Snoopy was in the process of decorating his dog house for the neighbourhood Christmas lights competition, one of her favourite parts. However, she just wasn't feeling it today. She looked up at the ceiling and exhaled a sharp breath through her nose. Her eyes scanned the room as she cocked her head, attempting to locate the source of the noise, or at least a general idea of where it could be coming from. 'What could it be?' she whispered, lowering the sound from the TV.

'I don't know, but I'm sure I could hear it last night while I was in bed too,' Ant added, putting his comic book down again. 'I thought it was coming from your room. I thought you were knitting.'

'Knitting?' Alli asked, pulling a face. 'When was the last time you saw me knitting?'

He shrugged. 'I don't know; I just thought you were.'

Alli didn't know if the noise had gotten louder, or if it was because she had become more aware of it, but it seemed to be coming from everywhere, all around them. From the walls, the ceiling, behind the couch. 'Where is it coming from?'

Ant nudged his sister, and she looked at him. He was wearing a mischievous grin. It was contagious. 'What?' she asked, fully aware of what he was going to say.

'Let's go and find it. I've read this same comic three times now, and it wasn't any good the first time around.'

Her eyes narrowed. 'What if the sound's coming from outside?' Her eyebrows raised as she finished the sentence.

He shrugged again. 'Well, it *is* Christmas, the first one without Dad. What's Mom going to do if she catches us outside? Cancel it?'

The grin on Alli's face got bigger. 'All right, but let's start *inside* the house, and then ...'—she shrugged, innocently—'if we don't find it, we can tell her we thought the ceiling was leaking and we wanted to find where it was coming from.'

'Where do you get your ideas from?' Ant whispered, looking up at the ceiling. He narrowed his eyes and looked at her. 'I think it's coming from the kitchen.'

His youthful but serious expression fell on her. She could see the mischievous twinkle in his eyes. He was desperate for adventure and wanted her to go along for the ride.

'Come on, then,' she whispered, getting up and tiptoeing towards the kitchen.

The noise continued to *click-clack, click-clack* as they made their way towards it. The constant rhythm was hypnotic, and Alli found herself swaying a little as she led her brother out of the living room. The closer they got to the kitchen, the louder the noise became. *It's got to be in here,* she thought, tightening her grip on Ant's hand. She didn't know if the sweat that was between their palms was from her or from him. She guessed it was her. Her mouth was dry, and she could hear her heart bashing the inside of her ears. *It must be my sweat,* she thought. As they crossed the threshold from the hallway to the tiles on the kitchen floor, she stopped. Ant banged into her.

'Shhh,' she warned with a finger over her mouth. 'Is it just me, or has the noise stopped?' she half mouthed, half whispered.

Ant cocked his head to listen before turning around and looking back towards the living room. 'It hasn't stopped. It's moved,' he announced, his voice too loud in the near silence. 'It's back in the living room.'

Alli listened too. He was right. The sound was now behind them, back where they had just come from. She squeezed his hand tighter as her bottom teeth bit onto her top lip.

They turned around. The game had just taken a new twist.

Slowly, they walked back into the living room. Again, the closer they got, the louder the *click-clack, click-clack* became. Ant pointed towards the couch. 'It's coming from behind there,' he whispered.

Alli noticed that his grip on her hand had tightened.

It was now coming from a cabinet behind the couch. It was only small, but as she had known from personal experience during games of hide and seek, there was enough room inside for a small person to hide. The intrepid pair moved the couch out of the way, neither wanting to mention that the temperature in the house seemed to have plummeted since they'd begun this adventure.

As Alli reached her hand towards the handle, all manner of demons and imps from Hell broke free of her imagination. She was more than a little disappointed in herself as a small whimper issued from her.

'What did you say?' Ant asked.

His voice made her jump. The wavering in it unsteadied her. He was seldom scared, even for such a young boy. She looked at him, suddenly not wanting to open the door. A dark feeling overcame her. It began in her stomach, then spread outwards. The cold was now physical, and she had to clench and unclench her fingers to get feeling back into them.

The *click-clack* noise continued.

'I don't like this,' Ant whispered.

She could feel him behind her, getting as close as his little body would allow. She was also acutely aware that he was only wearing his pyjamas and therefore must have been feeling the bite of the cold worse than her. That was when she realised she wasn't wearing much more either. The living room had been warmed by the fire in the fireplace that would have spread some heat out to other rooms, *or would normally*, only it wasn't today. Even though she could see flames dancing in the fireplace, they had a tinge of blue to them, and very little, maybe even zero heat coming from them.

'I'm so cold.' Ant shivered. 'Don't open that door.'

It was too late to heed his advice. She was too far gone, too near to the door to pull away. She *had* to open it; she *had* to know what or who was making that noise. A snowflake fluttered past her eyes, but she ignored it, thinking it was nonsense. *It doesn't snow indoors,* she thought, not entirely convincing herself of that fact.

As her hand touched the metal of the clasp, the cold bit through her skin, making her flesh stick to it. She inhaled through gritted teeth, trying to ignore the pain in her fingers. Her rampant curiosity was getting the better of her.

'Alli. I don't want to know what the sound is anymore. I just want to go and finish my comic,' Ant stuttered through his own chattering teeth.

One arm reached behind her and rubbed up and down on her brother's freezing skin, trying to warm him, while the fingers on her other hand rested on the latch to the door.

Click, Clack!

The sound continued, unhindered by the dramatic drop in temperature.

Click, Clack!

She concentrated, squeezing her numb fingers together and just about manged to turn the latch.

Click, Clack!

Holding her breath, she pulled on the small door.

It wouldn't open!

Click, Clack!

She tugged harder, feeling Ant's shivering body hugging ever tighter to hers.

Click ...

The door swung open.

The sound stopped.

The temperature of the room returned to normal, and goosebumps raised over her skin.

The cabinet was empty.

'It's stopped.' Ant whispered the obvious behind her as she felt him pull away from her. 'And it's not cold anymore,' he continued. 'What's happening, Alli?'

'I don't know.' She thought truth was the best policy right then, as she was as scared and confused as he was. 'You did feel that cold, didn't you?' she asked, second-guessing her goosebumps and the ugly feeling in her stomach.

'I ... I think I did,' he replied, stuttering. She could feel him still close to her but no longer touching. 'Where's Mom?' he asked, as if he was suddenly aware there were no adults in the room.

'She had one of her headaches. She went to lie down.'

'Do you think she felt the cold?' His face was telling her he was hoping her answer was going to be *yes*.

'The noise stopped. Why would it just stop like that? It's been around all day, and as soon as we get to this cabinet, it stops.' She was still looking in the empty space before her. She *knew* it had been coming from here, but there was clearly nothing in there to cause it.

'I don't know,' Ant replied. 'I just want to get back to my comic.'

Click ...

Both children froze as the gentle sound echoed around the room and their heads.

'Is that—' Ant began, but was interrupted by:

Clack ...

Alli looked back into the cabinet, making sure it was still empty.

It was.

Click ... clack!

She shook her head as she realised the noise was no longer coming from the cabinet.

Click, clack, click, clack ...

They both turned towards the kitchen. It was coming from outside. Alli was shaking her head. 'We can't,' she whispered.

'We have to,' he replied. 'What if it's the little girl I saw in Old Man Sharpe's yard? The one you saw in the woods? What if she needs our help?'

'Last time, I nearly died, Ant. I would have if you—'

'It wasn't me. Old Man Sharpe found you.'

'Yeah, but you—'

Click, clack, click, clack, click, clack ...

The sound was getting louder and, they both thought, faster.

'She might be out there in the snow. She might be lost, cold, scared.'

'Why would anyone lost or scared be knitting in the snow?' she asked, the voice of pragmatism.

Ant's face fell as if he hadn't thought of that.

'Do you think she's a ghost?' Alli asked, feeling stupid the moment it came from her mouth.

'Shh,' he scolded her. 'Don't say that.'

Without warning, he pushed his sister towards the door. Outside, the wind was howling, making it sound worse than it was. She touched the door and had a moment where she thought the strange cold air had come back to haunt them, but after she flinched from the breeze, she realised that was all it was. A cold draft blowing through the cracks in the door frame.

Click, clack ...

'Are we going to find the noise?' Ant asked. She could hear the fear and excitement in his voice, both of them vying for dominance.

'Should we?' she asked. Once again, she felt stupid that she was trying to get encouragement, or indeed permission, from her younger brother for something they'd been told not to do.

He ignored the question and just looked at the door. A small nod was all that was needed to get them moving.

'OK, get your coat on, boots, and snow pants too. We're not going out there without proper clothes. We have to make sure we know what we're doing. I don't want us to get lost like we did last time.'

The little boy with the air of a man years older than he was ran towards the closet where their coats and outdoor winter clothes were kept. 'Here you go. Put them on and let's find out where that noise is coming from.'

She could see that the fear, or most of it, had disappeared from his face, and excitement and adrenaline from this situation had taken over—they had won the battle. He threw her coat to her, followed by her boots and pants. 'Here you go, hurry up. She could be stuck out there, freezing.'

Alli looked at the door. Through the howl of the wind, the *click-clacking* sound could still be heard. It was too rhythmic to be anything but a person doing something that involved banging two sticks together. Without thinking too much about it, she put her winter clothes on over the clothes she had been lounging in. In a short while, they were both standing in the doorway, dressed and ready to go, set to explore the frozen wastes on Christmas Eve.

~~~~

'I remember now. We went out into the snow against the wishes of Mom,' Anthony said, leaning forward on the table. There was a look on his face, as if the memories were unfolding in his head. 'Were we grounded or something?'

I nodded. 'Yeah. After I got lost in the woods, Mom freaked. She threatened to cancel Christmas. Looking back now, I think it was more because of the lack of money and presents for us than anything else.'

Anthony replied by raising his eyebrows. I could tell he was about to say something, then he stopped. His face fell as he looked at me. 'Do you hear that?' he asked, raising his head.

'What?'

'Music. Are Mom or Grace playing music upstairs?' he asked, cocking his head.

I pouted as I cocked my head to listen. 'I doubt it!' However, I could hear a bugle playing from somewhere. It was faint but definitely there. A marching drumbeat was accompanying it. 'It's that fucking song I've been hearing everywhere. "Do You Believe the Magic," or something like that.'

'That's a spooky song,' Anthony replied, not looking at me. 'I never did like it.' He stood up and moved towards the kitchen door. 'It doesn't sound like its coming from upstairs.'

I spared a quick look towards the small cabinet door behind the couch. Thankfully, the music was not coming from there. As it continued, it became clear it wasn't a marching drum I could hear but the rhythmic *click-clacking* sound that had confused us so much earlier.

'It's coming from outside,' Ant said, laying his ear to the old wooden door.

'It can't be. It's pitch black out there, and probably twenty below,' I replied, making my way to the door. I put my ear to the wood, mimicking him. As I did, I realised he was right. The music *was* coming from outside, as was the *click-clacking* noise beneath it.

'This is too weird,' Anthony said. 'Everything's coming back to me now. The music and the noise.' He looked at me, and I could see the contours on his face changing, almost as if he was coming to terms with what he was hearing. 'Jesus, Alison, that was thirty years ago when we went out into the snow.'

'I think whatever we saw that night is calling us back. I think it's targeting Grace. She's the same age now as we were back then.'

'Well, as you were. I'm younger, remember.'

I looked at my brother, expecting to see him smirking, making light of the situation. I was dismayed, not to mention distressed, to see he was serious. He smiled, but to me, it looked forced. 'I'm just saying, you know.'

I nodded slowly. 'I'm scared too, Anthony. But with all the strange things that have been happening around here, without going all Scooby-Doo about it, I think we need to get to the bottom of it.' I moved away from the door and towards the closet in the hallway. I removed our coats. A heavy, cloying feeling of déjà vu descended over me as I threw Anthony's coat to him. *We've done this before,* I thought. *This exact same thing, on another Christmas Eve, thirty years ago*.

He caught his coat and began to slip into it. 'Where are we going?' he asked. I had an idea he knew exactly where we were going.

'We're going to follow that music and the clacking sound. We're going to find out what the hell is going on here.' *And what happened that night, all those years ago,* I concluded in my head.

'*Here it comes again … The promise and the awe*!'

I was nodding as the music continued to filter through. 'It's the same song. The one I heard when the hall changed around me. The same music I heard when Grace went missing. I need, even if it's only for my own sanity, to find out where it's coming from.'

'OK, then,' came Anthony's muffled reply. Despite the situation, I struggled to suppress a laugh as he stood in the kitchen with his coat hood pulled over his face, allowing him only the smallest porthole for him to see through. 'But do we really want to be doing this on Christmas Eve?'

'I think we have to.' I smiled, zipping up my coat. 'It'll be fine. Come on, let's go.'

'Are we going to be able to hear the music through these layers?' Anthony shouted through his hood.

'I've got a feeling that won't be a problem,' I said, pulling my hood up tight.

~~~~

'Are you playing music?' Ant cried out, his voice barely cutting through the wind that was screaming through the trees.

'What?' Alli shouted back at her trailing brother.

'That music. Is it coming from you?' he shouted.

She stopped walking and listened. The wind was screaming all around her, but the click-clacking noise was still coming from somewhere ahead of them. The eight-year-old girl faced into the squall of the Christmas Eve storm, her brother, two years younger, standing behind her. Both were listening through the wind. She exhaled in annoyance and began to undo her hood. The freezing wind clawed at her face like what she imagined a polar bear attack might be like. The wind screamed, yet there was something else, another noise beneath the shrieking weather and the impossible click-clacking. It was the gentle sound of the song that had been plaguing her all Christmas.

A baritone male voice crooning, '*Can you feel the Christmas magic?*'

It was followed with an eerie female back up, repeating, '*Can you feel the Christmas magic?*'

She thought the question was appropriate.

'It sounds like it's coming from over there,' she shouted, pointing in the direction of Old Man Sharpe's house. 'From where that light is.'

A golden glow, akin to a streetlamp, was illuminating the dark, stormy night in Mr Sharpe's yard. The shadows of the trees surrounding this secretive abode were blowing in the strong wind.

The dark of the night had turned them into silhouettes of savage monsters, beasts hungrily grasping, reaching for their next victims. For Alli and her brother. Everything about this felt wrong, but she knew it was something they had to do. Something was pulling her, them, towards this house. She didn't know if it was the odd light, the click-clacking, or the annoying music, but she knew she had to follow wherever it led.

Acting braver than she felt, she pulled up her hood and continued her mission, beckoning her brother to catch her up. The distance to Mr Sharpe's house wasn't far, but it was going to be a slog in this weather.

~~~~

'It's definitely coming from Old Man Sharpe's yard. There's a light on over there. He must be in,' I shouted above the screaming of the storm.

'Alison, this is ridiculous,' Anthony replied, also shouting over the banshee-like wind. 'Can't we just go back and enjoy Christmas Eve like fucking normal brothers and sisters do?'

I could barely hear him due to the cacophony of the trinity of the storm, the music, and the click-clacking noise.

'I can't,' I replied. 'I need to understand what's happening.' As I turned back towards the glowing light in Mr Sharpe's yard, I noticed the shadows of the trees. Something about them scared me. There was something that caused a memory to resurface, a memory from long ago. Like how they scared me then like they were scaring me now. I didn't have the luxury of time to dwell on questions that were developing, as something I couldn't explain was calling me towards the light ahead. I could hear the reassuring sound of Anthony struggling behind me.

That, too, brought a pang of nostalgia.

We'd made this journey before.

There was something else illuminated in the snow, or rather something that the light failed to illuminate, that caught my attention.

Footprints!

Small footprints!

My heart felt like it missed a beat.

Everything about the last time we'd made this journey rushed back at me.

'Whose prints are those?' Anthony asked as he caught up, pointing to the ground. He was playing with the pull on his hood, trying to open it a little more so he could speak. 'We didn't make them. They look like kids'.' He paused for a moment, and if I could have seen his face inside the hood, I know I'd have seen horror on his features. That same horror was on my face. 'You don't think Grace—'

'We made those tracks, Ant,' I replied, cutting him off mid-sentence. 'We made them. Don't you remember? Years ago, when we saw the ghosts.'

'Alison, you're scaring me now. What are you talking about?'

I leaned in, putting both my hands on his shoulders so he would be able to hear what I had to say. 'Thirty years ago, these exact same things were happening. Remember the little girl you saw on Halloween in the yard? Remember I went missing and the little girl in the light saved me?'

'Mr Sharpe saved you,' Anthony shouted back. 'We've been through this.'

I shook my head. 'No, he didn't. I'd have been dead long before you both turned up. The little girl in the light saved me. I told you about her, but you wouldn't listen. You have to listen now.'

Anthony grabbed me by the shoulders and brought my face close. I could just about make out his eyes through the dark of the hood. 'Alison, what's all this about? What's happening here?'

'Lisa,' was all I could say before turning away and heading back into the storm, towards Old Man Sharpe's glowing yard.

I was following two sets of small footprints.

~~~~~

'Who else is out here?' Alli shouted to Ant, who was lagging behind her. 'There's no way Mom's followed us.'

Ant looked behind him, back the way they'd come. There were four sets of footprints. Two of them were small, and two of them were larger, adult sized. 'Mom was asleep when we left. You said she had a headache. Do you think she's followed us? We're in big trouble if she has.'

Alli wasn't so sure the tracks were their mother's. She'd seen her taking pills, so she knew she would be asleep for at least a couple of more hours. The tracks belonged to someone else. She had her own belief who'd laid the tracks but thought it best not to mention it to Ant. She'd already gotten him into bigger trouble than he needed to be on Christmas Eve. 'I don't think they're Mom's,' was all she shouted before turning back towards the glowing light and the music. 'Come on, we're almost there.'

Ant was standing still. The only movement he made was a shiver that looked to be passing through his whole body. 'I don't like this, Alli,' he shouted. 'If those tracks aren't Mom's, then there's only one other person they could belong to.'

He was right. She had to give him credit for this. For a six-year-old boy, he was very intuitive.

'Is Old Man Sharpe out here with us?' he continued. She could tell by his voice, even over the wind, that it had taken more than a little bit of courage to ask that question.

She didn't answer. She just turned away and continued to trudge through the snow, towards the source of the light, the music, and the strange sound. *I hope not,* she thought. H*e gives me the creeps.*

~~~~

The light was getting brighter, illuminating our path. It was guiding us through the trees, helping us avoid any potentially dangerous trips on tangled roots or hidden rocks. It was turning the snow orange, coloured by the radiated glow of the unidentified source. The music continued. It hadn't gotten any louder, but the strong voice of the male singer had been replaced with a whispered voice of a female. *A young girl by the sounds of it,* I thought with a shiver as I continued to struggle through the thick snow drifts. The change had given the song an eerie, ghostly effect, and it made me feel colder than I already was, inside and out.

The smaller footprints continued for as far as I could see. I had a terrible thought that whoever they belonged to—I didn't want to think it might have been Grace—was within the source of the light. This consideration caused me to hurry my pace along. I had the reassurance of Anthony still behind me, his laboured but still strong breathing filtering through all the noises of this strange night as he followed me through the heavy drifts.

The house wasn't far away now. Just a couple of hundred yards ahead. I could just about make it out in the gloom of the night. The eerie illumination was giving it an odd lustre; it was tall, dark, and foreboding. All the windows were black. Not a single light shone from inside, a strange effect, especially on Christmas Eve. *But then there never were any lights from this house, Christmas or no,* I remembered.

The light began to pulse, and the click-clacking noise, the one that had irritated me in the house, rose again, despite the shrieking of the wind and the creepy music. I reached the snow-laden hedge that acted as a fence and opened the gate into the front yard. A bizarre feeling overcame me when I realised that before this trip home, the last time I'd been here, in this yard, I had been eight years old, on Halloween night. The time Anthony swore a vision of a ghostly girl had saved me from being detected by Mr Sharpe and believed that the same girl had saved my life in the snow. Now, here I was again, for the second time in as many days.

Stepping into the yard was like walking into an alien landscape. The thick snow on the ground and on the foliage around it was lit up orange. The light was coming from behind the house, casting long, thick shadows. I moved into the shadow of the house, following the small footsteps as they made their way around the back, towards the yard.

'Come on,' I urged my struggling brother.

'*Here it comes again ...*'

As the disembodied voice of the young girl whispered into my ear, I began to quicken my pace. Something was happening, and it was something I needed to witness.

'*The promise and the awe ...*'

~~~~

The light from Old Man Sharpe's yard was getting brighter, and the whisper of the little girl singing the now despised song was becoming increasingly insistent. Inside, if she was being truthful to herself, Alli was terrified. She had never been allowed out this late, never mind it being Christmas Eve, and never mind there being a storm. If their mother caught them here, there would be no Christmas morning for them, Christmas Spirit or no Christmas Spirit. But whatever it was, whoever it was out here, was calling her forward, pulling her towards something. It was something she couldn't fathom.

'It's here,' she shouted to Ant over the wind. 'She's pulling us here. I think she wants to tell us something.'

'Alli, I want to go home. Who's pulling you here? This is Mr Sharpe's house. We don't want to be here, never mind in the dark. Come on, Alli, let's go back.'

'The girl singing the song. I know you can hear her. She's the one making the click-clacking noise.'

'I can hear it, and I don't like it,' Ant whined.

Alli ignored him and continued through the snow, towards the back of the house. Towards the light.

~~~~

As I reached the corner of the house, I leaned against the brick structure for a few moments. I needed to rest, to get my breath back before I continued. The struggle through the storm had taken more out of me than I had thought it would, making me realise I wasn't as young as I used to be. Sparing a glance behind me, I watched Anthony emerge from the shadows.

'We're close,' I called.

To my surprise, he nodded. I was expecting an argument, for him to reason that we should give whatever this was up and return to the warmth and the comforts of our childhood home, to enjoy our last Christmas with our mother and forget all about the singing and the strange noises. Only I knew Anthony. He was witnessing everything just as much as I was, and I knew he was just as invested as I was. He would *have* to find their underlying cause.

'It's just around this corner; I know it is. Whatever's been causing all of this, playing with Grace's head, it's here.' I knew how I must have sounded. Anthony's analytical brain wouldn't be able to process the anxiety I was feeling, the elation and the excitement, coupled with an overwhelming terror.

'Alison, I need to know if you're OK. This is irrational, and for some reason, I've allowed you to drag me into it with you. We need to go back home, right no—' He didn't finish that sentence as he looked towards the source of the light. 'What the fuck?'

'What?' I asked snapping my head towards where he was looking. 'What is it? What did you see?'

'Who the Hell is that?' He pushed past me and stomped off into the stormy night, in the direction of the light.

'What did you see?' I shouted as I fought to catch up with him.

'There's two kids,' he replied, not looking back. 'Out here alone. That can't be right.'

~~~~

'It's so bright,' Ant yelled as he rounded the house into the yard, following his big sister. Both had their hands to their faces, attempting to shield their eyes from the glare. 'Is the tree on fire?'

'I don't think so,' Alli replied, removing her hand, allowing the light to filter into her eyes and become accustomed to the new source. 'I think it's just … glowing.'

'Glowing? Why? Trees don't glow.'

'I don't know. Come on.' Alli grabbed her little brother's jacket and pulled him along towards the radiant tree. He followed; he didn't have any other choice.

'Alli,' he shouted, the alarm in his voice evident enough for her to stop pulling him.

'What?'

'Look …' He was pointing back towards the house, where there were two silhouettes, talking as they rested at the corner. They looked like adults. One of them had his hands on the other's shoulders. 'Who is that? Is it Mom?'

Alli looked. There was something about the way the two figures interacted that told her it wasn't their mother. She shook her head. One of the shadows turned and looked directly at her. Her heart sank into the pit of her stomach. There was something eerie about them, about the way they looked at her, seeing her. For some reason, she knew this was not supposed to happen, ever. These four people were never supposed to meet or even see each other. 'No, I don't think so. Come on, we need to get to that tree now.'

She continued to drag her brother deeper into the yard and closer to the tree.

~~~~

'It couldn't have been Grace, could it?' I gasped as I continued my way towards the illuminated yard. 'I can't see any tracks. Are you sure you saw them?'

'Yeah. They were there; I'm certain,' Anthony replied, shaking his head. 'They looked at us. One of them dragged the other away.'

'Well, the snow must have covered their tracks pretty fast, faster than these other ones. I can't see anything.'

'Did you see them? Please, tell me you did,' Anthony pleaded as he followed me around the corner, catching up. As he rounded into the yard, he stopped, gaping at the sight before him.

I was already stationery, not quite believing what I was looking at.

The tree in the centre of the yard, the one where we had found Grace the day before, was pulsing with the eerie yellowish light. The warm, yellow throb was reaching across the yard, offering long shadows of the bushes around the perimeter.

There were two other shadows in the yard with them.

They were longer than they should have been.

My eyes were drawn to them. From their long heads to their elongated bodies, to their extra-long legs. At the end of the shadows were the solidified bodies of two children. One was taller than the other. The taller one was grasping the hand of the smaller one. They were both transfixed by something before them. Something I couldn't see.

Anthony sidled up next to me and took my hand. The sudden attention spooked me, and I jumped as his gloved fingers intertwined themselves around mine. I turned to see the welcoming site of my brother, my protector standing next to me. I gladly accepted his gesture.

'Who are they?' he whispered.

I smiled as I realised he was whispering so as not to disturb the scene. The music was resonating from somewhere, everywhere, through the air. It was whispering on the wind, but it was now only an echo of the former melody. The light was pulsing. Every time it did, the shadows of the children ebbed and flowed with it.

'I know who they are …' I whispered, answering Anthony's question.

~~~~

'Who is that?' Ant asked as a figure moved within the light.

It was just a silhouette, but Alli could tell it wasn't an adult. She instinctively knew it wasn't either of the figures they'd seen at the side of the house. There was only one shadow now, where previously there had been two. Whoever this was didn't look tall enough to be an adult. Alli guessed whoever it was—she was getting a strong feeling it was female—must have been about the same age as she was.

'*Alison.*'

The voice came from everywhere. It was on the wind, it was in the glowing tree, it was bouncing around inside her head. She was relieved that Ant had heard the voice too. He gripped her hand tighter as the voice called his name.

'*Anthony.*'

'Alli, I'm scared,' he whispered. 'Who is it? How does she know our names?'

As the silhouette stepped out of the light, Alli saw it was a young girl. *I was right,* she thought. *She* is *the same age as me.*

'Oh my God, she looks like you,' Ant gasped as he let go of her hand and pulled his hood down, hiding his eyes. 'She's the image of you.'

Alli removed her own hood and looked. The little girl did indeed look like herself. Her hair was a little darker than Alli's, but it was so similar. Where she wore her hair down, this little girl wore hers in old-fashioned plaits. Her clothing was also old-fashioned. She was wearing a long, dark coat that looked woollen rather than the fibres of the coats they were wearing. Her boots, although deep in the snow, looked old-fashioned too.

'Alison, Anthony …' the little girl said. 'Thank you for coming …'

Before she could finish her introduction, her head snapped to the left, back towards the house, and her eyes widened. She turned back towards them, but her face had changed … physically!

The side of her head was now swollen, distorted. Her left eye was darker than the other, and there was a heavy flow of blood running from her nose. She opened her mouth to say something, but all that came from between her lips was more dark blood; it looked fresh, thick, and plentiful.

It was the wound in her neck where the majority of the blood was pouring from. It ran like a dark waterfall.

Alli stepped back from the horror unveiling before them, taking Ant with her. He was more than a willing participant in this retreat. As they backed away, the girl raised her hands to them as if calling to them, asking them for help. More blood gushed from the wound in her neck, and Alli watched as her dark eyes began to roll back in her head.

Ant let go of Alli's hand as he looked towards the house. 'Old Man Sharpe,' he shouted.

Alli drew her stare away from the gruesome show to see what her brother was shouting about. Her already rapid heartbeat sped up further as the image of Mr Sharpe's frame, running through the snow towards them, became bathed within the yellow glare from the tree. 'Mr Sharpe,' she whispered, reaching out for her brother's hand again. When she found it, she pulled him towards her. 'Run.' It was the only word she could force from her mouth.

Ant was on the same page as her, and once he shook himself free of her grip, he was off like a shot towards the house, back the way they'd come.

They didn't get very far before they both stopped.

The two adults were back, and they were blocking their way.

They looked familiar, but Alli's freezing, petrified brain couldn't recall from where.

The woman and man, both dressed in brightly coloured coats that were like nothing she had ever seen before, stared at them. They looked as surprised as she was. The woman, her hood down, her hair tied back in a ponytail, reached out towards her. She opened her mouth to say something.

'Hey, you two … stop right there.' The loud voice cut through the wind.

For the first time, Alli noticed the music and the *click-clacking* sound had stopped. Mr Sharpe was gaining on them, waving his hands, shouting. Her gaze shifted to the bloodied vision of the little girl, now lying, slumped at the foot of the tree in the centre of the yard. The snow around her was stained red and was melting from its warmth.

There was only one decision she could make.

They had to make it past the two adults and get home. She grabbed Ant's hand and charged forward, fully intending to barge through the strangers, knocking them out of their way if she had to. As she charged, pulling her brother behind her, she braced herself for the impact of the woman.

Only it didn't come.

Instead, she passed through her.

A cold chill tickled her bones. It was colder and deeper than anything she had experienced this night, or any other night. It was the strangest sensation she had *ever* felt.

The cold stayed deep inside her.

She stumbled into a snowdrift when the physical barrier of the woman didn't appear, and Ant fell on top of her. As she lay, struggling to get up, she noticed the two strangers were gone, along with the light and the horrible vision of the bleeding girl.

Mr Sharpe, however, was still there, and was gaining on them, even in the deep snow.

'Come on, Ant. Get up,' she shouted as she struggled in the snow drift. Tugging on Ant's arm, she pulled him up, and the pair ran off into the night, into the direction of the safety of their home.

~~~~

I was almost thigh deep in the snow. The storm had either passed or was in one of those lulls that trick you into believing you are safe. The howl of the wind had receded but was replaced with a stronger, more rousing version of the song that had been playing almost constantly in my head.

'*Here it comes again ... open hearts and open door. In this season of joy and hope, let your true love soar ...*'

The light from the tree had given the lustre of daylight to the yard around it, strengthening the shadows of the two children.

'I know who they are ...' I whispered.

Anthony turned. He pulled his hood down, and I could see the confusion in his face. He was looking towards the children. 'I know them too,' he replied.

'They are us,' I whispered. Even through the noise of the song and the wind, he heard what I said.

'How is this happening? I ... I remember this.'

'They're looking at the little girl. The one in the light. The one with the blood pouring from her neck.'

'Oh my God,' Anthony mumbled. 'We were the adults!'

I nodded. 'We are. Any moment now, Old Man Sharpe is going to come running across the yard towards us.'

'Then we'll run,' Anthony continued.

'We'll run right through ... ourselves.' I turned towards my brother and, smiling, reached for his hand. 'I think we're finally going to get some answers. Answers to questions we've never thought to ask.'

All four of us stared at each other. I couldn't help but reach my hand out towards my younger self.

The two children's heads snapped to their left as if they'd seen something that scared them. Then the taller of the two, me, grabbed the younger one's, Anthony's, hand and pulled him away. I pulled him towards where we were standing at the corner of the house.

They ran.

We ran, but we also stood our ground.

There was an odd sensation as they barged through me. I steeled myself for an impact I knew wouldn't come. Instead, a feeling like numbness or pins and needles passed through me as both children disappeared.

'What the fuck just happened?' Anthony asked. I could hear breathlessness in his voice.

'We were chased out of the yard by—'

'Old Man Sharpe,' he finished, looking around for any sign of the man. There was none. 'Look,' he said as he pointed towards the glowing tree.

Within the light, there was a figure, a silhouette of a young girl. Initially, I thought it was Grace and took a step towards her. I felt Anthony's hand stop me. I tried to shake it off, to stop him from blocking my access to her, but something changed. I looked, and I saw it wasn't her, although the similarity was striking. 'Jesus, she looks just like …' I gasped.

Anthony's hand tightened around mine. I didn't need to finish the sentence.

The little girl stepped out of the light, onto the snowy ground around the tree. She didn't make any imprints as she trod through the virgin snow. Her hair was tied up in plaits, and I noticed they weren't blowing even though the wind was still fierce. Neither her long black coat nor her hair were affected by it. Suddenly, the wind died, and the night became still. Large, beautiful snowflakes began to fall gracefully from the sky as she approached. A warmth was radiating from her as the light coming from the tree sliced through the darkness of the newly still night. It enveloped me and Anthony in its warm glow, holding us in an embrace neither of us could fathom.

Anthony's hand tightened. It had become uncomfortable. I turned to look at him. He looked at me at the same time. Something about him had changed. At first, his expression was hard. I could see the muscles in his jaws flexing as he grinded his teeth, but they stopped as our eyes met. They softened, and a ghost of a smile appeared in the corners of his mouth. He just shook his head.

'I don't know,' I mouthed, anticipating his question. Turning my attention back to the little girl who looked so much like Grace, I opened my mouth. I wanted to speak to her, to ask her why we were here, why we had witnessed our younger selves from thirty years ago. The words, however, were stuck in my mouth.

The girl continued her advance. Her expression was unchanged. Her dark eyes were looking past us. *Almost as if we're not here,* I thought.

She made her way elegantly, gently over the snow, the yellow light following in her wake as she moved. *If she's not making footprints, then whose were the others we saw on the way over here?* I thought as the apparition passed by.

'I'm so glad you could make it,' she said. Or at least I thought that was what she said, as the voice was coming from behind her, from inside the light, inside the tree.

'Did she just speak?' Anthony asked. I could, hand on heart, honestly say I'd forgotten he was even there.

'I think so,' I replied, smiling. 'But I get the feeling she's not speaking to us.'

'Who else could she be speaking to?' Anthony whispered.

When we were kids, we had run straight home. We'd dried ourselves off and gotten into bed, ready for the Spirit of Christmas to come and bless us with gifts. Ready to forget what we'd seen, to forget about the ghosts, the footprints, and the light from the tree.

They were children. I envied them that. My thoughts wandered to what the *Spirit* brought us that year. I couldn't remember. I knew whatever it was, it would be small, as there hadn't been any money since Dad had died. I allowed the thought to dwindle as I watched the little girl flit past us, her eyes concentrating on something behind us, something we couldn't see.

Or at least I thought we couldn't see.

As I turned to follow her progress, I got the shock of my life.

It would not be the last shock of that night.

18.

DELORES HAD BEEN sleeping. The last few days had worn her out. She was tired, right down to her bones, *and maybe even further than that,* she thought. She was a lot sicker than she had allowed Alison, Anthony, and Grace to see. Since they'd turned up and made her very last Christmas complete, the pain had ramped up to almost unbearable levels. The relief Doctor Johnston, Browning's assistant, had given her was not enough to even touch the sides of what she was really feeling. The aches in her back were sapping her strength, and at times, she felt like her very veins were burning within the confines of her legs and arms. Even getting out of bed and making it downstairs was energy-draining labour. By the time she wrapped her robe around her emaciated frame, she was ready to get back into her bed and sleep off all her efforts. Just smiling and greeting her beautiful children and her gorgeous granddaughter zapped her. When Alison would ask her what she wanted for breakfast, the thought of eating greasy food, allowing it to slosh around in her stomach, made her want to retch. Even oatmeal was too much for her to contemplate.

Although she wouldn't admit it to her beautiful family, she'd had enough. She'd made her peace with this world and was ready to move on to whatever was next. She longed to pass through, to shake off this mortal coil, and leave the pain and sickness behind.

She wanted to see her husband again.

She longed to see Lisa too.

She hated to admit it, but she had been jealous of Grace.

Grace with her unlimited supply of enthusiasm, her beautiful smile, and her gorgeous dark eyes.

Grace with her unlimited access to Lisa.

A movement in the corner of her vision alerted her. She thought nothing of it at first, as the pain relief pills, which she took by the handful, often gave her visions of things that were not really there. However, something about this flicker told her this wasn't medically induced. With an effort she didn't think she had, she sat up in the bed. Her head swam as her blood took its time to activate the cells in her brain correctly. The room was cold, even though she knew Anthony had kept the heating on constantly since they had been there. *Money to burn,* she thought, rolling her eyes. However, this cold wasn't the regular cold she associated with deep winter nights.

This cold felt like she was outside.

The feeling was … energising.

She exhaled and marvelled at the plume of vapour streaming from her mouth. It felt like the frigid air was battling with the pain she was expecting to feel, and it was *winning.* Her legs and arms were surprisingly strong. She clenched her fingers, marvelling at the fluidity of her joints. She didn't feel sick. She didn't feel hungry either, and the absence of nausea caused her to smile. She pulled the covers back from her frail body and kicked her legs off the bed. She expected to be left breathless by the sudden activity, but it was the exact opposite. It left her feeling good, healthy, invigorated. *This is new,* she thought, standing up and stretching her arms. *Or is it old?* She turned. The flicker that had started this revival was still there; only now it was no longer a flicker.

It was a man.

He was wearing a long coat, and his dark hair was slicked back with some kind of product that made it shine in the strange light that was bathing him. His dark eyes were filled with wonder and joy, and the smile on his face belied the years it had been since she'd last seen him.

That felt like yesterday.

It could have been yesterday.

She turned away, ready to make her bed. To straighten out the blankets as had been her ritual and routine since before she could remember. But there was something in the bed stopping her from completing his task.

It was something she wasn't expecting.

'It's you, Delores,' the man said, his voice merely a whisper, but it was a voice Delores would have recognised anywhere, a voice she'd longed to hear for years beyond measure. As the words floated around the room, so did the music. The same music she heard every year around this time.

'*Here it comes again ... the promise and the awe.*'

She had always loved that song, but she hadn't been able to listen to it for so long. The memories it brought were just too painful.

'Toby?' she asked. 'Is it really you?'

The man smiled and held out his hand towards the frail woman.

D E McCluskey

19.

'GRACE,' I SHOUTED letting go of my brother's hand to dash towards the little girl in the red coat. 'Grace, what are you doing out here? Why aren't you at home in bed?' There was anger in my voice, but I was also feeling a kind of relief. Grace looked calm, relaxed. She didn't look cold, although the wind was whipping at her long hair, unlike the little girl's, who was standing next to her.

'Mommy,' she shouted over the wind that was picking back up. 'Mommy, this is Lisa. You can see her now, can't you?'

My eyes flicked between the little girls. I was amazed at how much they resembled each other. Lisa looked exactly like Grace, but from a different era. I now knew whose tracks we'd seen earlier.

'Wow,' I heard Anthony exclaim from behind me. 'Alison, both of these girls are the image of you when you were their age.'

I wasn't ready for that observation. 'What?'

'Look at them. They both look like you.'

I had to look closer, but I did finally admit that, in the yellow glow of the tree, these two almost identical girls did look like me. 'Grace, who told you to come out here?' I scolded, trying my best to sound stern over the sound of the wind. 'You're going to catch your death. You need to get home right now.'

Anthony moved forward to attempt to take hold of Grace's arm, but she stepped back. Lisa stepped with her. 'Lisa told me to come out here. She told me we had something to do. Something she wanted you to do, but you could hardly see her.'

'What? Grace, what are you talking about?' I asked, feeling anger and frustration building within me. The cold of the night was behind us now as all four of us were bathed in the warm glow from the tree.

'She's right,' Lisa said.

I felt a chill run all through me at the sound of her voice. I noticed Anthony's head jerk when she spoke too. I assumed he'd just experienced the same feeling I had.

'I asked her to come with me. There was something I needed to do, something that was long overdue,' Lisa said. Her voice sounded as if it were floating on the wind, blowing through the air rather than coming from the moving lips of the apparition before us. 'It was something I tried to do with you, Alison, but for some reason, you couldn't or wouldn't see me. You knew I was there, but when I appeared, when you finally gave in to me, you were ripped away at the last minute. Do you remember?'

'Old Man Sharpe?' Anthony whispered.

I wasn't sure if it was a question or a statement.

Lisa nodded. 'Mr Sharpe was chasing you. You both ran. Our connection was cut.'

'We … we had to. Our mom had—'

'Always told you to keep away from him,' Lisa interrupted.

'Mr Sharpe is a nice old man,' Grace said, looking from Lisa to her mother, and then to her uncle. 'He was very nice to us before, but he's so sad.'

'Before?' My eye widened. 'What do you mean before? Grace, where have you been?' I wanted my voice to sound stern, as if I were admonishing her, but I couldn't manage it.

Grace's face fell a little. In the shadows cast by the glow, she looked so much like the little girl next to her it was difficult to tell them apart. 'Lisa told you, Mommy. We had an errand to run. It's done now, and it's almost time for us to go home for Christmas. All of us.'

'Grace, you tell me what this errand was, and you tell me now; otherwise, you'll be in so much trouble.'

'I needed her,' Lisa said. This time, her voice was coming from her mouth, not the wind. 'I needed her help. I couldn't do what was required without her, or you. I couldn't do it on my own.'

I was losing my temper now. My eyes shot towards the little girl. I couldn't believe I was having a heated debate with … what could be a ghost in the middle of a snowstorm, on Christmas Eve night. 'And this errand was?' I asked.

'She needed to forgive me …' came a deep voice from behind.

20.

'I'LL NEED TO dress. I'm likely to catch my death of cold out there. It's freezing,' Delores said as she fussed around the bedroom. She was looking for something to put on, something to cover her frail, emaciated body. She didn't want him seeing her like this.

'You need less than you think,' Toby said. There was good humour in his voice. There had always been good humour in his voice. It was one of the things she'd loved about him. Heedless of what he'd said, she still wanted to wrap herself up in something. She spied her robe hanging on the door that led onto the landing. Taking pains to avoid looking at what was lying on the bed, she made her way over to it.

She heard him chuckle.

There was no malice in the laugh, and hearing it made her heart swell. He'd never had a bad temper, and he had always loved her. She knew that. It was the reason why she wasn't scared to see him now.

She hadn't seen her husband in thirty years.

'Why are you here? On this of all nights. Why tonight?' she asked, reaching the door. She was enjoying the pain-free movement of her limbs—for the first time in what felt like forever—but she was also worrying for her sanity. If she was seeing Toby now, tonight on the anniversary of Lisa's disappearance, then there must be a reason.

'I'm here with news, Delores,' he said, his voice as sweet and strong as it had always been. 'Joyous news.'

She felt his eyes on her, and she wanted, so much, to have the robe around her, hiding her thin, ravaged body from his gaze. She reached her hand towards it hanging on the back of the door, but it passed right through.

What? She pulled her hand back and looked at it. *What's happening?*

She looked down at her body, wanting to wrap her arms around herself; if she couldn't use the robe to hide behind, then she would use her hands.

What she saw amazed her.

The body of the cancer-riddled sixty-four-year-old woman was gone, replaced with the full, curvaceous body of a woman in her thirties. She looked up slowly and saw him. He looked exactly as he had *that* night.

The night Lisa went missing.

The night before everything had changed.

He was young, and he was handsome. He had never been a large, muscular man, but he was lean and healthy. He was wearing pyjama bottoms that were striped. She knew the stripes were faded blue, but in the gloom of the night, they looked dark. He was wearing hunting boots, and his coat was open, revealing the thermal vest beneath. *He was so handsome,* she thought with a smile.

He smiled back at her, indicating towards the bed. She knew there was something he wanted her to see there, something she needed to see.

Reluctantly, she tore her gaze away from the spectre of her long-dead husband. With every fibre of her being, she didn't want to look at the bed, but she also knew she had to; she needed to see it. The room was dark, and her earthly body was enveloped within the shadows of the room.

The knowledge of what it was, wrapped tightly in the blankets, didn't shock her. She'd known since the pain had gone away. It had been reinforced by the appearance of Toby.

She knew she was dead, and she accepted it.

Her body lay on the bed, cooling as she thought these thoughts. Even though it wasn't a shock, it still saddened her. She'd been so looking forward to Christmas morning. It was going to be such a great day, a fantastic day. She'd been determined to put the pain and nausea behind her and enjoy one last special day with her daughter, her son, and her granddaughter.

But now, none of that was going to happen.

A tear welled in her eye. She was amazed she could still produce tears; after all, she was nothing but a shadow of who or what she *had* been. 'Toby …' she uttered.

Something magical happened then, something she'd not been ready for.

And it was wonderful.

She felt arms that were not her own wrap around her. They squeezed her. A delicious flush ran through her entire … she didn't know what she should call it. Was it still her body? She didn't know. The only thing she did know was that a tingle she had not experienced in thirty years crept through her.

It was the most wonderful Christmas present she could have ever received. If she hadn't known she was dead, she might have sworn this feeling was arousal. The arms were so strong and so familiar. They were unmistakably Toby's.

She could smell his cologne as his warm lips touched hers. This time, there was no questioning the feeling. It *was* arousal. It wasn't sexual, but it was emotional. She'd longed for this, dreamed of it. No other man had held her like this; no other man had kissed her since his departure. She simply hadn't wanted anyone else.

She didn't want this to end. The physical connection between them was … *what?* she thought. *Sublime* was the only word that came to her.

Eventually, he pulled away. She tried to follow him, desperate for the connection not to end.

'We have to go,' he whispered. 'There's a lot to do.'

'Where are we going?' she asked, her eyes still closed from his embrace.

'I have news.'

She opened her eyes and gazed on the face of the man she had loved forever. 'News? What is it?'

'I found Lisa.'

'Lisa ...' she whispered. 'You found her.' It wasn't a question.

'We have to go. There's something you need to witness, something you need to know.' He took her hand. 'We need to go now.'

'But my coat ...' she protested.

Toby smiled and shook his head. 'You don't need it, my sweetheart.'

He had always called her his sweetheart, and hearing it now melted her.

'You don't need anything anymore. Come now, we have much to do.'

Toby Wynne led the ghost of his wife, Delores, wearing nothing but her nightgown, through the house and out into the deep cold of the most magical night of the year.

21.

I TURNED IN the darkness. The shock of hearing another voice out in this cold, cold night startled me, and I felt my head spin, so much so that I almost fell. Anthony caught me mid-stumble and stopped me from toppling into a deep snowdrift.

Lisa was looking towards the source of the new voice. A smile had taken over her face as she welcomed the owner into the bright circle of warmth around the tree.

'Mr Sharpe,' she announced. 'I'm glad you could make it.'

'I wouldn't miss this for the world,' he replied, his baritone echoing through the night. 'Not even death could keep me away from this.' His voice was filled with humour and satisfaction.

I took a step backwards, allowing him to step into the light. Anthony had done the same. He looked old, older than he'd looked in the shopping mall … *Was that only yesterday?* I thought, shaking my head as he passed. He was wearing only a thin set of pyjamas and an old tatty tartan bathrobe. His feet were bare, but I noticed he, too, was not making any prints in the deep snow. I pulled Grace closer to me, away from the much-feared old man. Anthony wrapped his arm around her too.

'It's OK, Mommy. I was with him before. Lisa needed to see him, and she couldn't go without me. We were there when he passed.'

I was horrified. 'You were where?' I asked, not sure I'd heard her correctly.

'Me and Lisa, we were in his house. She had to tell him something. Something he needed to hear before …'

'Before what?' I asked, holding my daughter at arm's length, looking in her eyes.

'I needed to tell him he was forgiven.' The other girl's voice was coming from the wind again. I turned away from Grace to see Lisa looking at me. I pulled my daughter close again. Her head wobbled like a ragdoll's as I realised I'd used considerably more force than I meant to.

'You stay away from us, from her. She's my daughter. Who are you to take her out of her home and into the home of a … a dangerous old man?'

'She's your sister.'

Yet another voice came from behind me.

'Mom?' I heard Anthony gasp. I spun and saw him staring wide-eyed into the night.

I spun again, the other way, wanting to see who he was talking to.

A woman much the same age as me was walking through the snow towards us. She was followed by a man, a man I recognised, but for that moment, I couldn't for the life of me think where from.

Slowly, recognition dawned on me, but I couldn't believe what my eyes were seeing in the dim light of the tree. I glanced towards Anthony, and in my heart, I knew what I was thinking was true. He was crying. The tears on his cheeks sparkled in the storm.

'Mom? Mommy, is that you?' My breath was caught in my chest, and my head was spinning again.

The woman in the nightgown, her long dark hair not blowing in the wind, her bare feet not making any prints in the snow, smiled at me.

I knew that smile. I had loved it my entire life and would for the rest of my days.

It was my mother.

'Grandma,' Grace shouted, trying to wriggle free of my grip. I couldn't let her go. It may have been selfish of me not to allow her to run into the snowy night towards the ghostly figure of her grandmother, but I needed something to ground me, to stop the madness of the moment, of this situation, from overwhelming me, dragging me into its spinning abyss.

Grace was that anchor.

'Let her come,' Delores said as she looked from me to her granddaughter. The smile on her face was beautiful, filled with love and youth.

Grace began to wriggle again, but I continued to hold her tight. I felt a touch on my hand and looked up to see Anthony; he was smiling. 'Let her go,' he whispered. I looked at him, a million questions forming in my head. 'Let her go. That's Mom, and I think the man behind her … is Dad.'

I knew it was, but I hadn't been willing to entertain the idea that I was in a yard in the middle of a snowstorm, surrounded by the ghosts of four people.

'Let me go to Grandma, Mommy. Please?' Grace pleaded, wriggling more than ever. I watched as the vision of my younger mother held out her hands towards her.

'Let her come,' she whispered.

'I … can't,' I gasped. 'I don't want to lose her.'

'You won't lose her. Let her go,' the little girl's voice whispered on the wind. The little girl who I just found out was my sister.

I closed my eyes and reluctantly let her go. Grace ran through the snow towards the ethereal figures. Contact was made as if the woman was really there, and I watched as my daughter buried her head into my mother's chest. Delores looked up and smiled at me and Anthony, her two children. She signalled us to come to her too.

Anthony's hand was on my shoulder, coercing me forward.

I went.

I was happy to do so.

As I wrapped my arms around the younger version of my mother, and my daughter, I felt the strong arms of Anthony caress me too. Then there were more arms. One pair were strong, the arms of an adult, the other were small and feminine, those of a child. I closed my eyes as I melted into the family hug.

Three generations of love passed between us from beyond the grave.

~~~~

Eventually, the hug ended, and we moved apart. I had to wipe the tears from my eyes, as they were impeding my vision. I smiled as Anthony did the same.

'Why?' was all I could think of asking. 'Why is this happening? Mom, are you …'

'Dead?' Delores finished for me. 'Yes, I am,' she said with a smile, nodding. 'Please, no tears for me, though. Look at me. I'm here right now, with all the people I have ever loved in my life.'

'Why is Mr Sharpe here?' Anthony asked, looking at the old man in his pyjamas. 'And who is this little girl?'

Lisa stepped forward. He took an involuntary step backwards, and the little girl laughed. 'Don't be afraid, Anthony. My name is Lisa.'

At the sound of her name, he frowned.

'I'm your sister.'

'My sister?' he repeated.

Her smile broadened. 'Yes, your big sister.'

He looked up towards Mom and then at me.

Delores was nodding. 'This is Lisa,' she said.

'Lisa?' I asked. 'As in Grace's imaginary friend, Lisa?'

'Yes,' she answered. 'Your sister, who is not so imaginary after all.'

I was lost. I didn't know if I was coming or going. I could scarcely tell which way was up and which way was down. 'I … we don't have a sister.'

'You did …' The little girl stepped forward. Her face was serious, but there was a sadness that was barely beneath the surface.

'Did?' Anthony asked.

'Yes, you did,' the man who had been introduced to us as our father said. 'Your sister disappeared thirty years ago this very night. We searched and searched for her, but we never found her body.'

I noticed Old Man Sharpe had dropped his head as my father spoke. There was a story here, and it seemed that, like it or not, we were going to hear it.

'It started on Christmas Eve,' Lisa said. 'I was—'

'No, it didn't,' Mr Sharpe interrupted, his deep voice insistent. 'It started years before that, even before you were born. It began as a personal attack in Not Bob's, in town. I was drinking in there with an old friend from college. He was passing through town on his way to Canada. He stopped over for a few days to catch up.'

Mr Sharpe had the attention of everyone in the night.

22.

HE WAS STAYING at my place before joining the Greenpeace movement up in Canada. He wanted to help stop the cull of wolves and bears. He was trying to stop history repeating itself.' Mr Sharpe paused for a moment; a small smile broke on his lips. 'He was a colourful character, and more than a little flamboyant. He liked to wear colourful clothing, and he talked with a lisp.'

Anthony nodded. 'Everyone in town thought he was gay, didn't they?'

The spirit of Mr Sharpe looked at him, his eyes devoid of humour. He nodded slowly. 'He *was* gay,' he continued. 'None of that nonsense bothered me in the slightest. Everyone should be free to live their lives how they want to live them. Live and let live was always my motto, but there were elements in the town who were, shall we say, not as tolerant as others.'

Anthony was still nodding.

~~~~

The barroom was long, there were tables on one side where diners could sit and eat cheeseburgers or fried chicken with fries, swilling them down with beer, milkshakes, cokes, or unending supplies of strong, dark coffee. The bar ran the length of the room. There was a long mirror where drunk or sober customers could check themselves out while ordering from the numerous beers on tap or from the multiple bottles of booze on display, by the glass, the bottle, or pitcher.

Early evening on a Friday usually found the bar filled with after-work drinkers and socialites, but not tonight. Due to the extreme weather, Jon, the owner and bartender of Not Bob's Bar and Grill, was considering closing up early. He hadn't had more than five customers in at any one time the whole day.

He looked over to one of the booths and saw a young couple who were dangerously close to each other. *First few dates are always the best,* he thought with a smile. Then he looked over to another booth in the far corner. A semi-regular was there, drinking beer with another man. He didn't like the look of the other man. *Looks like a fag,* he thought, his mind crossing the line from good thoughts about sitting in the warmth of his house, his wife and kids out of the room so he could drink and watch TV.

I don't like the way that schoolteacher is sitting so close to him either.

The man who Jon disliked had long, dark, curly hair that had been pulled back in a ponytail. There was a growth of beard on him, but it looked like it had been painted on as opposed to growing where and when it wanted … *like it should.* The lines were a little too straight for Jon's liking. The colourful sweater he was wearing was a little too tight. *He's one of those fag hippie types,* Jon thought as he polished another glass to within an inch of its life. *How the fuck did he squeeze himself into those jeans?* he marvelled as the guy got up and made his way towards the restrooms.

Jon shook his head as the man breezed past.

'Hey, Jon! Cold enough for ya?' The voice broke him out of his thoughts. He blinked and turned towards the customer with his regular smile on his face. The one that said, *I'm happy to serve you, but I'm just as happy to kick your ass.*

'Harry,' Jon greeted the customer through gritted teeth. 'How's it going, man?'

Harry Sharpe nodded as he rooted through his wallet. 'You know how it is; getting by.'

'Friend of yours?' Jon asked, indicating towards the men's rooms.

'Yeah.' Harry nodded, fishing out a five-dollar bill. 'We went to college together. He's just passing through on his way to Canada. Give us another two beers, if you would, buddy.'

'Are you sure your friend doesn't want anything ... fruiter?'

'What?' Harry asked.

Jon shrugged. 'Nothing. I was just wondering if you might have wanted to try out some of the new *fruity* cocktails. A Pina Colada maybe, or a Blue Hawaiian?'

He'd put some serious emphasis on the word *fruity*.

Harry narrowed his eyes as he regarded the bartender. 'No, thanks,' he answered, shaking his head. 'Beers will do fine.' He paid for the drinks and returned to the table. As he sat down, his friend exited the restrooms. Jon watched him walk over to the tables. He gave him a small nod as he passed. The man responded by tipping him a wink and a smile.

Something inside Jon, something that was always there and was seen frequently, far too frequently for his wife and kid's sakes, snapped.

He slammed the glass he was cleaning on the counter as the man shuffled back to his seat. A red mist was beginning to cloud his vision as adrenalin surged through his veins, making his heart beat faster. The growing rage within him was almost at tipping point. His hands were shaking as he seethed through his teeth. He saw the young couple get up. The man left a few dollar bills on the table as the lady put her thick coat on. Then they left, leaving him alone ... *with these two fags,* he finished in his head.

Stepping out from behind the bar, he made his way over to the booth where they were sitting, far too close to each other for his liking. He also didn't like the way they were laughing and joking. *Probably about sucking dick,* he thought with a nasty snarl.

'Drink up. I'm closing shop,' he barked as the two men looked up at him.

'Can we just finish these off before we go?' the fag asked him. The very fact that he—it—even had the audacity to talk to him enraged him.

'No. I said we're fucking closed. Now get out of my bar.'

'Jesus, Jon. What's up with you?' Harry said, placing his beer on the table. 'We'll be out of your hair in a few minutes.'

The small but wiry man loomed over them.

Jon's face was turning pink. 'I've always thought there was something strange about you. Spending all your time with those kids,' he hissed at the schoolteacher. 'You should be ashamed of yourself. Call yourself a fucking man?'

'What did you say?' Harry asked.

'I asked you nicely to leave. Now I'm fucking *telling* you to leave.' He still couldn't bring himself to look at the other man. 'Go, now, before I have to …'

'Have to what?' the other man asked, pushing away from the table, getting ready to stand up.

Oh, don't do that. I'll kick your faggot ass from one end of this room to the next, Jon thought, stepping back a little, allowing the man room to stand up. 'Throw you out,' he finished slowly.

As the stranger stood, he looked him right in the eye. They were both about the same height, but Jon looked older, mostly due to ill living. 'Are you leaving, or what?' he asked slowly.

'Simon, don't,' Harry said grabbing his arm as he, too, stood. He then turned his attention to Jon. 'What the fuck's up with you? I've been drinking here for years. There's never been any trouble.'

Without taking his eyes from the other man, Jon answered. 'Mr Sharpe, I've been serving you for years, and I've always thought there was something … odd about you. Now, would you and your *friend* here'—the word *friend* was spoken in a mocking feminine way—'please leave my establishment?'

'Come on, Simon. I've got a bottle back at my place. We'll finish it off there,' Harry said, putting his arms into his coat.

'Gladly,' Simon replied, turning around to grab his coat from the back of the booth.

Fucking faggot, standing up to me like that. I'm not taking that shit. Jon, who'd drunk a bottle of Kentucky Bourbon the night before and had been about a whisker away from beating his wife again for having the audacity to cook him fish when he wanted steak, was done with this *shit.* He'd wanted to beat Shelia so much, but knew if he had, there would have been no excuses this time. She would have left, and he would have probably ended up in jail. Now, however, it seemed fate had delivered him a new option. He'd been given the opportunity to deliver his rage on someone more deserving than his wife. *A fucking faggot,* he spat within his own head.

As Simon turned to get his coat, Jon balled his hand into a fist and swung it at the back of his head. It connected cleanly. Simon fell forward, banging his nose on the table where their half-finished drinks rattled and fell onto their sides, swilling the floor.

'Fuck,' Jon shouted as he shook his hand out in front of him. He hadn't expected hitting the back of this guy's head to have hurt so much. 'You want some more of that, you stinking faggot? Do you?'

Harry stepped back as Simon straightened himself up from the table. There was blood over his face, and it looked like one of his eyes was about to swell.

Jon smiled. 'See what happens when fucking nancy-boys come around here drinking in real men's establishments? Now get the fuck out, or you'll get worse.'

Simon wiped his nose with his hand and looked at the blood. He grabbed his coat and pushed past the bartender. He pushed a little too hard, knocking him back.

'What the fuck?' Jon raged, grabbing Simon by the hood of his coat and jerking him back. 'Don't you fucking *dare* push past me like that. I'm not one of your fucking boy—'

In one swift movement, Simon spun underneath the man's grasping hand, grabbing the other man's arm in a two-handed grip. He exerted a little pressure, and Jon buckled. *What?* This was his only thought as his own weight rebelled against him and he felt himself falling onto the floor. It was Jon's turn to mash his face, and the crunch of the cartilage in his nose sounded louder in his head than it did in real life.

Blood flowed from his nose. He could taste it running down his throat and see it close up mingling with the spilled beer on the floor.

He struggled but couldn't move.

At that exact moment, almost like a cliché in a small-town film, the door to the bar jingled and three men walked in. All of them wearing uniforms and badges.

The fracas was broken up in a matter of seconds.

Then the lies began.

'Thank God, Sheriff,' Jon sputtered through his bloody face. 'I caught these two doing God only knows what in one of my booths. I asked them to leave, as this is a family establishment, and this one, this … gentleman attacked me. Sucker-punched me, Sheriff.'

The older man with the badge looked at the two bloodied men and then at Harry, his eyes giving away his recognition of the teacher. 'Is this true, Mr Sharpe?'

Harry shook his head. 'No, Sheriff … it's not.'

'You should have seen the things they were doing, Eric,' Jon spat. 'It was unholy, I'm telling ya. Fucking queers! Shouldn't be teaching our kids, shouldn't be anywhere near them, I'm telling you.'

~~~~

'And that was all it took. One man's hate, ignorance, and bias, and my name was ruined through town. I went to jail for a short while, some trumped-up assault charge they couldn't prove. And I lost my job as a teacher,' the ghost of Old Man Sharpe continued his tale. 'Oh, they let me out when it came to pass that Simon was ex-military. He was a gay man, but no one in the army knew or would back that, as he was an exemplary soldier. They let him out too, and he asked me to go to Canada with him.' The ghost of the old man shook his head. 'I couldn't go. Everything I had was here.

Eventually, when they found out that Jon was regularly beating his wife and selling stolen goods from behind his counter, he went to prison. They let me back into my job. I'm not a homosexual, not that it mattered, but my reputation was gone, shattered. I was ruined. But I had my house and some savings my parents had left me.'

My head was bent low. I couldn't look the man in the eye. 'We treated you like the boogieman of the town. You were the subject of all the horror stories told around campfires for years. No one really knew why.'

The old man blinked, it was long and laboured, then he nodded.

'We embellished those tales,' Delores said, stepping away from her husband's embrace. 'When Lisa went missing, the first thing we did …'

Harry Sharpe looked at her. His face was old and withered, older than it should have been. He wiped tears from his face as he spoke. 'You had every reason to.'

Everyone was looking at him now, human and ghost alike.

He took a moment to swallow before continuing.

'I had a lot to do with your misery throughout the years. I destroyed your life in a frantic attempt to save mine. I couldn't go to prison. I would never have survived it. I'd come to grips with being ostracised by the town, but I didn't think I could have survived another scandal.'

It was an odd thing to watch a ghost cry, but that was exactly what me, Anthony, and Grace were doing.

'It wasn't my fault. I didn't do anything …'

Everyone was silent.

'What are you talking about?' Toby asked, putting his arm around his ghostly family.

Lisa turned to him on his embrace. 'You need to listen to him, Daddy. He's telling the truth. It wasn't his fault. It was mine.'

'What wasn't?' Toby asked, looking at Mr Sharpe.

'Christmas Eve, thirty years ago,' Mr Sharpe continued, his eyes dripping tears.

Mom and Dad were looking at him. Their expressions were hard to read. I was holding Grace again, tighter than I had been earlier. The light from the tree was keeping us warm, but I felt I needed to hold her as close as I could. Anthony came in too, wrapping us both in his clasp.

'You went out to look for her. You were out all night. You caught a chill, one you never fully recovered from. All of that, it was my fault.' Mr Sharpe sobbed. 'It was *all* my fault.'

'What did you do?' Delores whispered, her face unreadable.

'He didn't do anything, Mommy, honest. It was my fault.' Lisa broke away from her parents and ran to the old man. She flung her arms around him and hugged him. 'I tried to tell you that I forgave you. I tried, but I couldn't come back to you. I just couldn't. Then, when Alison reached my age, I had a chance, but we couldn't do it. I'm just happy that I finally could through Grace.'

Lisa turned to face our parents. There were tears in her eyes, but her face reminded me of two, maybe even three other people. Myself, my brother, and my daughter. *She really is my sister. The sister I've never known.*

'It was Christmas Eve. The snow was thick, like it is tonight. I was in my favourite place in the house, the warmest place I could find,' Lisa began.

'The cabinet in the living room,' Delores finished. It wasn't a question.

The little girl smiled and nodded. 'I was listening to you and daddy talking. You were whispering, but I could hear you. It was about money. I knew there wouldn't be any Christmas presents that year. I'd heard you worrying about putting food on the table, mentioning something about another mouth to feed.' Lisa moved her gaze from her parents and cast it towards me and Anthony. I felt a strange sensation passing through me. It wasn't every day you were addressed by the ghost of your sister, one that you didn't have any knowledge of. 'You were a baby, Alison, and Anthony …'—the ghostly girl smiled, and there was real sadness in it—'well, I never met you until the year Alison turned eight.'

I squeezed my brother's hand and was glad to get it returned.

'I'd taken it upon myself to learn how to knit. I was doing chores around the neighbourhood and saving all my money for yarn. I wanted to make gifts for Alli and the new baby. Just so they would get something. I wanted to keep the spirit of Christmas alive for you.'

'Where were you doing the chores?' Delores asked.

'She would come around to my house and dust and clean for me,' Mr Sharpe replied. 'Since I lived alone, I wasn't the best housekeeper. When I removed myself from the community, I taught myself to knit,' he shrugged. 'It passed the time of day. I would give her a few cents each time she cleaned for me, or I would teach her how to knit. She was an excellent student.' His smile was kindly.

Dad and Mom were both shaking their heads.

Neither of them knew anything of this.

'So, while you were talking, I was hiding and knitting …'

23.

'I DON'T CARE what they're saying down at the plant, Toby, I don't care. All we need is enough food to get us through the winter. We can't get by on what we've got in the bank,' Delores said while standing by the kitchen sink. She was supposed to be washing the dishes but was mostly just bashing them about in the soapy water.

Toby was sitting at the table. His head was in his hands, and he was shaking it. 'I don't know what to do, Dee. The plant is shutting down due to the intense cold snap. They won't pay me if I'm not working.'

'But it's not your fault, is it? Surely, they have to compensate you somehow.'

'I'm not in the union, Dee. They'll only pay union members. We couldn't afford the dues, remember?'

Delores turned around, stripping off the bright-yellow gloves she was wearing. Once they were off, she rubbed her hands on her bulging belly. 'What are we going to do? I haven't gotten much for Lisa for Christmas. She'll have some new shoes and a small doll but nothing else. We don't even have any candy.' She leaned on the sink and looked up to the ceiling, sighing. 'I hate this.'

Toby stood and went to his wife. He wrapped his arms around her and leaned in for a kiss. 'I'll figure something out,' he whispered. 'Even if it means getting a job at Not Bob's … I'll figure something out.'

'You won't get a job at that place.'

Something enraged Toby then, and he turned away from his wife. He bashed his fists onto the table so hard that it rattled the glasses still on it. 'For Christ's sake, woman. What *do* you want me to do?' he half shouted, half whispered.

Lisa was hiding in the cabinet. Her father had fixed a little light in there because he knew it was her favourite place. As she heard him blaspheme and the bang and rattle of his anger, she flinched. She hated when her parents argued. They very seldom did, but when they did, it was normally about money.

She had a little radio in there with her, and as her father shouted, she turned up the volume, attempting to drown out the raised voices.

One of her favourite songs was just finishing. It was a Christmas song about one of Santa's reindeer with a bright red nose. The programme had been on TV earlier that day, and she and Alli had sat together to watch it.

She loved Christmas.

The next song was one she didn't really know. It sounded a little like a church song more than a Christmas song. But it was better than listening to them fight, so she continued listening to it. A trumpet rang through the speakers, and female voices began singing her a question. '*Do you believe the magic?*' they asked as a marching drumbeat and a deep male voice took over the vocals.

As the song wore on, she grew to like it more.

'*Do you believe in Christmas magic?*'

She peeked through the opening in the cabinet door and saw her mother looking towards where she was hiding. She thought she could see a glint of tears in her eyes.

She was right.

She wanted to go and hug her, to stop her from crying, but she knew there was nothing she could do to cheer her up right then, so she picked up her knitting and continued working on Alli's present. She was making her a pair of thick, warm gloves.

She'd nearly finished them and was excited to give her them tomorrow morning for Christmas. But the thing she was most excited about was the present she was making for the baby. She knew it wouldn't be here tomorrow morning, but she thought that he or she still needed a gift.

Mr Sharpe had given her a little booklet with a pattern in it for a star made entirely from yarn. She could hang it over the baby's crib, and they could all look at it and understand the true spirit of Christmas. It was the thought of this present that had gotten the butterflies in her belly fluttering. *Mom and Daddy will be so happy,* she thought, smiling. *I* can *feel the Christmas magic,* she answered the man in the song.

By the time the song had finished, her mother and father had taken their conversation into another part of the house. She had liked that song, so she tuned through the radio stations, trying to find it again.

It didn't take long until she succeeded.

She hummed away to herself as she resumed her work.

After an hour or so, the gloves were done. Pride swelled within her as she held them up, admiring her handiwork. She put them to one side and picked up the unfinished star. She'd worked extra hard shovelling snow for Mr Sharpe for a few extra nickels, enough to afford the bright yellow yarn needed for this project. Mr Sharpe had given her a little extra, as he said he needed some yellow yarn too.

A smile spread on her face as she continued to knit, taking her instruction from the pattern, enjoying the *click clack, click clack* of the knitting needles banging together as the star began to emerge.

The afternoon wore on into the evening. She'd ventured out of the cabinet a few times to play some Christmas Eve games and to help her father with some Christmas chores.

Other than the small fight, it had been a beautiful day.

'Well then, little one, it's time you went to bed. You don't want Santa coming down the chimney and finding you still awake, do you?' her father said, turning off the TV.

'Daddy …' she protested playfully. 'I've got some questions about Santa.'

Her father's eyes widened as he put his finger to his mouth. 'Shhhh,' he whispered, indicating with his eyes towards the sleeping baby in her mother's arms. 'You can't ask questions about Santa on Christmas Eve.'

Lisa rolled her eyes and nodded, the smile on her face telling him she hadn't really wanted to ask the questions anyway. She gave her mother a big kiss, then she kissed her stomach, as had become her custom, before kissing her little sister on her head.

Unbeknown to any of them, this would be the last time she ever performed this little ritual.

She took her father's hand and followed him up the stairs.

He read *The Night Before Christmas* to her, as was another custom, and then kissed her on her forehead. 'Goodnight, sweetheart, sleep tight,' he whispered as he turned her light off and closed the door behind him.

That was the last time she saw him alive too.

Satisfied that her father had gone back downstairs, she snuck out of bed. She retrieved her knitting, which she had hidden in her closet earlier for this very occasion.

The gloves were finished, but the star still needed some work.

She put her radio on, the volume set very low so as not to attract attention to what she was doing. A grin broke on her face as she heard her new favourite song playing.

'*Can you feel the love around? On this, the day of days*!' She was humming along as she pulled out the remaining yarn.

There wasn't much left. In fact, there was very little. She was going to miss completing the star by a long way. Frowning, she put the incomplete gift onto the bed and looked at it. *What am I going to do? I can't give the baby an unfinished Christmas present.* Then she remembered she'd bought some yellow yarn for Mr Sharpe with the extra money. Surely, he wouldn't have used all of his.

She looked out of her window at the dark trees outside. The snow was thick and was still falling, but there was no storm. That had blown earlier but was now long past. She knew the way to Mr Sharpe's house like she knew the back of her hand.

I hope he's still up, she thought as she fussed around her room. She found her boots and her long black coat. But she couldn't find her snow pants or gloves anywhere. She thought about putting the ones she'd made for Alli on. They were a little small, but she figured she would only be gone for twenty minutes, tops. When she was back, she could lay them out, and they would be dry and warm for tomorrow's unveiling.

Grabbing the unfinished star, she stuffed it into her pocket and left her room.

The house was silent.

It was eerie, but there was a nice feeling about the living room, as the fresh smell of the Christmas tree wafted through the air. There was also a smell of cinnamon, which was her all-time favourite. With a smile and butterflies dancing in her belly, she opened the front door and slipped out into the cold night.

Again, for the very last time.

The wind was biting. Even through her new gloves and her long black coat, she could feel the probing fingers of ice poking their way through the fabrics, eager to sink their long sharp nails and teeth into the warmth of her skin.

Her destination wasn't that far. It was less than a quarter of a mile through the trees, then she would be at the hedges of his yard. She put her hands deep into her pockets, lowered her head into the oncoming wind, and quickened her stride.

The moon was out, as the clouds had dissipated after the storm, so her way was well lit. She toyed with the half-complete star in her pocket.

There was a light in one of the windows of her destination, and it heartened her, even though the walk was proving to be harder than she'd thought it would have been. Eventually, she reached the hedges and opened the gate. The snow wasn't anywhere near as bad inside the yard, mostly because she'd spent long hours through the week shovelling it with Mr Sharpe. She reached the big old oak tree in the centre and rested against it for a moment. She knew the back door, less than fifty feet away, would be open. She'd been welcomed to let herself in on many occasions.

Once she had her breath back, she continued the final leg of her mission.

She could see the door, and the light inside it illuminated the room beyond. The fire was burning, meaning Mr Sharpe would still be up. *Good,* she thought.

The door was indeed unlocked, and as her hand turned the handle, it opened with ease.

As she stepped inside, the warmth hit her immediately.

As did the smell of alcohol.

'Mr Sharpe? Mr Sharpe, are you home?' she called into the seemingly empty room. She could hear the cackling of the fire and another noise. It was an odd noise for a grown man.

It sounded like sobbing.

Lisa was of two minds on what her next course of action should be. She needed the yellow yarn to finish the star, but the sounds of sobbing were scaring her. She wondered if Mr Sharpe was all right. She'd never seen him crying before.

As she crept deeper into the house, the crying got louder. She approached the doorway to the living room with caution. Wrapping her fingers around the jamb, she peered inside.

Mr Sharpe was in a chair in front of the fire. Next to him, on a small table, stood a mostly empty bottle of brown liquid that Lisa identified as *booze*. She didn't know or care what kind it was. He was holding a sheet of paper in his hand. Holding it as if he had been reading it but had finished.

His eyes were closed, and she could see tears glistening on his cheeks. His whole body jerked in time with each sob. She'd never seen him like this before. He'd always been the big jolly old man, quick with a smile and a laugh, and usually with one or two interesting facts about trees and plants.

She looked behind her at the open door to the yard. She longed for it, for the escaping from seeing her friend like this, but she was torn, firstly for her concern for him, and secondly for the need for the yellow yarn.

'Who's there?'

His voice scared her more than anything else about this situation.

'I know someone's there. Who is it, and what do you want? Can't you all just leave me the *fuck* alone?'

His voice was loud and angry, but it was also high-pitched and slurred. It didn't sound much like the Mr Sharpe she knew so well.

'Haven't you taken enough from me that you have to break into my house? If I get my hands on you, I'll break your fucking necks,' he screamed.

She was not used to hearing such cussing, certainly not from Mr Sharpe, and tears began to well in her eyes. She hid herself behind the wall as she heard him getting out of his chair. A bottle, she guessed it had been the one on the table next to him, fell. It didn't smash; it just rolled along the hardwood floor. He grumbled something she couldn't hear properly. Blood was pumping through her ears, drowning out the majority of the other noises.

She was petrified.

She didn't want Mr Sharpe to *break her fucking neck;* all she wanted was some yellow yarn.

'I'm warning you. I've got a gun, and I know how to use it.' The slurring growl of the angry man filtered through the rush of blood through her head. She could hear him now; he was behind the wall, angry and mumbling. She didn't know if he owned a gun. She'd never seen him with one, but that didn't mean he *didn't* have one. She decided that the yellow yarn would have to wait for another time, maybe when the shops opened again after Christmas. She could ask her mother or father to take her into town and get some. They wouldn't mind, not when she told them what it was for.

Not wanting to be in this house any longer, she decided to make a dash for it rather than feel the wrath of Mr Sharpe and his potential gun. She liked her *fucking* neck just the way it was.

As he emerged through the door, looking red-faced and angry, Lisa sprang from the wall. She ran towards the door she'd left open. So fixated on her escape was she that she didn't realise the floor was wet from the snow she'd allowed to blow into the house.

As she ran, she lost her footing.

~~~~

'Lisa? Is that you?' he shouted as he saw the little girl speed towards the door.

He watched, wide-eyed, as she fell. He was helpless to stop her momentum.

Everything that followed then, for him, happened in a hideous slow motion. There was a crunch as she stumbled into the door. There was a tinkle of smashing glass as her head collided with one of the thin panes of glass.

He watched her fall.

Her head smashed through the small pane.

In his mind's eye, he watched it happen over and over again. He saw the jagged sliver cut through her throat as the weight of her body pulled her down. He saw it pierce her skin, cut through her neck, and finally tear her carotid artery.

Blood spurted high. It sprayed his windows and the curtains before pooling on the hardwood floor.

He fell to his knees, ignoring the pain in his kneecaps as he hit the floor. The body of Lisa, his only real friend in this world, lay sprawled on the floor in his house. Her limbs were twitching as a horrible pool of dark red spread beneath her.

'Lisa …' he sobbed, running to her, lifting her from the floor, the blood of his friend covering him, dripping from his hands.

He turned then and saw her.

He didn't know if it was Lisa he saw in the room, watching the turn of events. It looked like her, but she wasn't dressed the same. The little girl looked at him. Her small, scared face was wide-eyed, and her mouth was open in what he thought would soon be a scream.

No scream was forthcoming.

He was thankful of that minute of mercy.

He held out his bloody hands to the little girl. He wanted to tell her this was an accident, that it wasn't his fault. He wanted the little ghost to fix Lisa, to make her better, to bring her back.

As he sobbed, the little girl faded away, and he never saw her again.

24.

'LISA …' THE GHOST of Mr Sharpe whispered into the night.

Delores and Toby were staring at him, shaking their heads, disbelief dripping from them both.

'You were there?' Toby whispered.

Mr Sharpe hung his head, nodding.

'And you didn't do anything to help her?' Delores asked, her youthful mouth hanging wide as the horror of this revelation revealed itself to her.

'I did. I did everything I could. I tried to stop the bleeding. I really tried, but the glass had gone in too far.' Harry's face was contoured in a grimace. He looked like a different man. 'Half … half of her face was gone, just gone, from the impact. There was nothing—'

'He really did do all those things,' Lisa interrupted. 'I was dead minutes after the glass cut into me. He tried and tried. I was there; I watched him.'

'I saw him too,' I whispered.

Mr Sharpe looked at me. In his eyes, he didn't see me as the grown woman before him; I knew he was seeing me as the petrified ghostly little girl in his house, the one he was reaching out to. 'You did, didn't you?'

Toby took a step forward. His eyes were blazing as they focused on the old man. 'I went to you. I went to your house looking for her.' His hands were balled into fists. 'You bastard, you told me you hadn't seen her for days.'

Mr Sharpe took a step backwards, away from the threat. There were fresh tears in his eyes. 'I know. I've lived with that decision, with that lie, every single day of my life for the last thirty years. I have beat myself up over it, blaming myself for what happened to her, and to you. I wanted to make it up to you, to tell you what happened.' This was directed at Delores. 'But you wouldn't let me. You carried on believing what the town said about me. You believed that I could do horrible things to the little boys and girls in my care. I found your children lost in the snow. I wanted—I tried to help.' He dropped his head back onto his chest. 'But I couldn't. My guilt was too deep.'

'What did you do?' Delores whispered. It was such a soft sound, but it carried on the wind. She put a hand to her mouth and took in a deep, shaky breath. 'What did you do with our daughter's …' She paused as if the thought of her very next word might kill her all over again.

Lisa stepped into her mother's embrace, and I watched as my mother's arm wrapped around her, pulling her close.

Mr Sharpe's eyes flicked towards the tree that was glowing.

Delores's unfinished question hung in the wind as her and Toby's eyes followed his. 'Oh no,' Delores sobbed and fell to her knees at the base of the tree. She began to scrabble in the snow, but of course, there was no displacement.

'You can't dig,' Toby said, putting his hand on her shoulder. 'We're not of this realm anymore.' He looked up at Mr Sharpe. His head was shaking as his wife ignored him, continuing to dig through the snow.

'Why? Why tell us, me, you didn't know where she was? Why tell me that and then dig her a makeshift grave in your yard? You know what happened to me because of looking for her.'

Mr Sharpe nodded. 'It was the note. The one that had been pushed through my door. I don't know who wrote it, but I do know why. Every town has a boogieman, a scapegoat to cast their sins onto. In our town, it was me.'

Lisa stepped forwards. 'What was in the note that made you so upset?'

Mr Sharpe looked at the little girl, more tears welling in his eyes. 'It said that *they* knew what I was doing to the children. Disgusting, dirty things. It was Jon Billingsworth, the owner of Not Bob's. He was out of prison by then and back in town. He was angry because he'd taken a beating from a, how he called it, faggot. He never did get over that. He told everyone that me and Simon had tried to rape him or something stupid of that ilk. He spread it all around town. I'm not sure everyone believed it, not coming from a convicted wife beater, but enough did, enough to sow the seed of doubt into the town's heads. I had gone to jail for it. I lost my job. I lost my friends ...'

It was Toby's turn to hang his head.

Mr Sharpe looked at him. The welling tears broke free from the lids of his eyes. 'I know what I did. I *know* it was wrong. But if I'd have called the police, or even an ambulance, there would have been questions. What was an eight-year-old girl doing in your house, alone on Christmas Eve night? What did you do to her? How did you kill her? I would have had no chance. I would have been put away in a high-security facility in no time. I had to think fast, and I'd already half dug a hole by the tree earlier in the year because I was thinking of planting more plants.' He closed his eyes again, his eyeballs visibly shifting beneath the lids as if reliving a nightmare, which was exactly what he was doing.

Delores looked at the tree, then at Lisa, who was standing next to it. The snow had melted around her. 'Is she ...' She paused as if she couldn't bring herself to finish the rest of the question.

'Yes.' Lisa nodded. 'I am.'

The golden light that was bathing them was emanating from the small patch of ground where she was standing. She stepped out of the area, and it opened up. The ground began to dig itself, creating two small mounds of ruddy earth on either side of it. Everyone, solid and ethereal, stepped closer to peer inside.

Golden light radiated from a dark, dirty piece of cloth that could have been a black coat. Inside were dirt-stained off-white bones.

Human bones.

Lisa's bones!

'What's causing the light?' I asked. The question was not directed to anyone in particular.

'It looks like it's coming from the pocket of her coat,' Anthony replied, pointing at a fold in the coat. He leaned in after removing his glove. I watched as his fingers wriggled around inside the pocket.

He removed something.

Whatever it was, it was glowing, shining. It was the source of the radiance that had saved them, that had kept them warm in the various storms they had encountered.

Everyone was drawn to it as he lifted it out of the ugly hole.

Lisa was smiling.

He opened his hand, and the light beamed even more radiant than it had moments ago.

'Merry Christmas, Anthony,' Lisa whispered to her brother. 'I made that for you.'

He looked at his ghostly sister. His face was unreadable in the illumination, but the shining in his eyes told me a whole different story. 'Why does it glow?'

She smiled. 'It's my anchor. It's how I've been able to come back.'

'That's where she took me, Mommy,' Grace said. I pulled her close and held her for a moment. 'I wondered why it was glowing. Now I know.' As she looked at me, there was a smile on her face. It was a happy smile.

'It was my reason for leaving the house that night. It was why I was in Mr Sharpe's home. It was why I died. I didn't want anything bad to happen to Mr Sharpe. He hadn't done anything wrong. I didn't want him to get into trouble. I knew if I could come back to tell him I forgave him, then maybe he wouldn't be so sad. The only way I could do it was through a little girl, one who I shared family with. One who was the same age as me when I died.'

She looked at me again; her smile had spread wide across her face, lighting up her eyes. I guessed it wasn't because of the golden light coming from Anthony's hands. 'That's why I reached out through you, Alison. I thought I could use you to get to Mr Sharpe. You could see me, but you couldn't believe in me. You had Anthony as *your* anchor; he grounded you. Your fear and mistrust of Mr Sharpe was too strong by then. It blinded you to me.' She then directed her smile towards Grace, who smiled back at her.

Oh my God, I thought, *they do look so alike.*

'So, I reached out to Grace. You're an only child and would be more open to seeing me, to interacting with me. You helped me obtain my goal. You helped me forgive Mr Sharpe.'

'Why didn't you tell us we had a sister?' Anthony asked our mother. 'There was never any indication that there had ever been anyone else.'

Delores swallowed. Her head dropped, and Toby held her a little tighter. 'It was too hard for me, for us, to talk about. Your father and I decided to hold her memory in our hearts. We didn't want you to be sad that you never got to know her.'

'Our memories of her were perfect, and our sadness that she was gone was complete.' Toby looked at his wife, then back to Anthony. 'We'd planned to tell you about her when you were older. The plan was to tell you and give you photographs of her …' he said, looking at me, '… together.'

'But it never happened. We never got to tell you. Your father was taken so soon, and my grief …'—Delores stalled for a moment, swallowing her sob—'for both losses. It was just too much for me. It was easier for me not to talk about it. It's a decision I've regretted every day of my life, and for that, I apologise to you, all of you.'

'A lot has happened here tonight,' Lisa whispered.

It sounded strange, listening to such a grown-up conversation coming from a small girl.

'Many wrongs have been righted. I forgave Mr Sharpe. Mr Sharpe confessed to why he buried me and didn't tell anyone about me. Mother, you've told my sister and brother about me, and now, I need to apologise to Grace. I'm sorry for dragging you into all of this. It's a lot for a seven-year-old to grasp. I thank you for allowing me to use you like I did.'

Grace was smiling. 'You don't have to apologise. I love you being my best friend.' She looked up at me. 'I told you Lisa was real, didn't I?'

'You did, baby, you did. I'm so sorry for not believing you.'

'Our time here is limited. The veil between our worlds runs thin this time of the year, it's what has allowed us to make this connection, but it's time now. We must cross over.'

The glow from the half-completed, filthy woollen star in Anthony's hand began to glow brighter. He looked from the light to the young woman who was his mother. 'Mom, are you really …'

She was smiling. 'Yes, Anthony, I am. Don't grieve for me. Look, I have everything I need here.' She indicated towards Toby and Lisa. 'For now, anyway. I'll miss you three, though, more than you can possibly imagine.'

'Four,' Anthony said taking a step forward.

'Four?' Delores asked.

He lay the star on the ground and searched deep into the pockets of the waterproof pants he was wearing. He pulled out his phone and held it out to the spirit of his mother. 'This is Rosie,' he stuttered.

I watched as he held the device, the one with the photograph, to Mom and Dad. Sobs were wracking through his body. 'She's … she's your new granddaughter.'

Delores's eyes widened. She stepped up and looked at the picture. A tear spilled from her eye and dripped down her cheek. 'She's—she's beautiful,' she stuttered, wiping the rest of the tears that were now falling. 'Look after her and look after each other. Will you do that? For me?'

'For us,' Toby said, wrapping his arm around his wife and daughter.

'And for me too,' Mr Sharpe added.

'We will,' Anthony said, pulling in a shaky breath. 'We will.'

Grace ran to her grandmother and hugged her. I copied her, as did Anthony. Finally, Lisa and Toby moved in to complete the family reunion.

There were multiple instances of *I love you,* and many tears were shed. After a short while, we broke away. The light that had been pulsing from the star began to strobe. Delores, Toby, and Lisa began to walk towards it.

We watched, me, Grace, and Anthony, holding onto each other, as the rest of our family disappeared into the diminishing light.

Delores stopped, just once, and turned back. She held out her hand. Mr Sharpe smiled and nodded before walking towards her, accepting the invitation.

All four of them disappeared into the bright golden light.

As they did, what was left of the waning illumination flickered before disappearing completely, leaving me, Anthony, and Grace cast back into the darkness of the night. The cold hit us instantly, and I hurried to put up the hood to my coat. I then helped Grace to wrap up too.

A small spark of the light remained, and it bound us all together in its warmth. We followed that light back to the safety of the house that we always had and always would call home.

It was to be a Christmas none of us would ever forget.

25.

THE FUNERALS OF Delores Ann McEvoy Wynne and Harry Sharpe were two very different affairs.

Delores's had a healthy attendance of the good folk of Kitchowa. She had been a popular and respected member of the community. This was evident by the small church being filled, fit to burst, by townspeople wishing to pay their final respects to a good woman. There was even a healthy crowd outside who couldn't get into the warm church. Such was the love for the woman and the respect that had been paid towards her.

The eulogy was beautiful. The pastor had known and loved her very much. He gave a poignant and humorous account of her life and how she had touched the lives of all the people present and many more who hadn't been able to make the service.

Afterwards, the people flocked to her children. They hugged us, sharing their tears, their smiles, and their stories before spending an enjoyable afternoon in a local restaurant.

Mr Sharpe's funeral, on the other hand, was a very quiet affair. It was attended only by the pastor, Anthony, Grace, and me. There were no other mourners to offer anecdotes about his life, but there were tears. The three of us celebrated him and his lost, sad existence with a meal in the same restaurant we'd celebrated Mother's.

We celebrated alone.

26.

AFTER A FEW days of dealing with the legalities of Delores Wynne's estate, Grace and I went home to Minnesota, and Anthony went back to Toronto.

There had been an oversight in the registering of the adoption, and Richard and Rosie hadn't been able to travel to the United States from Canada. So the hugely anticipated meeting of my new niece had to be put off.

We arranged to visit Toronto and our new family when the weather broke for spring.

Even though we'd lost our mother and Grace had lost her beloved grandmother, we parted in good spirits. We had grown. It was no longer only me, Grace, Anthony, and Richard against the world; we now had Toby, our father, Lisa, our sister, and Mr Sharpe, our friend … not to mention the excitement of Rosie becoming the newcomer into our lives.

We might have buried Delores, but the events of that Christmas Eve out in the snow had given us all the closure we needed to allow our mother, and our assorted ghosts, to rest in peace.

27.

'ALISON.' RICHARD BEAMED as he opened the door. 'Wow, you look fabulous. Have you done something to your hair?'

I ran my fingers across my head and laughed. 'Well, you know, it's not every day a girl gets to meet her new niece, and cousin, is it?'

'Uncle Richard …' Grace shouted, darting out from behind me to give her uncle a huge hug. Richard had no other course of action but to lift the girl off her feet and swing her around before carrying her into the house.

'Uncle Anthony,' she screamed again. Richard put her down as Anthony came down the stairs. More hugging and swinging ensued.

'I'm so sorry about Delores,' Richard said as he picked up the two suitcases I'd dragged from the car. 'She was a lovely woman. I'd have loved to have been there, but …' He indicated up the stairs with a nod of his head and a grin that stretched from ear to ear. 'You know. I hear you had quite the adventure. Two funerals and all kinds of shenanigans.'

As a family, we had decided to keep what happened in Mr Sharpe's yard to ourselves. It would have been too difficult to explain to anyone else, even someone as close as Richard, about what really happened. So I knew he was talking about the death of our mother.

'He told me that this little feisty one kept running away and getting lost, that you had to go out and find her in the snow on more than one occasion.'

Grace was laughing and blushing as she sat on Anthony's shoulders.

'That's true. She put the fear of God in us a few times, I'll tell you that. Anyway, I'm not here to talk to you two rough boys all day. I believe I have a niece to meet?'

Richard grinned again. 'Yes, yes, you do. She's right up there in the first bedroom. She's waiting for you.'

Anthony put Grace down, and the moment her feet hit the floor, she was up the stairs in a flash.

I followed, only nowhere near as fast.

The bedroom was golden. The paint was a deep yellow with golden undertones. The curtains were gold, and the ceiling was painted a slightly lighter shade of gold than the walls.

'We were going to go with red, you know, for Rosie, but Anthony insisted he had a newfound appreciation for this colour. I wasn't overly happy about it at first, but as we began to paint it, I found that I fell in love with it. It's—'

'Warm,' myself and Anthony interrupted Richard's speech.

He looked at us both and pulled a face. 'That's what I was going to say,' he laughed. 'Anyway. Alison, Grace. I would love you to meet … Rosie!' He indicated, with obvious pride, towards the white crib in the centre of the room.

As I entered, my eyes were drawn towards something hanging over the crib. At first, I couldn't tell what it was, but as I got closer, it became obvious.

I felt the itch of tears dripping down my cheeks.

Hanging over the crib was a half-competed knitted star.

'I don't know where he got that thing,' Richard whispered, trying to hide his voice from his husband. 'It's got to be the ugliest thing I've ever seen, but he's been adamant we hang it there.'

'Grace, come here,' I said, wiping the tears from my eyes. 'Come and see what Uncle Anthony has hung over the crib.'

Grace ran in. She stopped when she saw the star, and her face broke into the biggest, most joyous smile I had ever seen her pull. 'The star?' she shouted.

'Yes,' Anthony said from just outside the doorway. 'The star.'

'He calls it the Spirit of Christmas,' Richard said, looking between us all as if he was the only one in the room still sane.

'The Spirit of Christmas?' I repeated. 'I love it.'

Anthony walked over, and all four of us hugged as we looked into the crib at the small baby inside.

Rosie Delores Lisa Wynne looked up at us all and smiled.

D E McCluskey

Do You Believe (Christmas Magic)

Words and music by
Johnny Plaid, Anthony Bolland & E J McCluskey
© Played by Plaid 1968

Do you believe the magic?
(Do you believe the magic?)
That's in the air tonight.
It illuminates our hearts and minds.
(Hearts and minds)
A bright and blinding light.

Do you believe in Christmas magic?
(Do you believe in Christmas magic?)
That sings to us this day.
It beats a time with our childlike hearts
(Childlike hearts)
Love never goes away!

Do you believe?
In the promise and the awe ...
Do you believe?
Open hearts, open door ...
In this season of joy and hope
Let your true love soar ...
(Believe ...)

Can you feel the love around?
(Can you feel the love around?)
On this, the day of days
A feeling passing through the years,
(Through the years)

To set our hearts ablaze …

To set our hearts ablaze …
(To set our hearts ablaze)

Love never goes away …
(Love never goes away)

Like a bright and blinding light …
(A bright and blinding light)

Do you believe?
In the promise and the awe …
Do you believe?
Open hearts, open door …
In this season of joy and hope
Let your true love soar …

Do you believe?
That Christmas brings you more …
Do you believe?
Open hearts, open that door …
In this season of joy and hope
Let all your love soar …

Let all your love soar …
(Believe)

The Season of Secrets

Author's Notes

OK, so in the first instance, I might need to apologise to my long-term readers for this novel. I'm sorry I decided to go for a happy ending. I promise, sincerely, it won't happen again.

Honest!

This story came out of the blue. It came from a place somewhere in my love of cheesy Christmas films. Now, I know I'm a horror writer and a psychological thriller writer, and yes, I did write *Zola* and *Cravings* ... but there is something about those horribly acted and poorly written Hallmark films that I just HAVE to watch them all through the year.

I usually start right about September ... and I'm usually sick of them by the end of November, every single year.

Anyway, I remember watching a film years and years ago. It wasn't a Hallmark one, but it was a ghost story. It was about a little girl who had been killed in the 1970s in the basement of this old house. The boy living there in the late 1990s kept on hearing the same song, ghostly song, over and over again.

Did you ever hear a dream, walking ... like I did, or something like that.

Anyway, the handyman turned up and was whistling the song, and the boy knew then that he'd been the one who had killed the girl.

You don't need to watch it now, it was awful anyway, yet the idea of the film stuck with me for years (if not the title), and I kind of based this story around the haunting melody of a song. I really wanted to use 'Do You Hear What I Hear,' probably the Bing Crosby version. However, because I'm a lowly indie author, I wouldn't be able to stump up the cash to use the copyrighted lyrics … so I wrote my own.

'Do You Believe? (Christmas Magic),' *Words and music by Johnny Plaid, Anthony Bolland, and E J McCluskey.* Jonny Plaid doesn't exist, Tony Bolland is my mate who I wrote *In the Mood for Murder*, *Sing Sing Sing for Murder*, and the upcoming *Swinging for Murder* with.

EJ McCluskey is my dad.

And the haunting melody was born.

The original title of this was The Spirit of Christmas, but I thought it might only appeal to readers seasonally, so I changed it to The Season of Secrets, after considering Do You Believe? after the name of the song.

This story gets me all the time too. Every time I did a run through it to mould the story, correct typos, and whatnot, I always ended up with a few tears in my eyes … So, I wanted to dedicate this one to Lauren and her swinging brick.

So … to the thank you section.

Lisa, my ever-loving, ever-patient, and ever-rolling-her-eyes editor, as I try, yet again, to set a novel in the USA. All she ever does for me is fix Americanisms and tell me a million times that American kids don't do this or don't do that. So, thank you, Lisa … you are a force to be reckoned with.

Got to thank my whole family … who are all so supportive.

I have to thank the multitudes of support I get from various Facebook groups and all the TikTok stuff that I don't really understand.

I have to thank my proofreaders, Kelly Rickard and Lauren Davies, and my hardcore ARC and street team (I sound like I know what I'm talking about here).

Thank you to The Shippy Writers too; I honestly think we need a better name.

And most important of all … TO YOU!!!

Thank you for reading my words and, for the most part, enjoying them too. So remember, people, the Christmas you get … you deserve!

So be good and be nice … and go and please review this book for me.

Dave McCluskey
Liverpool
September 2023

More books by the author:

Novels (DE McCluskey)

The Twelve
In The Mood For Murder
Sing Sing Sing For Murder
CRACK
Z: A Love Story
TimeRipper
Butterflies
Mutant Superhero Zombie Killing Disco Zombies from Outer
   Space (with uzis)
The Contract
Black Feather Fever
Glimmer (Glimmer Saga #1)
The City of the Fireflies (Glimmer Saga #2)
The Throne of Glimm (Glimmer Saga #3)
The Boyfriend
Dark Knightmares
Reboot

Novellas (DE McCluskey)

Zola
Cravings
The Special Stuff
The Stinky Stump
The Grinkle Nonk
All Of These People Are Going To Die #3
A Prelude For Murder

D E McCluskey

Collections (DE McCluskey)

Guardian
The Christmas You Get, You Deserve
Ink

On Going Series (DE McCluskey)

Brownmoor #1
Brownmoor #2

Graphic Novels & Comics (DE McCluskey)

Doppelgänger
Deathday Presents
Short Sharp Shocks
The Something Wicked Years
Wooden Heart
Three Days in the City
The Adventures of Mace Masoch

Novels (Dave McCluskey)

A Seagull's Tale
Olf

Graphic Novels & Comics (Dave McCluskey)

Interesting Tymes
Interesting Tymes x 2
Edward D'Ammage Presents: The Wedding
Olf
A Christmas Carol – in rhyme
Santa's Lost Boot
The Hangry Hamster (Grace McCluskey)

Printed in Dunstable, United Kingdom